ONLY TEN CENTS

Copyright

This is a work of fiction. Names, characters, places and incidents are products of the author's imagination or are used fictitiously. Any resemblance to actual persons, living or dead, or to events or locales, is entirely coincidental.

A Note from the Publisher . . .
Only Ten Cents was originally published in 1894. This edition has been reproduced with every effort to retain the flavor of the original with minor changes to update spelling and punctuation. You'll find this book reflects many of the feelings and attitudes prevalent at the time of its original publication. It may contain references that reflect mores and opinions that directly conflict with today's prevailing sentiments.

ONLY TEN CENTS

Isabella Alden

CHAPTER 1

Where it Came From

S HE was a pretty little girl, with fair face and blue eyes and a fluff of golden-brown hair that curled all about her temples, because it would not lie smooth, but insisted upon curling. You would have liked her face from the first, and would have turned to look at it again if you had a chance; but I suppose you would have said, as many said when they looked at her: "How very pale Nettie Beldon is!" And then, if you had known her well and had been in the habit of seeing her often, you would have said, as so many of her friends said: "Poor Nettie grows paler and thinner every day!"

It was all true; nobody understood it better than Nettie's mother. Every morning she studied her little girl's face carefully to see if the night had left her looking more wan and tired: and often she had to turn away quickly and wait several minutes before she could make answer to something which Nettie had said, so as to hide the tears on her face and the tremble in her voice. Nettie was fading. Yet she had a very quiet, peaceful look, as she sat there in her large, queer wheeled chair, quite unlike the ordinary ones in which people sit. There was a reason for this, too; although Nettie was only twelve years old, it was almost five years since she had taken a step; and during those years most of her waking time had been spent in that wheeled chair, which was so built that she could push herself forward on a level all about the room, and even out on the bit of a piazza. But they were afraid to have her do that lest the wheels should get beyond her control and run over the steps. So she had to content herself with that one room. For a few months past she had apparently been quite contented with it; had taken very few rides about the room, for she had so little strength now that it seemed like a hard day's work to cross the room even in her chair.

"It is very pleasant here by the open window," she would say, smiling on her mother. "I like to watch the people going by, and the horses, and everything. A cunning little dog passed this morning, and looked up at me and seemed to nod. I suppose he said *Good-morning!* It sounded like *Bow-wow*, it is true, but if I understood his language it would be *Good-morning, little girl! What do you sit there all the while for?* I like to watch for him, mother; he is a friend of mine."

This will give you a glimpse of one of the ways in which Nettie passed her time, and interested herself in all that was going on. It was a poor plainly furnished room in which she sat; you would have thought there was not very much to interest one, though Nettie found a great many pleasant things in it. It was the front room of an old-fashioned house which had belonged to Nettie's grandfather. That particular room had been set apart long ago as Nettie's own—hers and her mother's; for at night her mother never left her; and she stayed with her daytimes now, as often as she could. They were long days when she had to be away—for Mrs. Beldon and Nettie were all of the family who were ever at home in the daytime. Robert was only ten, and in winter they managed to send him to school; but through the long summer he was cash-boy in the one large store in the village, and did as much as he could toward helping to support the family. Sarah was eighteen, and was assistant in the primary department of the public school; it was her salary which enabled Mrs. Beldon to stay at home with Nettie. She was a sewing woman and used to go out every morning. While Nettie was so that she could leave her she stayed away all day, and sewed steadily for a dollar a day. They did not call themselves very poor; they said they were a great deal better off than some people. Ever since Robert was eight years old he had earned a little each day toward supporting the family; and as for Sarah, if she had not been one of the best scholars in the High School she could never have gotten her position.

"We shall do very nicely this year," they used to say cheerily, in order to comfort Nettie. Yet she being a wise little girl, thoughtful beyond her years, knew as well as though they had told her, that by the time the rent and the doctor's bill were paid, and the choice fruits and the high-priced meats and other luxuries which he constantly ordered for her, were paid for, there would be very little left to live on. It required the most thoughtful management and the most sacrificing care to keep them from debt. Oh, Nettie understood. Sometimes when she sat there in her big chair all alone it made the tears come into her great blue eyes and roll sorrowfully down her pale cheeks, to think how much money she cost them. Didn't she know that the very chair in which she sat cost forty dollars! And that they were *two whole years* saving the money? They had done extra work, and gone without needed clothing, sometimes, to save enough to buy the chair. It had been a great luxury to her, and a great rest to her aching back; but when the cold winter days came she looked at it sometimes mournfully, and one day in a burst of confidence she told it that if it could turn into some flannel wrappers for mother, and a pair of thick-soled shoes for Sarah, and a good warm overcoat for Robert, she would be willing to lie in bed all winter. However, they would not have been willing to have her.

But I began to tell you about the room in which Nettie spent her days. It was a good-sized room, and the walls were freshly white-washed every spring and fall, so that everything about Nettie might be as bright and clean as possible. The floor was covered with a neat matting, in pretty plaids of straw-color and green; and in the center was a large bright rug which had a history full of interest to Nettie, for she had made the rug herself. A great deal of work it had been, but there had also been a great deal of pleasure about it; it had taken up many of the long, long hours. It was made of woolen strips cut about half an inch wide, and sewed together like carpet-rags. Oh, the balls, and balls, and *balls* of red and green and blue and yellow and black that Nettie's patient fingers had cut and sewed and wound! All the neighbors in the village knew about her ball; not a little girl came to call on her but brought a roll of woolen patches—bits of bright red flannel from the children's new skirts; bits of blue or pink opera flannel left from the dainty dressing-sacques of some pretty young lady; sometimes large pieces of black cloth or dark blue cloth, or mixed gray cloth, left from "Joe's" coat or jacket, or "Fred's" new trousers. Everybody remembered her; so the balls grew. After a time she began to crochet them into strips about six inches wide, and two yards long. She had a very large crochet needle with which she made her strips of whatever colors she pleased. As they were finished her mother sewed them together firmly; then a collection was taken among her friends, of worn-out woolen stockings and socks; they poured in from all over the neighborhood, as soon as it was found that Nettie wanted them. These she raveled and made a pretty wavy fringe of the yarn, which was sewed on the two ends of the rug. When all was done a brighter, neater piece of work to lay upon a floor, the Beldon family thought could hardly be imagined.

"It is so soft and thick and warm," said Sarah, touching it with loving hands.

"Yes, and so bright!" said the mother. "Just the thing for Nettie to rest her eyes upon when the days are dull and cloudy; and to think that she made it herself, every stitch of it! I declare, I am proud of you, Nettie."

And Nettie smiled and looked pleased over it all. She did not tell anyone, not even Sarah, to whom she told most things, how many tears had been dropped all over that bright rug, because of the thought that she could never step her own feet on it. Poor Nettie! Yet she shed very few tears when people could see her, and tried to be as bright and cheery as she could before her mother.

"It is hard enough," she told herself, "without me crying. I won't let her know that I shed a tear, and I won't cry if I can help it. I don't mean to cry anymore; I ought to be a real thankful little girl. My back does not ache nearly so hard as it used to, and I have ever so many nice pleasant things to look at."

Then she would gaze about her room with satisfaction. The clean white walls had many pictures on them; not such as you are in the habit of seeing on your walls: but pictures which had been carefully cut from magazines and illustrated -newspapers which from time to time had been sent to Nettie by some of her friends. They had no frames, but were fastened with a little mucilage to the walls, and were sources of never-failing interest to Nettie. Some days she would lie for hours together among the pillows in her wheeled chair—which was so built that it could be fastened back when she wished, to make a sort of couch. In this way she would study her pictures, and imagine stories about them until she had as many as five different stories for the same picture. Besides the pictures there was, in the window seat, a pot of ferns whose graceful waving leaves so beautifully green, were watched with utmost care and interest.

"They are better than flowers," Nettie used to say, "because they would drop off after awhile, but the ferns stay."

Certainly, as she told herself, she had many things to be grateful for; although, as I hinted, you would have called the room poor and plain. You would have thought the white curtains at the windows coarse, as indeed they were; but Nettie thought them beautiful. They were so white, and had such pretty, graceful vines trailing over them, and such cunning little ball-tassels on the ends of the cord which looped them back. There were two south windows in the room, and in winter the sun shone in warm and bright, making the colors of Nettie's carpet brilliant, and rejoicing the heart of her one plant.

It was a winter afternoon; the snow lay thick on the hills around, and the sleigh-bells jingled merrily. Nettie sat looking out into the bright sunshine and the cold, clear beauty spread everywhere, and thought her sorrowful thoughts. She was quite alone, and so decided that she could afford to look as sober as she pleased for a little while, with neither mother nor Sarah to feel worried about her. Sarah was at school, of course; on these short winter days the schoolroom claimed her until it was nearly dark; and her mother had gone to finish a piece of sewing for a woman who was in a hurry for it. She was to go from there to the store to get some necessary things; so it would be late before she reached home, and Nettie would have plenty of time to think her thoughts.

I am wondering if you could imagine why they were sorrowful thoughts? You think perhaps I have given you reason enough for her sober face. You think it would be very hard to sit in one chair all day long and never take a single step—never to see any other room than that, except the little bedroom which opened from it into which Nettie could wheel herself if she chose, though she could not help put herself into the bed. But it was not on this account that her face was sad this bright wintry afternoon. There were times when she could not help envying the boys and girls as they trooped merrily by with their school books, or slid gracefully by on skates, or flew by in handsome sleighs; but today she hardly thought of any of these.

Instead, her face had grown grave over a barrel which she knew
was being packed, at least the girls were getting ready to pack it,
to go hundreds of miles away.

In order to explain this I shall have to say that Nettie,
helpless as she was, belonged to a society. Yes, you are right; it
was a Pansy Society: seven girls belonging to the Sabbath-school
class which Nettie had always called her own—though she was
a wee creature, less than seven years old, when she attended it—
had organized themselves into a Pansy Society. They met every
week under their teacher's lead and spent a pleasant hour
together. One week it was a prayer meeting, when the teacher
gave them a little talk about some Bible verse; another week it
was a sewing society, another it was a temperance meeting, and
on the fourth Saturday of the month it was a missionary
meeting; but always the Pansy Society.

Of course then they were pledged, every one, to try every
day to do some kind and pleasant thing for others; and many
were the kind words and pleasant acts they had succeeded in
doing for Nettie. Quite often, if it happened to be what Nettie
called one of her "well days," they met with her in her own little
room, where there were not enough seats for them all, without
going to the neighbors' to borrow a chair or two. But they all
seemed glad to come, and sometimes told her, as they kissed
her good-bye, that they always had better meetings at her house
than anywhere else; and Nettie looked forward to these
Saturday hours as the very brightest in the history of her weeks.

Now about the barrel. The missionary part of the society
had become very much interested in a Sunday-school in a
Southern town. A young woman who used to be a teacher in

their own Sunday-school had married and gone there to live, and it was she who had written to the superintendent's wife a story of their mission Sunday-school, where they gathered each Sabbath a company of people who were very poor and ignorant; so that some of the girls who were as old as twelve and fourteen did not even know how to read. The Pansy Society had become deeply interested in these girls, and having heard from Mrs. Carpenter that they were going to have a Christmas-tree in their mission school, and that it would be the first Christmas-tree that many of them had ever seen, they resolved to pack a barrel with all sorts of pretty and useful things, and send it in time for the tree. Of course they had been very busy indeed since this plan came to them, and only the day before, two of them who had called on Nettie had reported that the barrel was almost filled, and that they had "just the loveliest time" getting the things together! Their mothers had helped, and they were sending half-worn dresses, and aprons, and sacques, and shoes, and all manner of things besides; toys and books, and pictures, and ever so many pretty little things that they had made.

"We are dressing dollies," one said. "Oh, dozens of dollies! We got them real cheap, you know, at the toy store; some of last year's set that were shop worn; but they are ever so pretty, and we girls did have such fun dressing them! We thought of meeting here one week, just so you could enjoy the fun of it, but your mother said we would better not, for you were not quite so well as usual, and she was afraid the excitement would bring back the pain; so we just came to tell you about it this afternoon, and show you two or three of the dollies."

Then they had opened their baskets and displayed the treasures, and Nettie had exclaimed over them, and admired their dresses, and their hats, and their pretty curly hair, and been as bright and glad and pleased as a little girl could be. Now as she sat alone, thinking it all over, in spite of her resolution not to cry any more, the tears would gather in her eyes every few minutes, and now and then one of them would get the better of her and roll slowly down to her chin.

"Poor child!" Mrs. Beldon had said to herself with a sigh, as she went out of the door. "Poor brave little girl; she doesn't think mother knows how badly she feels, and she doesn't think mother knows the reason; but I do. I know all about it."

CHAPTER 2

What it Bought

I F I could only get her a little something to give!" Mrs. Beldon continued, thinking her sorrowful thoughts as she walked slowly down the street. "But I've turned things upside down to try to find something that we could spare, and I don't seem to have a thing this time. Poor Nettie doesn't wear out clothes like other girls, or outgrow them, so that I have any to give away; and I need every penny this winter. Yet it does seem too bad that she couldn't have a hand in it! If I should say anything to Sarah I believe she would contrive it somehow, but I don't know; it seems to me that Sarah has about all on her hands and heart that she ought to have. Maybe I will see something that I can buy—just a trifle that will do to send. I can spare ten cents, poor as I am, but I don't know what could be bought for ten cents to go in a barrel for a Christmas-tree. I suppose there are toys, but Nettie would like something that was going to do a mite of good. I know my little girl like a book; she longs to be helping somebody, and she cannot understand how she helps her mother." Then this poor mother brushed away the tears, because she knew only too well that the time was coming when they would have to live without Nettie.

It was so nearly dark when she came home, that she drew the curtains and lighted the lamp before she showed any of her purchases to Nettie, for this was one of Nettie's pleasures, to be shown every little thing that came into the house; if it were nothing more than a spool of thread it interested her, as having come from the outside world, the beautiful world where the boys and girls spent so much of their time. Sarah had not come in yet; she had examination papers to look over tonight, and would be unusually late, Robert told them. Then he buttoned his jacket, which was not warm enough for cold weather, tightly around him, drew down his cap—which was getting too small for him—as closely as he could, pulled on his mittens which his mother had knitted, and tramped off for the milk for Nettie's supper, and Nettie and her mother were alone.

"I have got something ever so nice to show you," Mrs. Beldon said, shaking the fire and adding fresh coal to make it curl up in blue flames, and shading the light from Nettie's eyes, while she looked at her carefully and discovered traces of tears, which Nettie thought she had quite hidden. "Something which I think you will like. I saw it at the store, and I couldn't help buying it for you, it was so cheap."

"Something for me, mother?" said Nettie, and she tried to look and feel interested. "You are always buying something for me. I wish it could be your turn once in a while."

"Nonsense!" said Mrs. Beldon briskly. "What do I want, pray? Not dresses, I can tell you; I am so tired of them that it doesn't seem to me that I shall ever want another of my own. I had a real fussing time with that wrapper this afternoon. Mrs. Smith never knows exactly how she wants a thing until after it is fixed; then she knows to a dot that she wants it entirely different from the way it is. But never mind Mrs. Smith. Wait till I get fresh water in the tea-kettle, and look after the apples in the oven, then I will show you something pretty."

Sure enough, by the time the tea-kettle had begun to sing, and the apples, which had burst all their skins, had been taken up and set to cool, Mrs. Beldon produced and untied an interesting-looking roll, and spread it out in triumph on the little stand which she drew up in front of Nettie. "There, isn't that pretty? It is exactly like the things I used to work when I was a little girl. I haven't seen one of them in I don't know how many years, yet I used to make them ever so often. When I saw it lying there on the counter I thought of you right away, and thinks I to myself: I do wish I could get one of those for Nettie to work for that barrel."

Nettie raised herself a little from among the pillows, and an eager look began to come into her eyes, while a delicate pink flush appeared on her pale cheek. "For the barrel, mother? Something that I can make?" She looked curiously at the cardboard spread out before her—very familiar material to her mother, but new to Nettie.

"What queer little dotted stuff!" she said. "What is that marked on it? Letters? Why, mother, does it read something?"

"Yes, indeed it does," said the mother triumphantly. "Here, let me hold it so that you can make it out. They are not very plain, you know: just a pattern to be worked. Take pretty blue or pink, or some kind of worsted or silk, and work the letters so that they stand out bright and clear. They are as pretty a thing as one need have. My, how many of them I used to make when I was a little girl!" She slipped a piece of paper under the cardboard, and then held it in the right light, so that Nettie could read quite distinctly: "Blessed are the pure in heart, for they shall see God."

She read slowly, picking out the words that wound in and out amid a sort of scroll-work.

"Why, mother, how very pretty! And how very queer! I never saw anything like it before."

"I have," said the mother. "Once I worked this very motto for my grandmother, and she had it framed and hung in her room. It hung there for years. I don't know what became of it at last; it was sold, I suppose, when all the things were. Grandmother set great store by it: she used to say she was going to keep it for her great grand-children; if she had, it would have been yours, Nettie. But there wasn't anything kept; what were not burned were sold. Never mind, I would rather you would make one for someone else than to have one of your own that I had made, any day. Don't you think you would like to work this, and put it in the barrel for some of those poor girls to hang up on their wall? They would like it first-rate, I know."

"Could I work it, do you think?" asked Nettie doubtfully. "Why, it is all full of little holes where the letters are, isn't it?"

"Of course," said her mother briskly. "Those are the places where the needle goes through, back and forth, a real pretty cross stitch. *Do* it? "Of course you could. It is a good deal easier than some things you have done, and I can show you how exactly. I was going to get some worsteds to work it with, but I thought perhaps Sarah could attend to that better than I. Then I thought you would have your own notion about what colors you wanted, too; they don't cost a great deal; you can have any colors you please. It will be as pretty a thing to send away down South as you could possibly have."

When Sarah came home she expressed her pleasure in the motto; perhaps not so heartily as her mother, for Sarah knew that it was very old-fashioned.

"Still," she said to herself, "it is Bible words, and they are very pretty when they are worked. I don't know why it would not be a pretty thing to go out there among those poor children." By the time she had reasoned this out she spoke joyfully to Nettie: "It is just the thing, dear. Think it will hang on some little girl's wall, perhaps, and comfort her when she is trying to be good, and remind her when she feels like letting evil thoughts get possession of her heart, how important it is to keep it pure. I will get you the worsteds tomorrow, or perhaps this evening. Robbie can go out with me, so that you can have tomorrow to work at it. Yes, that will be the best, because they are getting the barrel ready very rapidly now. What color do you think you would like?"

And before she had even taken off her rubbers, or put away her things, she drew a chair by Nettie's side, and together they studied the letters in the scroll-work, and settled what shades would be the best. Nettie grew eager and interested; she could imagine just how the motto would look when it was finished and hanging on some white wall, telling its own story.

"It is like a little piece of a wall-roll, isn't it?" she said to Sarah. "I read in a Sunday-school book a few days ago about a wall-roll that a woman looked at—a sick woman—and the verse kept her all day from being cross, when she had a dreadful pain in her side. I was thinking, Sarah, that I ought to have a wall-roll sometimes, to keep me from being cross."

"Are you ever cross?" asked Sarah, stooping and kissing her. "If you are you hide it down in your own little heart, and nobody sees it. I have often and often wondered how you could be so patient, and thought if it was I that had to sit there day by day I could not do it."

"Oh, yes, you could," said Nettie, "because, you see, you would have to, if it was you; and as for being cross, I am cross inside often. And look at the words, Sarah: 'Blessed are the pure in heart.' It isn't being 'pure in heart' to have a cross inside."

"But the heart tries very hard not to let the cross come outside," Sarah said, with another loving kiss. "I know all about it, Nettie. Or no, I don't; I can't know half how hard it is, but I can imagine enough to make you a wonder to me, because you are so patient and good."

Then Nettie smiled lovingly on her grown-up sister, and said to herself that she certainly would have a very naughty heart indeed if she wasn't thankful for such a home, and such a mother and sister.

Then she studied the motto again. "It ought to have a frame," she said reflectively, "and be a real picture. How I wish it could be framed; but then, of course, we can't do that, can we, Sarah?"

"I am afraid not," said Sarah cheerfully. "Frames cost a good deal of money, you know."

"Yes; I didn't expect one for a minute. I am afraid this cost a good deal of money. Mother, how much did you have to pay for it? You couldn't afford to buy it, I am afraid."

"Yes," said Mrs. Beldon briskly, "that is the nice part of the story that you have not heard yet. I must tell you about it. I had been wondering what we would get for your barrel, and had counted out my money and made all my plans; and I said to myself, 'If there is a thing which can be bought for ten cents that is worthwhile for Nettie to send, why, I shall buy it; we can spare so much for poor people, I guess.' But I was rather down-hearted, because I could not think of anything which would please you, that could likely be bought for ten cents. I was thinking about it all the while I was getting my spools of thread and my tape and things at the store, and all of a sudden I saw on the counter this motto, so like old times that it seemed to me I had gone back to my childhood. I seized hold of it as if it were an old friend and read the words, and I guess my eyes got pretty dim looking at them, for it is the very same verse, you know, that used to hang in my room. I said to the clerk, how much is this? 'That?' he said, looking thoughtfully at it. 'It is the only one we have; it got packed away in an old box, among some goods that we used to keep a long time ago: we have been straightening out things for the last few days, and came across that. They used to be in great demand, you know, but they have gone out, this many a year.' 'Yes,' I told him, but the words read just the same that they did when they were in fashion; they hadn't gone out. He laughed, and said most people forgot about the words, and only looked at the way they were put; and then, if you will believe it, he said if I wanted to give him five cents for it I could have it; he was sure he didn't know what the thing was worth."

"Five cents!" said Nettie, in great delight. "Why, mother, such a pretty thing, and so large for five cents!"

"Yes," said Mrs. Belden complacently, "and they used to cost thirty and forty cents, and some of them that had a great deal of fancy work about them were as high as fifty. I remember it distinctly, so you can imagine how pleased I was to get it for five. Now I have five cents left for something else. If that would only frame it."

"Oh, but there are the worsteds to buy," said Nettie.

"Sure enough! And you want three or four colors, don't you? How lucky I was not to spend it on a frame."

It snowed a little that evening, but nobody said anything about it to Nettie. "Just a few big flakes," Sarah said in the kitchen to her mother, "and Robbie and I don't mind it any more than if we were snow-birds, do we, Robbie? I think I would better go; I shall not have time to go out in the morning and come back again before school, you know, and I am afraid Nettie will be restless tomorrow unless she can be at work on the motto. Besides, they want to send that barrel off on Monday, and she would have to work too steadily if she had to do it in one day. So we will just skip around to the store, and if we get wet, why, we will change our clothes when we come home."

"I haven't any clothes to change," said Robert, as he stamped bravely through the new-fallen snow at Sarah's side. "I have on the only pair of trousers I have at present."

"Never mind, if you get wet you can skip off to bed. You will not mind going an hour earlier for the sake of giving Nettie a pleasant time tomorrow, will you?"

"Of course not," said Robert, and on they went.

CHAPTER 3

Work That Grew Out of It

THE motto proved to be very interesting work. Nettie learned in a few minutes how to do it; then her only trouble was that it was hard to lay the work aside and take her usual rest. In the afternoon she had company. Mrs. Beldon went across the road to her neighbor, Mrs. Stone, to help her finish a little dress which was to go in the barrel, and Carrie Stone came over and took her place beside Nettie, bringing her work, which was a pretty, soft hat that she was trimming with velvet.

"I wish I could have a peep at the little girl who is going to wear this hat," she said, holding it up at just the right angle, and studying it critically. "I don't know whether to make that trimming higher in front or not; it all depends, you see, on the kind of girl who is going to wear it. And another thing, I don't know but this green velvet would have looked better than the color I have chosen. It is great fun to send them hats and things. Don't you think so, Nettie?"

"It is very nice," said Nettie, "to be able to do it. Is that the hat you wore last summer, Carrie?"

"Yes," said Carrie; "it's an old thing, of course, but mamma thought it would do for those children away down there, especially if they are as badly off for clothes as Mrs. Carpenter says."

"Why, I think it will be lovely," said Nettie. "It looks almost like a new one just out of the store. You ought to be a milliner, Carrie, you have such a talent for trimming hats."

Carrie laughed a little scornfully. "I am fond of fussing over hats," she said, "but I should not like to be a milliner; I aspire higher than that. I am going to be a school teacher, I think, or a music teacher; I should delight above all things to be a music teacher; but it does cost so much to take lessons. Papa says each term that he does not know as he can afford it any longer. What are you going to be, Nettie? Oh! I forgot. What a mean, careless question for me to ask you. I was thinking for the moment that you were Anna Potter."

"Never mind," said Nettie gently. "Of course you cannot always remember; besides I am going to try to be something myself. I have thought more about it since I have been making this motto than I ever did before, and I am truly going to try to be pure in heart."

"You dear little thing," said Carrie, who was nearly two years older than Nettie, and felt at least five years older, "you are that already; you will not have to try."

"Oh, no!" said Nettie earnestly. "I am very far from that. Sometimes I am as glad as can be that even mother cannot see my heart; it is just full of unhappy, fretful thoughts. You can't think how much trouble I have had over this barrel, because I could not help get things for it. I knew I couldn't, you know, or at least I thought I couldn't; but it seemed impossible to put it away and be contented. I told myself that it was just dreadful to be so poor that I could not buy so much as one little thing, so as to be counted in with the class; I even cried about it, Carrie, though I did not let mother or Sarah know. I am sure I don't know how mother found out that I cared so much, only mothers always seem to find out everything; I kept it all in my heart. What a snarled-up looking heart I must have! And then mother came home with this lovely motto and showed me how to work it, and I felt right away as though I did not deserve to have such a thing as that happen to me, after I had been cross about it."

"What an odd little creature you are," said Carrie. "I tell you what it is, Nettie Beldon, I wish I was half as good as you are, then I should be contented. I don't think it matters much about being cross in your heart if you can keep it to yourself. Dear me, I never succeed in keeping my crossness in. Only this morning I was in such a rage! I slammed the door so that Mamma called me back three times to shut it quietly. And it just seemed as if I couldn't shut it without slamming. I got so provoked at Aunt Susan. She is the most provoking old aunt that was ever made, anyway—always poking at me, finding fault with something I do or don't do, as if it was any of her business! I am not her girl, and I do wish she could remember it, and mind her own affairs. There now, you see how I talk; I get cross just as soon as I begin to think about Aunt Susan. I was awfully cross at her this morning. I even told her that I wished she lived a hundred miles away, and that I needn't have to see her again for six years. Yes, I did, as true as you live! Mother scolded me for it, and that was what made me slam the door. If you had to live with Aunt Susan you would understand how it was, and not try to keep the 'cross' all inside. I might do it if I lived with your mother and sister Sarah, for I think they are both too lovely for anything; but Aunt Susan is another matter, I can tell you."

"I don't know," said Nettie gently. "I don't suppose any kind of living is easy down here in this world; things go all criss-cross sometimes even when you are alone, and have no one to fret at. I never slam doors, of course, but perhaps I would if I could get to them; and I think it makes a great deal of difference what you have in your heart, because if it didn't, what would this verse mean?"

"Oh, the verse?" said Carrie. "I don't know. I don't pretend to understand Bible verses; they mean too much, all of them. I am sure if I ever succeed in getting good-natured outside I shall not trouble about my heart."

"But I don't believe you ever will get good-natured outside unless it begins inside," said Nettie. "Don't you remember Miss Schuyler's allegory at that last mission band we had here? How the little girl had a poison plant in her heart, and tried to make it blossom roses?"

"Miss Schuyler is too fanciful," said Carrie. "I never did understand her. Would you put this bright steel buckle on this hat, or do you think it would look too much fussed-up for that kind of a little girl?"

"I don't know," said Nettie. "Don't poor little girls like 'fussed-up' things? I should like a buckle on my hat if I were going to wear one." Then she wondered how she should get back to the subject from which Carrie had so heedlessly turned. She wanted so much to ask her, now that they were alone, if she remembered the promise they all made to Miss Schuyler, nearly three months ago, to read a few verses in the Bible every day, and to pray a prayer right out of their own hearts at least every morning. The verse that Miss Schuyler had given them was what she called their motto prayer: "Create in me a clean heart, O, Lord, and renew a right spirit within me." How could Carrie be praying that prayer, and yet say that she would not be troubled about her heart if she could act right outside? It was the heart which troubled Nettie most. She realized so fully how much easier it was, at least for a person who lived the quiet sheltered life she did, to act right than to have right thoughts.

"Carrie," she began timidly, "you remember our motto prayer, don't you, that Miss Schuyler gave us? That has made me think a good deal about trying to keep the heart right. Doesn't it help you?"

"No," said Carrie, frankly, "I don't know that it ever helped me. To tell the truth, I forget about it most of the time. Oh, I say the prayer over whenever I think of it, but I don't see as I am a bit different from what I was last fall. There is a great difference in people, anyhow; some are naturally gentle and good-tempered, and all that, and some are quick. Mamma says I always was a quick-tempered little thing—went off like gunpowder at the slightest touch. If I had a gentle disposition like yours it would be different. You ought to see the hat Laura Saunders is trimming for that barrel. It is going to be a real dowdy thing; I wouldn't give it to one of the little Dutch children down the lane, but she seems as set up about it as possible. She says it has a real feather on it—a real rooster's feather, I guess; it looks like that, anyhow. Oh, there are some funny things to go in that barrel! I guess the people will laugh when they get it, or else they will curl up their noses. I should, if I were poor, and such trash was sent to me. I think we ought to send real nice things to people, if we send anything. Now this hat of mine is old, to be sure, but I have trimmed it up real nice, so that nobody need be ashamed to wear it. I could wear it myself on a pinch, if I were a poor girl and needed it. Well, Nettie, I have finished my work, and I believe I will have to go; I want to run in and see how Maud is getting along with her things. We girls are each going to trim a hat, and I want to see if any of them look prettier than mine. I don't believe it; they did not have as nice materials to begin with."

So Nettie was left alone to think. She was forming the last letter of the word "heart," and the sentence stood out beautifully now: "Blessed are the pure in heart." Could Carrie be trying to be pure in heart, and talk about it so lightly? And she had broken the promise she made to Miss Schuyler.

"Perhaps I should be just like her," said Nettie, "if I could fly about as she can, and had so many things to think of. Perhaps that is the reason God does not let me get out of my chair. Then why does he let Carrie? Perhaps it is because he is going to take me in such a little while to see him, that makes me feel different from the others. But then, they ought all to try. Oh, I don't know anything about it; but I wish I could have said something to Carrie. I wish I could do something for somebody to try to help them. I wonder if this motto will help anybody? If it is only a pretty thing to hang on the wall and look at, that won't do any real truly good. I must pray," said Nettie, her face growing graver yet, but settling into a quiet look of satisfaction. "I must pray about it a great deal, and I must get mother and Sarah to pray, and Miss Schuyler and the girls. I must get them to ask Him to use the Bible verse—his own Bible verse—to help somebody to get pure in heart. What a beautiful thing that would be to do! Then in a long, long while, perhaps after I have been in heaven ever and ever so many years, somebody will come up to me and say, Are you Nettie Beldon? And when I tell her I am, she will say, 'Well, an angel just told me that you were the one who sent that motto to our school, "Blessed are the pure in heart, for they shall see God," and it made me want to be pure in heart, and I tried, and here I am in heaven.'" At this point Nettie dropped her needle, and clasped her hands in an ecstasy of delight.

By the middle of the next afternoon the motto was done, and bound around the edges with a bit of blue ribbon which Sarah had secured for it, nobody but herself knowing just how. The next thing was to pack the barrel. Mrs. Beldon took an hour out of her busy life and went to help, more especially so that she could describe to Nettie minutely all the various treasures which were tucked within it, and look herself after the motto, to see that the box which held it was placed where it could not be crushed. It certainly was a very interesting barrel, indeed. In addition to the clothing— all of it useful, and some of it very pretty—which the mothers of the girls contributed, and the extremely pretty hats, and shoes almost as good as new, but outgrown, which came in from various sources, there were ribbons and bits of lace for dressing dolls, and toys of all descriptions. The effort had begun, as I told you, with the girls of Nettie's class; but it had grown and grown until they almost failed to recognize their work. Different members of the Sunday-school heard of the plan, and asked if they might send something, and it ended in the very youngest of the children bringing each his or her toy to contribute.

"There is no barrel that will hold all the things," said the packing committee, looking around them in astonishment at the piles and piles of goods which were to be crowded in. It proved in the end that they sent two barrels and a small box.

"The more the better," said Mrs. Brewster, pushing with all her might on a package of stockings, to make them settle down into their place and take less room; "I was reading about that Sunday-school only last night. There is an article in *The Times*, quoted from one of their Southern papers, and they do need help tremendously, now that's a fact. You see, it is a city made up very largely indeed of people from the North, who go off in the spring and come late in the fall, and don't care very much about the people, anyway. They are not the class, I guess, who work very much among poor people; they just come down there to eat oranges, take rides through the pine woods, and have a good time generally, and expect to go back to their own fixed-up churches and Sunday-schools whenever they get ready. They don't care much about other people; that is the way it looks to us here, anyway. I am glad we have got so many things to send; the committee will know how to dispose of them."

I don't know as it would be possible to describe to you the excitement there was in a certain house in that far-away city when those barrels finally arrived. They made a quick journey; on the sixth day from the time they were rolled into a freight car in the town where Nettie lived they were rolled out at their destination, and set upon the platform in triumph. The day they started it was so stormy that most of the girls who had intended to go to the depot to see that the barrels were tenderly handled, were obliged to give it up. It not only snowed, but the wind blew, sending the snow with great whirling eddies into people's faces, and piling it up in drifts in the most unexpected places; more than that, it was so cold that the people said they did not see how it could snow; and the steps of the house where the barrel was packed were so slippery that Johnny Webster, one of the boys, lost his footing and came down the steps as though he had been a sled sliding down hill; and the boys who were waiting for him on the sidewalk below laughed, one of them with all his might, while the other exclaimed, and inquired anxiously if he were hurt. Two women who were passing stopped to inquire, and also to assure him that he ought to be careful, "Those steps are very icy."

"As if I didn't know that!" said Johnny, rubbing his sides in dismay; and as the women moved on he gave his attention to the boys. "I think it was awful mean in you to stand there laughing, just because a fellow has rolled downstairs."

"What hurt does laughing do?" asked good-natured Tim Brady, shaking his sides again. "It keeps me warm, and I saw you wasn't going to be hurt much; you were just coming down bumpity-bump, as a sleigh does when it comes to pitch holes, you know," and Tim laughed again at the recollection.

CHAPTER 4

How It was Received

I T is a real horrid day!" said Susie Porter, who had rounded the corner but a minute before, and stopped to inquire if there were any bones broken. "It seems too funny for anything, to think of their sending off little white dresses and summer sacks and things in those barrels. I don't believe there is summer anywhere this time of year."

"Pooh!" said Johnny. "Much you know about it. They go a-walking in the woods, and take their suppers along; and they eat their dinners out on the piazza sometimes right in the middle of winter. My father has been down in that country, and he knows all about it."

"I don't believe it," said Susie stoutly. "It is a good deal warmer than it is here, maybe, and I suppose there isn't any snow—the geography says there isn't—but it is cold, of course, and if they eat their dinners out on the piazza I believe they do it just to say they did, and are cold all the time. I don't believe those white dresses and things they sent will do a speck of good before the first of May, anyhow. That is a whole month earlier than we can wear white dresses here."

And although Johnny, with his wider knowledge, tried to make Susie understand the probabilities of a tropical climate, she scoffed at it all. She had lived in four different places in her short life, and had never seen a December which was not cold, and more or less stormy and slippery and disagreeable, and she did not think that there was any place in this country, anyway, that wasn't so. If only Susie could have gone with the barrels, or been in town the day they arrived, how astonished would she have been. The little lake—one of the many which beautified that part of the world—looked so blue, and still, and lovely, lying in the golden sunlight, and the water-oaks, and the little willows, and magnolias, and palm branches were so green and glistening. And the mocking-birds which flitted from branch to branch sang such lovely summer songs, and all the air was so still and balmy: it would have been almost impossible to realize that it was December, and that there were eager people in many a house along the banks of that river talking about a Christmas-tree; wondering what it would be like, and what fruit would grow on it for them.

Susie knew all about Christmas-trees; she had helped the boys hunt for them in the woods many a time, and clapped her mittened hands, and jumped up and down to keep from freezing; but a Christmas-tree when the birds were singing, and the river was flowing by, and some of the orange-trees were in bloom, and flowers and sunshine were everywhere, and the people were saying, "Oh, dear, how warm it is" would have been a bewildering experience to Susie.

They had a great time unpacking those barrels and trimming that Christmas-tree. Trimming the church, indeed, so that it would do justice to the tree. Miss Southey, one of the teachers, a young lady who was picking flowers in December for the first time in her life, brought her hands full of them to help trim the pulpit, and wished at least a dozen times while she was at work that her old pastor, who would probably have to plunge through snowdrifts to reach his pulpit on Christmas Day, could see the lovely things she had spread about her. Then Mrs. Carpenter called to her to come and assist in marking the dollies, and toys, and clothing.

"We have quantities of it," she said eagerly. "There is more than enough for a present for each child. I believe each one can have two; something useful, and something pretty. Do look at these hats, Miss Southey, aren't they lovely? The girls in that society I told you of made those. Won't they be just the things for some of the children in your class? I noticed a little girl among your scholars last Sunday who wore a shabby old sunbonnet. Won't her eyes, grow large, though, when she sees this hat, for instance, all trimmed up in velvet? And look at those dollies! Aren't they too cute for anything? Here is a fashionable lady, and here is one beside her dressed in the olden style. I don't know which is the cunningest, for my part. What a time we shall have marking all these things so as not to create heart-burnings and start any number of quarrels! Here is a box. Dear me! how carefully it is tied up; there must-be a very special treasure inside."

It was Nettie Beldon's box, from which eager fingers were untying the pink strings that had been so carefully wound about it by Sarah's deft fingers. At last the cover was off, then a fold of paper, then a fold of cotton.

"Dear me!" said Mrs. Carpenter again. "How very precious this must be. I am quite trembling with excitement, aren't you?" And then was revealed to them Nettie's cardboard motto.

Mrs. Carpenter laughed until the tears started. "The idea!" she said, when she could speak. "What a ridiculous thing, done up as if it had been real lace, or porcelain, or something of that sort. One of those old-fashioned cardboard things that went out I don't know how many years ago. They can be bought for a mere song in places where they can be bought at all. What a thing to send to a mission Sunday-school away down here! Who do you suppose will care for it? Isn't that exactly like some people? They want to have the name of sending something, no matter how worthless it is.

"It is very neatly done," said Miss Southey, taking Nettie's precious card in her hand, and looking at the careful stitches around the edge, and at the careful shaping of each letter, very neatly done indeed. "Some little girl has sent it, Mrs. Carpenter, who thinks it is a treasure, perhaps; and really it is Bible words, you know."

"Oh, of course! But the question is, who have we that will care for such a thing? If it were painted and framed it would be something worth having. I shouldn't mind having it myself, then; but those old cardboard things! I don't know what do with it. I wonder who could have sent it? Why, here is the name on the box—Nettie Beldon. Oh, I know now; she is a poor little hunchbacked girl. I saw her once; she can't walk at all, I believe. I suppose they have let her send it just to amuse her, though it does seem to me they might have gotten her a dollie an inch long to dress, or something that would have been worth sending. What shall we do with it, Miss Southey? There isn't a child who will want it instead of these toys and things."

"Oh," said Miss Southey, "let us hang it on the tree. It will look pretty among the branches this evening, and perhaps we shall find some way to dispose of it."

"Well, we can tell the child we used it for an ornament, and we will hope there are some people so benighted as to consider it ornamental. I do think these are the most hideous things; so stiff, you know. I wonder that people ever thought them pretty, though, in my early childhood, I can remember that it was quite fashionable to work them."

"I never saw any," said Miss Southey, studying it curiously. "I don't know why it is not a pretty idea; we print Bible verses and hang them on our walls, sometimes—I always thought it a pretty custom—why not work them carefully? Who knows, Mrs. Carpenter, but it may accomplish some good in the world?"

"I am sure I hope it will," said Mrs. Carpenter, laughing; "but I haven't myself, the least idea what to do with it. There might be some old grandmother somewhere, if we only knew where, who would like it for the sake of the association; but as for the children, they got beyond that sort of thing long ago. It is just like Nettie Beldon, though, to work it; she is a little old-fashioned creature, a pretty-faced child, and the family are poor. I suppose this came into her possession in some way, and she had nothing else to send. Oh, we will stick it up, as you say, for ornament, and write them a glowing account of how lovely it looked." And she laughed merrily as she fastened it with pins to the long arms of the lovely pine-tree.

Then the dollies were arranged—how charming they looked in their beautiful dresses, or their quaint old-fashioned ones—and the balls, and tops, and kites, and jackknives, and shoes, and handkerchiefs, and gloves, and pin-cushions, and I don't know what all, were marked and hung. It was a long puzzling task. Mrs. Carpenter and Miss Southey, and others of the committee, who gathered soon afterwards, worked industriously all the long bright day, and only succeeded in getting the last thing hung as the sun slipped away behind the pine-trees, and the sudden darkness, which in that climate follows his departure, fell upon the Southern day.

"There," said Mrs. Carpenter, "the sun is gone; now in five minutes more we shall not be able to see our hands before us. But we are all done, aren't we? Isn't this the last thing, Miss Southey?"

"Yes," said Miss Southey, holding up a belated dollie; "I believe the last child is provided for, when I get this young lady seated. There are a number of dollies and a few garments left. It seems a pity to have anything left. I suppose there are poor children in the neighborhood who will go without presents. If we only knew who they were!"

"Oh, we will keep them," said Mrs. Carpenter. "They will do for presents with which to reward new-comers in the future. They will be very nice stock in trade. How I wish the lamps were lighted so we could see the creation of our hands. It will look very lovely, I think. I am charmed with the presents; most of them have been just what we needed."

"Yes," said Miss Southey again, speaking in an absent tone. Her eyes fixed once more upon the motto, at which she had looked from time to time, during the afternoon. Just before the sun set, it had streamed in, and resting on the motto seemed to glorify the words, "Blessed are the pure in heart."

"They are wonderful words," said Miss Southey to herself. 'Pure in heart'—how much it covers. I wonder if anybody ever is really pure in heart?' I should like to be. What a wonderful life it must be: and then the reward is so wonderful—They shall see God.' It must be something different from seeing him at the judgment: everybody will do that. This is a kind of seeing that will bring joy with it, perhaps, though I do not know how anybody can think of seeing God and not be afraid. I wish I understood the verse. Perhaps I would better take the motto myself and hang it in my own room, and see what it will say to me."

But all this was shut up in her own heart. Mrs. Carpenter had pointed out the motto to the members of the committee, and had laughed over it so much that Miss Southey began to have almost a feeling of affection for it, or protection. She could not help thinking of the poor little hunchbacked girl, who sat always in her chair, Mrs. Carpenter said, and who had made it, and sent her heart with it, perhaps.

"Poor little thing," said Miss Southey. "I believe I will find out just what her address is, and write her a letter telling her how pretty her motto is to me: and I won't say a word about how the others despise it. I wish I knew somebody, some dear old lady to give it to, who would love it."

It was a very interested audience which gathered later in the evening, to see the wonderful blossoming tree, laden with such fruit as they had never before imagined upon a tree. Young men and young women, and large boys and girls, and little boys and girls, young mothers with their babies, and little dots just old enough to toddle around, all swarmed and crowded and pushed to the front as far as they were able, and were one and all so astonished at the tree, so eager to study its fruits, so eager above all to possess some of them for themselves, that it was almost impossible to hold at least the younger ones in check while the singing and the recitations and the speech-making went on. In fact, right in the midst of the superintendent's most eloquent sentence little Fannie Norton's excitement became too much for her.

"Only see that yellow-haired dollie with blue eyes and a blue sash," she said. "Isn't she just too lovely?" and threw back her head against the mortified girl behind her and laughed outright.

For a moment the superintendent frowned, then he looked at the eager little face and spread-out hands, and smiled with the audience, and resolved, like the wise young man that he was, to cut his speech short, and not torture those poor little creatures any longer. And at last, at last, it was time to gather the fruits. Then such excitement as there was! You must imagine it, for I am sure it could not be described. Name after name was called, and as the happy owners slipped out of their seats, and went their way down the aisle and returned again presently, sometimes with a dollie clasped in both loving arms, sometimes with a new hat mounted on a triumphant head, sometimes with both hands so full of treasures that the owners had to elbow their way through the crowd in the aisle, their faces would have made a study for an artist. Such queer, quaint little people, some of them.

There was Tiny Bolter, for instance, whom everybody knew as the best scholar for her age in the district school, and whose sweet grave face looked actually pale with excitement as she came down from the tree with an open book clasped lovingly against her heart, while her right hand grasped a fan. "A real truly fan, that open and shut, and was just precisely like the one Miss Southey carried on Sunday." So Tiny thought. Had she not admired that with all her might for weeks and weeks?

Following close behind her was an odd contrast; Gretchen, a little German girl, whose parents had come across the sea and settled0 a few months before in this Southland. Gretchen was dressed after the fashion of her grandmother, with a very long dress, and a very wide white collar, and very wide cuffs on her queer wrists, and with a curious little half cap, half bonnet, on her head. A pretty picture was Gretchen, and she carried her treasure, whatever it was, clasped in both hands. It looked so small, that although the audience stretched their necks on both sides they could not determine what it was. Gretchen was so utterly absorbed in studying the little wires connected with it, and the bright cord that hung from it, that she forgot the presence of everybody, and walked down the aisle not looking to the right nor the left, thinking only of her lovely little knitting-machine—only she did not know that was the name of it. In no such frame of mind was Harry Jenkins, who, starting at the same time down the other aisle, held a great painted ball in both hands, and was so embarrassed by the size of the ball and the number of people looking at him and laughing, that he actually put the ball to his mouth in a fit of absent-mindedness, and tried to bite a piece out of it, as he would out of a great orange.

CHAPTER 5

Where It was Left

SITTING apart from the merry groups, watching with keen eyes every movement that was made, was an old, worn, wrinkled woman, with a mouth sunken in to show where the teeth once had been, with a bonnet as old-fashioned in its way as little Gretchen's, from which drooped a queer, long, old-fashioned veil. The bonnet strings were tied under her chin in a very old-fashioned bow, and altogether, no queerer picture for the artist's pencil could have been found than old Mrs. Jenks, who surprised everybody by coming out to the Christmas-tree. She lived in a forlorn house a long distance from the room where the Sunday-school gathered, and which the people called a church, though it looked very unlike the churches to which you are accustomed, and she never came out to the Sunday services.

"Keep boarders," she explained, her face looking more sallow and wrinkled than ever, as she talked with the ladies who were in search of Sunday-school scholars. "I keep boarders myself; that is about all that I can do. They are railroad hands, most of them, and they eat like all possessed; especially Sundays, when they ain't got anything else to do, 'pears like they eat up everything I can get together. It takes me from morning till night to fry, and bake, and stew, and scrub, and fuss for them men; I ain't been to meetin' in—I don't know *when*. My house is always full, and I am always at work, and I ain't no children to send to the Sunday-school, which is a mercy, for I never could get them ready if I had: and I ain't got things to wear to go myself, if I had time to go, nor the strength to get there if I had the things." So they had been obliged to leave Mrs. Jenks to her dreary life: yet here she was at the Christmas-tree. Her face looked as wrinkled as ever, and her mouth set in such queer puckers that one not acquainted with her would have thought she was offended at the whole thing, and was pursing up her lips against it. Poor Mrs. Jenks! Some of the gay groups looked at her curiously, giving her a passing thought, and that was all. Nobody spoke to her—why should they? What was there that could be said to Mrs. Jenks?

Miss Southey looked at her timidly for a few minutes, and wished she knew some pleasant word to speak to her. How old and worn her face looked.

"I wonder why she came?" said Miss Southey to herself. "She is not in sympathy with this thing, surely. She must have came out of curiosity, to see what foolish things we would do in the name of the Sunday-school. Poor old creature! I suppose she never saw the like in her life before."

Oh, dear Miss Southey, you are very much mistaken! Once Mrs. Jenks was a little girl with brown wavy hair, and eyes that were bright, and lips that were always breaking into a laugh, and she wore a pink calico dress with short sleeves, and nankeen pantalets, and had her hair braided down her back, and was called one of the prettiest girls in the row; and she went to Sunday-school in a little red school-house, away off among the snowy hills of Vermont—tramped there through the snows in winter, sauntered there through the green meadows in summer, and loved every foot of the road, and every bird, and flower, and twig, yes, and snow-bank, that she met on her journey: and they had a Christmas-tree, once; a wonderful Christmas-tree! And Mrs. Jenks went down the aisle, just as some of the little girls do that she is watching now; went down at the call of her name, and got for her present a sampler worked for her by her own mother, with all the letters of the alphabet upon it; capitals, and small letters, and figures, and her own name and her mother's name. And Mrs. Jenks has that sampler yet, folded in a sheet of tissue paper that is yellow with age, and smells of lavender, packed away at the bottom of a box, which in its turn is away at the bottom of a trunk that she seldom opens. And Mrs. Jenks thinks of the sampler tonight, and of the brown-haired girl, and of the children who were with her, and of the mother who had dressed her to go. She set her lips firmly, in those hard lines, so they should not quiver: and she dropped her veil lower over her queer bonnet, because she felt that her dim eyes were growing dimmer, and she was afraid somebody would see the gleam of tears. Poor Mrs. Jenks! Miss Southey looked at her, and then at Nettie's motto banging high on the tree. No name was on the motto; they had not been able to find anyone whom they thought would want it.

"What if I should give it to Mrs. Jenks?" said Miss Southey. "Who knows but that it might speak to her heart? Surely she has a heart, if she does look so hard and sallow and old. I have almost a mind to get it down and write her name upon it, and have it called out."

Oh, Miss Southey! If you had only been entirely a mind to do that sweet, kind thing, what might it not have done for Mrs. Jenks? But no, after a few minutes thought Miss Southey shook her head. "I would better not," she said. "Don't know her at all, and I don't know how she would take it. Perhaps she would be offended at having her name called out; they say she is a queer, hard old woman. Perhaps she would make fun of the verse, and of poor Nettie's work; I cannot have any more people sneering at poor little hump-back Nettie. We will let the motto hang." And so Miss Southey lost her opportunity to do something which might have set the angels in Heaven to singing, and turned and gave her attention to the boy who "didn't want no present."

This was none other than Tommy Dorn, who stood with his hands in his pockets, and his hat drawn well over his face, and a scornful look in his eyes, watching the proceedings from afar. He had not crowded up to the front, he had refused to take off his cap and "be treated like a gentleman," as one of the officers of the school invited him to do.

"I don't want no present," he had said to the boys, who asked him eagerly what he expected to get. "I don't expect nothin'; I don't want nothin'."

What was the matter with Tommy Dorn? A very ill-mannered, sullen little boy, you would have called him surely, if you had overheard his words and seen his face. Yet Tommy Dorn is an illustration of the fact that we must not be too hasty in our judgments in this world. He was not behaving very well, it is true: that was because he had never been taught to behave any better; but down in his heart, away down where nobody could see it, was a sense of honor stronger, a great deal, than filled the heart of the curly-headed, well-behaved little boy who sat in the very front row, and waved his hand jubilantly when his name was called.

Miss Southey had been going down the aisle to carry a dollie to a little creature who was wedged in between grown people, and was too shy to come for it herself, and she heard the loud-spoken, almost contemptuous words, "I don't want no present, I tell you, and I don't expect none!" She turned and looked in the direction of the speaker. In a few moments she came quietly to his side.

"What is the matter, Tommy?" she asked, speaking low. "What is the reason you do not want any Christmas present tonight?"

"'Cause," said Tommy, and he thrust his hands further into his pockets.

"Of course," said Miss Southey, good naturedly, "there is a cause, I haven't the least doubt of it; I was asking you to give it to me. Don't you like our presents? Don't you think the tree looks pretty?"

"'Course," said Tommy; "red and pink and blue things always look pretty when put together. I never see them on a tree before, but they shine and look pretty."

"It is strange fruit to grow on a tree, but what I do not understand is, why a boy with such good judgment as yours shouldn't want some of it for his own."

"What's the use in wanting things?" asked Tommy.

"Why, one use is," said Miss Southey, "that it is a step towards getting them sometimes. If I want a thing very much, and there is nothing to hinder, I generally set about trying to get it."

"'Course," said Tommy, his common sense convinced by this logic, "but s'pose there is things to hinder?"

"Even then it depends upon what the things are. If they hinder me when they ought not, and I can get them out of the way, why I set about it, and get them out of the way as soon as I can: but if they ought to hinder, and convince me by their being there that I ought not to have the thing, why, that is another matter: of course my good judgment tells me then to give up and try for something else."

There was a flash of acquiescence in Tommy's eyes which interested Miss Southey. "Is there something in the way of your having a present tonight?" she asked, determined to get at the truth of the mystery.

"Yes'm, there is," said Tommy, in his most decided tone; "and it ain't one of them things that is going to get out of the way, neither; I won't be so downright mean as that if I never get no presents off a tree: and I never did, and I don't expect to."

"Tell me about it, Tommy," said Miss Southey. "Tell me the things that are in the way, won't you? There are special reasons why I would like to know."

"'Taint nothin' much," said Tommy, "only I ain't been to Sunday-school, not in six Sundays, maybe more than that. I could have come if I had a-wanted to, but I went off a-fishing and a-rowing, and things, and didn't come: and now I ain't going to be so low-down mean as to come tonight and expect a present off of that there tree, and expect to have my name called out just as if I had been there. I don't expect it at all; I told all the boys so, and I don't want none neither, 'cause there won't be no sense nor reason to it."

"Do you mean, Tommy, that you would not think it honorable in you to receive a present?" said Miss Southey, and there was a curious little ring of gladness in her voice: she was so surprised and pleased to find this little germ of honor in the heart of a boy, where she least suspected it. Poor Tommy had not much encouragement in his forlorn home to be honorable about anything.

He turned and looked at her with a sort of wondering gaze when he noticed that little tremor in her voice. But his own was gruff enough as he answered, "I s'pose that's the word. I don't know your high and mighty words. I call it low-down mean to take a present when you don't deserve it, or to want one, and I don't mean to neither."

"But, Tommy, suppose a teacher in the school who knew you very well, knew you had been away from Sunday-school for two months, and knew where you had spent your Sundays, and that you could have come if you had wanted to, yet for all that had felt as she was trimming the tree as though she wanted to have you come tonight, and had picked out a bright new jack-knife with four blades, and a white handle, and had tied a card to it with your name on it, because she wanted you to get it, wouldn't that make a difference? It wouldn't be low-down mean to take such a present as that, would it?"

Tommy stared, and was silent for several seconds. Then he asked, almost fiercely, "What would she want him to have it for?"

It was Miss Southey's turn to hesitate; only for a moment, then she spoke briskly. "She wanted him to have it because she thought he would like it; she thought perhaps he had never had a knife, and that he was old enough to have one, and would like it, and perhaps when he got it and thought about it, how the teacher remembered him enough to want him to have it, it would make him feel as though he would like to go to Sunday-school again just to please her, and that next Sunday and the Sunday after when he wanted to go fishing or rowing, instead he would come up here to the school, because he knew she was watching for him and would like to have him; that's the reason she did it."

"Well," said Tommy, his eyes gleaming now suspiciously, "if anybody should ever do a thing like that to me it would be a bargain, that's all, only I don't expect nobody ever will." At that particular moment he heard his name sound through the building in a clear tone from the platform, "Thomas Dorn."

Miss Southey watched him make his way through the crowded aisle, with a wonderful smile on her face. What a fortunate thing it was that she had stood near Miss Wheeler when she wrote Tommy Dorn's name on a card, punched a hole in it, and tied it fast to a splendid four-bladed knife, as she said, "I am going to give this knife to Tommy Dorn to see if it won't coax him to come to Sunday-school. He has not been here for five or six weeks, and I don't think there is anything to hinder but his own sweet will. I have heard of his going fishing in the meantime on Sundays, too. Sometimes it seems almost a premium on bad behavior to give presents to such children; but, after all, if I can catch my fish with a four-bladed knife, don't you think I would better do it?"

Miss Southey had heartily agreed, and now had a pleased feeling that she had been permitted to help catch the fish. "He said it was a bargain," she repeated laughingly to herself, "and he looks like the sort of boy who will stick to a bargain. I believe Tommy is caught."

CHAPTER 6

How It Reached Swamp Lane

THE evening was over at last; and the next morning came the clearing away. Only a few of the committee were present to help, and of those few some could stay but a short time; so it chanced that Mrs. Carpenter and Miss Southey were left alone together to do the last things.

"Here are three dollies left," said Mrs. Carpenter, "and a cunning little mug, marked 'For a good girl,' and a fat pincushion stuffed with ... sand, I should think, by the weight of it, and that ridiculous cardboard motto. What shall we do with them all? These dolls and things were marked for the Robie children, and it seems they have moved away; been gone for three weeks, and I knew nothing about it. What a changing population we have to do with! One might as well teach a flock of pigeons. I will put the dolls along with the pincushion and cup, and other little things that were left, to give out as occasion suggests, wouldn't you? But what about that motto? Have you any ideas concerning it?"

Some of the sentences Miss Southey had not heard. Her attention had been attracted by a little noise near the door. Turning, she had come in contact with a pair of great dark eyes looking out from under a queer sunbonnet. The little girl who wore these stood gazing into the room. She had rested her pail on the back of one of the seats and leaned her arms upon it, and was staring at the Christmas-tree as if fascinated by its sight.

"Look at that child," said Miss Southey, in a low tone. "Did you ever see such eyes? She is perfectly amazed. Evidently she was not here last night. Do you know her? I cannot fix her face at all; it doesn't seem to me that I ever saw her before."

"I never did, I am sure," said Mrs. Carpenter. "Dear me, what eyes! Perhaps she is one of the aforesaid pigeons, just flown here."

"Then we can kidnap her for the Sunday-school," answered Miss Southey. "I mean to try. Come in, little girl, and see the tree, if you want to. Did you ever see a Christmas-tree before?"

"I've seen lots of trees," said the newcomer, advancing with slow and cautious steps into the middle of the room, "but I never saw one that grew in the house before."

"Nor one that bore such fruit, I dare say?" said Mrs. Carpenter, good naturedly. "Why didn't you come and see it last night when it was all in bloom? It was the prettiest sight you ever saw in your life. Who are you, little girl? Where do you live? Do you go to Sunday-school?"

The little girl stared as though some of these words had a new and strange sound. Recollecting herself presently, she said, "I live down in Swamp Lane, and my name is Alvira Miranda Bruce, and they call me Vira for short."

"I should think they would want to," exclaimed Mrs. Carpenter, exchanging glances with Miss Southey. "Well, Alvira Miranda, do you go to Sunday-school anywhere?"

The child shook her head. "I'm going to the schoolhouse round on Bond Street by and by," she said, "when ma can get me some clothes ready; but it don't keep Sundays."

Then Miss Southey took up the conversation. "Oh, but we don't mean that kind of a school, where they learn to read, and spell, and write; we mean Sunday-school, where the children sing, and have stories from the Bible taught them, and have picture papers and cards. We had this Christmas-tree last night for our Sunday-school, and gave each scholar a gift from the tree. Wouldn't you like to come to such a school as that?"

Alvira Miranda stared and said nothing.

"Suppose we let her choose a present from these things that are left?" said Miss Southey, speaking low to her friend. "I would like to see what sort of choice the child would make."

"Very well," said Mrs. Carpenter, "try it; she will choose the dollie, without doubt, or possibly this little red mug. Isn't it pretty? I wanted to give it to that cute little Lettie Parsons, but I knew her heart would be broken if she hadn't a dollie; and she needed a pair of shoes, and of course it would never do to give her three presents. Explain to the child that she may come and make her choice, and that we will enter her name on our roll and expect her at Sunday-school next Sunday, which will probably be all the good it will do us; the family may move out of town before that time."

Miss Southey turned back to Alvira Miranda. "Did you have a Christmas present?" she asked. "Last night was Christmas

Eve, you know, and this is Christmas Day. Why, you ought to have wished us a Merry Christmas. What did you get for a present?"

"I don't get no presents," said Vira, with a grave face, but in a most matter-of-fact tone. "Ma used to have presents when she was a little girl, she says. But I don't have none, never. Ma can't get presents for me; she ain't got no money for nothing. Pa gets drunk most all the time, and don't have no strength to work."

"Oh, poor little girl!" said Miss Southey. She seemed all the poorer, and her life the harder, because she could tell these terrible things about her father in a quiet, matter-of-course tone, as if this was an every-day matter, so common to fathers that no one need be surprised; and for the matter of that she was right—it is common enough; but how hard it seemed to hear a little girl tell of it in that way!

"Poor child!" repeated Miss Southey. "Then you certainly need a present from the children's tree. Come here and select one that you would like. You may have whatever one you please from these things."

Then the eyes were worth looking at. They seemed to grow larger, and deeper in color, with every step which Vira took, slowly and cautiously, towards the wonderful tree.

"For my truly own?" she asked, as though she could not possibly believe in the words she had heard.

"Yes, indeed: for your truly own, to keep for always. Here are some dollies, and a pincushion and a mug; you may have your choice. Which of them would you like to take home?"

Apparently there was not need for the slightest hesitation in this regard. Vira paused in front of the treasures, and said in very distinct tones, "I want that picture."

"Picture!" repeated Mrs. Carpenter. "There is no picture here, child. What do you mean? What one do you want?"

"That," and Vira's soiled forefinger pointed unmistakably to the despised motto.

The ladies exchanged astonished glances. "Is it possible," said Mrs. Carpenter, "that you would rather have that than this pretty red mug that you could drink out of? Or a dollie that you could hold in your arms, and take to bed with you at night?"

The child nodded. "I want that," she said simply.

"Well, of all things in this world!" said Mrs. Carpenter. "Who would have expected it? Miss Southey, do you think the child can understand that she could have one of these lovely dolls, if she chose?"

Then Miss Southey tried again. "Do you understand, Vira, that you have a right to choose a dollie, if you want to, and take it home with you and keep it always? Or that you can have this red mug, which says on it in gilt letters, 'For a good girl'—I hope you are a good girl, Vira—and that it would belong to you by right?"

"I don't want them," said Vira; "not if I can have the picture. I like pictures most, and I've wanted one always. I don't care for dolls; they ain't no account. They can't talk to you, nor look at you, only stare; they can't even cry. I would rather have a real live baby. Miz' Perkins, she lives in Swamp Lane right next to our house, and she has got a real live baby, just as pretty as it can be. It can laugh, and cry, and do lots of things. It is enough sight better than a dollie; and dollies get broke, besides. I had one once, and I loved it. Pa., he broke it one time when he was drunk—broke it all to pieces. I never wanted no more dollies, and I'm not going to love them anymore; but I would like a picture first-rate."

"Did you ever see such a queer child?" asked Mrs. Carpenter. "Well, I am sure we will be glad to get rid of that motto. Wrap it up, Miss Southey, please, and let her take it. There is no accounting for tastes. I wonder what she means to do with it?"

Miss Southey took down the motto with careful, almost regretful hand; it seemed hard to have Nettie's motto go to a drunkard's home. A dollie or a mug would be so much more appropriate, she thought.

"Can you read?" she asked the little girl, who was watching every movement.

"Some," said Vira, nodding her head. "I can spell out words, if there is anybody to pronounce them. Ma, she can pronounce them; she knows how to read first-rate, but we ain't got any books to spell words out of now. We had some, but pa, he sold them for whiskey: we ain't got a single one. That is why I like this picture; it's got words on it. I like to spell out words and pronounce them."

"Poor little girl!" said Miss Southey, and this time she spoke loud enough for Vira to hear. "Shall I read these words to you? Or no; you will like to spell them out, and have your mother pronounce them, perhaps. That will be best. And, Vira, won't you come to Sunday-school next Sunday? I have a class of little girls; cannot you come and be in my class?"

"No," said Vira. "I can't come next Sunday, nor the next; and I don't know when I can. Ma has got to get clothes before I can come anywhere. This is the only dress I have got." And she held up a ragged fringe of skirt, to show its poverty. "Ma, she is going to get washing, just as soon as she can, and get me some clothes so I can go to school. I don't know about Sunday-school. I s'pose she will let me go. Do they spell out words there?"

"Oh, yes!" said Miss Southey. "We spell the words when we cannot read them without spelling. I think you would like Sunday-school. I will come and see your mother, and ask her about letting you go."

"All right," said Vira, keeping her perfectly grave face; and without so much as a "thank you" for her Christmas present, she seized it, and make all speed out of the building.

"This is the wildest little specimen I have seen yet," said Mrs. Carpenter, looking after her. "She is odd looking, and oddly dressed, and uses odd language; she doesn't seem to belong to any type, does she? What in the world do you suppose she wanted of that motto? What will she do with it?"

"She wants to *spell out the words*," said Miss Southey, smiling sadly. This young woman was not very much used to poverty. She had never in her life heard a child talk as Vira did. But she wrote the long, high-sounding name in her note-book, and the residence, "Swamp Lane," and shivered as she thought of the over-crowded condition of the portion of the town thus suggestively named, and said to herself that she would go and hunt out this child at her first opportunity, and see what could be done toward getting her ready for Sunday-school.

Vira, meantime, trudged home. If you have never seen the small cabins in which the very poor live, I think it might be hard to describe one to you. But I want you to have a picture of Vira's home. It was made of rough pine boards. Inside, the boards had once been whitewashed, but were now so smoked with pine knots and tobacco as to present a worse appearance than though they had never been whitened at all. The floor was bare and unpainted, and very dirty; the two small-paned windows had lost three lights of glass, and their places were supplied on chilly mornings and evenings by the crown of an old hat, or a bundle of gray colored rags, or sometimes a wad of brown paper. There was no closet or cupboard, and no substitute for one, except a row of shelves midway between the window and the stove. These shelves were of unpainted wood, and looked almost as much soiled as the floor. Scattered over them, without regard to order, were the few dishes which this forlorn family possessed. Three or four cracked plates, two cups—one with the handle gone, the other with a row of nicks around its edge—two or three sorrowful-looking cracked dishes which Mrs. Bruce called "sass" dishes, two worn-out spoons, and three knives and forks completed the list. Under these shelves on the floor, leaning up against the dirty wall, were a few cooking dishes: a grimy sauce-pan, a wicked little black kettle which shone with grease and neglect, and a worse dish, if possible, called a "spider." As for the tin pail which Vira swung by one hand, while she held her treasure in the other, it did duty in various ways—went for the half-pint of milk in which they indulged on holiday occasions, brought water from the pump at the corner, went for a pint of molasses—when money enough could be raised to secure that amount—boiled the water for the tea which they drank three times a day, and at certain hours it became the dish-pan in which the few dishes were occasionally washed. In short, no more useful member of society ever existed than that four-quart pail.

About the furniture of the room, besides the dishes and cooking utensils, and the ugly little stove which was gray with age, and had lost a hinge from its oven door, and had a piece burned out of its side, and all its covers cracked, there was a table of unpainted wood, very dark with grease and smoke and neglect; there were three chairs, one of them without any back, one with a rickety leg. There was a wretched bed in the corner, the bed-clothes of a sort which would have made you shiver. Beside it, lying on a cot frame, was a ragged and soiled comfortable folded for a mattress, and a very ragged quilt folded for a spread, and no pillow at all. This was Alvira Miranda's bed.

Now you know everything there was in that room. No, I have forgotten an old tub, and a shovel, and a rusty tin pan, and a box half-full of all sorts of refuse.

CHAPTER 7

What It Did To the Wall

IT was to such a home as this that Vira carried Nettie Beldon's motto.

"For mercy's sake, child, what made you gone so dreadful long?" was her mother's greeting. She stood in the doorway ready to meet her. "Where is the molasses? I have been that distracted to know what I would get for dinner."

"I didn't get no molasses," said Vira. "He said he hadn't got none. It wasn't true; I saw it in a barrel all the time: but he says he ain't got no molasses at all, not a drop, and that he ain't going to have any more."

Mrs. Bruce sighed heavily. "I expected that," she said. "He ain't going to have any more for us till we can take the money along to pay for it. I don't know as we can blame him. We have got it three times now, without a cent of money, and it stands to reason that a man can't be giving away his molasses that he has to pay for. But what we are going to do, I don't know."

"Look at that, mother," said Vira, who had set down her pail in the middle of the room, and, seating herself on the floor beside it, had with eager fingers untied and unwrapped her treasure. "Just you look at that! Who cares anything about molasses when we've got this! It is my very own, truly, to keep for always."

"My land!" said Mrs. Bruce. "Wherever did you get that? I used to make them things when I was a little girl, just as true as you live. They was going out then, and was kind of cheap, and I had a good many of them. I made them for all the rooms, and the hall, and everywhere. And I declare for it if I didn't have one just for all the world like that. Well, if that isn't queer, words and all! I didn't use them colors in making it, and the fancy work all around the letters was different, but the letters was most of them just the same; and I worked it criss-cross, just like that. If that doesn't beat me. Where did you get it, Vira?"

"It was give to me," said Vira. "It came off a Christmas-tree. They had a Christmas-tree down in that great building on the corner of Bond Street, and I peeked in and saw it. They had dolls, and mugs, and things—and this picture. There was two ladies there, and they called to me to come in and pick out what I would like. They said I could have one thing for my truly own, to carry home; and I picked this out in a hurry. They didn't want me to have it exactly, I guess. They tried to make me take a doll, or a mug, or something, but I stuck to it. They said I could have anything I wanted, so I stuck to this. Ain't it a beauty, ma? I've wanted a picture with words on it ever so long, and I have got it."

"It's a dreadful pretty thing," said her mother, with a far-away, sorrowful look in her eyes. "What are you going to do with it, Vira?"

"I'm going to put it up on the wall, like I see them pictures in the saloon."

"Humph!" said her mother, putting her hands on her sides, and looking gloomily at the picture. "What's the use, Vira? It will go for whiskey before tomorrow night."

"It shan't!" said Vira fiercely. "I'll hide it somewhere. I ain't going to have this go for whiskey; that's the reason I wouldn't take the mug, nor the cushion, nor none of them things. And I wouldn't take the doll, because it would get broke when pa gets into one of his tantrums. I don't care for them anymore, anyhow, now that I have got the baby. But I ain't going to have this picture sold for no whiskey. I will hide it."

"I should like to know where," said her mother forlornly. "You can't bury them kind of things in the ground, and if you could he'd find it. When he gets crazy for whiskey there's no place where he can't find them. But I don't know but this is safe enough. Rum saloons don't take to them kind of pictures, I don't believe. I don't know as he could get a glass of whiskey for it."

Vira had no answer to make to this; she was busy hunting pins enough about her ragged dress to pin her picture to the wall. She succeeded, for her rags were literally pinned together on her. They fluttered in the breeze as she leaned against the wall, fastening her treasure to it. Then she stood back, with a complacent air, and looked at it. Then, for the first time, she slowly and laboriously spelled out the word, "B-l-e-s-s-e-d." This was too much for her; she had to appeal to her mother, who pronounced it at once in two syllables, "bless-ed." Then she went on carefully, "a-r-e t-h-e p-u-r-e i-n h-e-a-r-t f-o-r t-h-e-y s-h-a-l-l s-e-e G-o-d." She dropped her voice over the last word, and spoke it with a touch of reverence. Then slowly, and with the wonder gathering in her large eyes, read the sentence once more.

"What does it mean?" she demanded, at last.

"Oh, land!" said her mother hastily. "I don't know. Don't you go to bothering me with your questions, or I shall go crazy outright. It's enough for me to tell you what the words spell, and a great wonder that I can remember that."

She drew a long sigh as she spoke, and brushed back from her temples the hairs which were gray before they ought to have been. A hard, sad life did Mrs. Bruce lead. Vira was not noticing her at all, had not heard the long-drawn sigh with which she finished her sentence; she was gazing at her picture.

"It makes the wall look dirtier," she said at last, in a tone of grave conviction.

"Yes," said her mother; "it does so. That is because it is so clean."

Vira seized the skirt of her ragged dress, spit on a tag of it, and applied it to the wall. More dirt was her only reward for vigorous rubbing.

"It won't wash," she said sorrowfully. "I thought maybe I could wash a place big enough to go with the picture, but it makes it look worse than ever."

"It wants to be washed with whitewash," said Mrs. Bruce. "That is what was done to this whole wall once."

"Whitewash!" repeated Vira. "What is that? Where can we get some?"

"Humph!" said Mrs. Bruce. "That's the question! I don't know, I am sure. I don't know what you and me are going to do, Vira; we can't even get molasses to eat with our corn bread; and I can't get any work. I have been around this morning to all the places I heard of. They don't want any washing done, nor cleaning, nor anything. There was one woman had the impudence to tell me if I would go home and clean myself, I would stand a better chance of getting other people's cleaning to do. If she hadn't another rag to put on her while she cleaned these, I wonder what she would do? I had a mind to ask her, but I didn't. I don't know what is to become of us, Vira, now that's a fact."

For the first time since she had pinned it up, Vira turned from the picture, and gazed thoughtfully at her mother.

"Don't you worry," she said at last, with a vague idea of giving comfort, "something will happen; something always does before we starve, you know. Who cares for his old molasses? If he don't want to let us have any, he needn't: we can eat corn bread without molasses; I have, lots of times. The lady who did up the picture—she was the youngest and prettiest, and she had a nice voice; it goes along soft and easy, like music that the band plays on moonlight nights away down on the square. I like her—she said she was coming to see you about my going to Sunday-school, and having clothes. And something will happen, you see if it don't. We have got to have whitewash put around this picture; the wall looks just awful dirty where it is. Could you put it on?"

"I reckon I could, if I had it, and a brush to put it on with, and something to stand on to reach up to it."

"Why, you wouldn't have to stand on anything to reach as high as this picture; you know it don't look so dreadful black anywhere else, and you could reach to that. I wonder where they keep it? I mean to find some somewhere. Say, mother, will you try to put it on?"

"Oh, land!" said Mrs. Bruce. "What's the use in having one patch clean and all the rest dirty? I tell you, I haven't got any brush, child, and no way on earth to get a brush, nor to get lots of other things that I need more than that."

"Well," said Vira, resorting to her unanswerable remark, "we'll do it somehow; something will happen. Say, mother, I wish you could tell me what these words mean. What is the good of reading them over when I don't understand one bit about it? Where does it come from? Where did they get it?"

"Get what, Alvira? You do beat all for asking questions."

"Why, the words. Who made thom up? Did that lady make them up, and put them on there, do you suppose?"

"I don't know who put them on there, I am sure, but of course she didn't make them up. Didn't I tell you I had one when I was a little girl, with just them words on it? They are from the Bible, child."

"The Bible," said Vira, with that little touch of respect again in her voice. She had heard of the Bible. "Then it's true?" she said, after a moment's pause. There was a note of inquiry in her voice, and she waited for an answer.

"I suppose so," the mother said, speaking like one from whom the words were forced: "at least folks where I lived when I was a little girl used to think that the words of the Bible were true."

"Blessed are the pure in heart," read Vira. "Mother, if you made a thing like this, and had these same words on it, you must have known what they meant, didn't you? Didn't you ask anybody about it?"

"I didn't ask a hundred questions about it, as you do, I'll be bound," said Mrs. Bruce. "But, of course, I knew in a general way what it meant; all children did in those days."

"Then tell me in a general way what it means. What is a *pure heart?*"

"It is a clean heart, child, of course; when a thing is pure, it's clean."

"Clean," repeated Vira thoughtfully: then after a moment: "What is meant by heart?"

"Why, it means thoughts, of course," said poor Mrs. Bruce. "What else could it mean? The thing inside of you that thinks and feels, whatever that is."

Then there was silence for several moments, during which Vira stared at the picture on the wall, while the mother turned, with a sigh, to note the point which the yellow sunshine was reaching on the floor, telling her only too plainly that it was drawing near the hour for the midday meal; and she wondered what Jim would say to cake made out of corn meal and water, with no molasses to eat on it. Yet that was every article of food she had in the house.

"Blessed are the clean inside," read Vira slowly, thoughtfully, then glanced toward her mother. "Mother, how can it mean that? How do you get them clean? You can't take them out of you and wash them, like you can clothes, and dishes, and things." Whereupon her mother declared, with an emphasis which Vira understood and knew she must respect, that it was utterly out of reason to ask her any more questions about the thing; that she didn't understand it, never had, and never expected to. It was a Bible verse, she was sure of so much, and "pure" meant clean. For the rest, Vira must find out the best way she could, and not bother her any more about it; she had trouble enough.

It was not in Alvira Miranda Bruce's nature to give up a thing on which she had set her heart. She decided that there wasn't any use in asking questions of mother, for the present, at least, but that she certainly should, somehow or other, "find out what them words meant." Meantime, she would bend all her energies toward finding ways and means of whitening that part of the wall where the picture hung.

While she was hastily putting down her corn-meal mush, which was not very palatable without butter, or sugar, or molasses, to say nothing of milk, which was a rarity in that country that seldom fell to Vira's lot, she had a bright idea. The man, Nero, who tramped by the cabin almost daily, on his way to and from work, was a whitewasher. Many a time she had seen him walking along, with his pail of white mixture on one arm, his whitewash brush under the other arm, and his clothes dotted from head to foot with white flakes.

Now, while the mush went down in as hasty mouthfuls as its heat would allow, Vira thought, "Why not ask Nero about it? Surely he would know where whitewash could be had. And maybe be would lend her a brush, and show her how to put the stuff on the wall. But I don't believe I need any telling about that," said the wise young woman. "What could there be to do, but put the brush in the pail, and splash it on the wall? I s'pose I could do it just as well as not, if he would lend me his pail a little while—just long enough to make a big white patch for the picture to lean against. I think he might do that; he looks good-natured. I mean to ask him, anyhow."

This much settled, Vira took a very large mouthful for the last one, pushed her backless chair from the table, seized her sunbonnet, and was off. It had occurred to her that she happened to know where Nero was at work that day; she had seen him in a house she had passed on her way home, perched on a step-ladder, brushing away at the kitchen wall. She had no thought of asking permission to go on her errand. She had nothing to do at home, and her mother did not care how she spent her time, so long as she did not get "drownded" in the river, nor hurt on the railroad crossing. Truth to tell, her mother was so nearly crushed by trouble, and hard work, and hunger, that she seemed to think very little about Vira. But it was only seeming; the poor mother loved her little girl with all her heart. The trouble was, she did not know what to do for her, or with her. There was certainly nothing in the dreary home to interest the child, and her questions on all sorts of subjects so disturbed, and at times actually frightened, the mother, that it was a relief to get rid of her great wondering eyes, and be left alone.

"Jim," as she called her husband, did not come home to dinner. There was a sense in which this was a relief. For Jim, though rarely cross, was sometimes very stupid by that hour of the day, and hard to manage. And he did not like plain mush, without anything to help make it "go down."

CHAPTER 8

Superior To Circumstances

THE first knowledge that Nero had of Vira's presence was when she uttered a little exclamation of dismay over the fact that he made a misstep and almost lost his balance. When he had regained it, he turned to the end window, from which the exclamation had come, and saw the little girl perched in it, gazing up at his work with wonder and admiration in her face.

"Hi!" he said, looking down at her. "Where did you come from, little girl? What you s'pose you want?"

"I want to see you," said Vira gravely. "I want to see how you spread that stuff on, and what makes it stick. Where do you get it, anyhow?"

"The stuff? Oh, I get the lime, and mix it up. It is easy enough to spread on after you know how; but I tell you what it is: old Nero Caine near making a bad job of this. If I'd-a tumbled down on the floor that time, I'd have broke some bones, sure! I'm not so spry as I used to be, now that's a fact. I'm getting awkward and bumptious."

"Oh, dear! Does it cost a heap of money?" asked Vira, her eyes now fixed on the white mass in the pail.

"What, the whitewash? Well, considerable, when you take that and the pails and the brushes into account, it's not a very paying business. Whitewash brushes are the costliest things and they will wear out, spite of all I can do to take care of them. They wear out mighty fast. I ain't never got rich at the business, and I worked mighty hard, too, all my life. Do you think of going into the business, little girl?"

"No," said Vira slowly, "only I want a patch on our wall made white, dreadful bad. It wouldn't take but just a little, and I was thinking when you got your work done someday, if you would lend me the stuff and the brush, and let me fix just a little place on the wall; it wouldn't take but a little bit of stuff."

Nero, who had come down from the step-ladder, now dropped his brush into the pail, and turned and, stared at his visitor. "Just one patch?" he said. "Why, how big a patch? Is it a piece of wall that has been mended? It takes a powerful lot of whitewash for them kind of things."

"No, no," said Vira, "it's an old wall, very black and dirty; the ugliest wall you ever saw. But I just want one place in it fixed for a picture I have got."

"For a picture?" repeated Nero, growing more and more bewildered. "They don't white-wash pictures, little girl, and they don't commonly whitewash patches on walls, because it makes the other part of the wall look meaner than ever. Where do you live, and what is your name?"

"My name is Alvira Miranda Bruce," said Vira, with great dignity, "and I do want to whitewash a patch on my wall, so that the picture on the wall will have something white around it."

"Alvira Miranda Bruce. Ho, ho! Are you Jim Bruce's little girl?"

"Yes, I am," said Vira shortly, "and I have got a picture that I want to put some white around. Couldn't you just lend me your brush and white stuff tonight when you go home?"

"I can't make you out," said Nero, shaking his head. "You couldn't handle this brush, little girl, not with them hands. It's the heaviest kind of a brush, and when it gets all wet with whitewash it weighs a good deal. And then the stuff has to be put on smooth and even, or it will look all streaked, and worse than ever. And then just one patch on a wall … Why, it would look mighty queer. What is the picture that you want to fix up for?"

"It's a picture full of letters and words," said Vira, "and I don't care how queer it would look; a white place all around it would look better than the black dirty wall where it is now. I got it pinned up, and it is just as white and the black wall all around the edges looks horrid: and it is bound all around with ribbon, too: and I know a nice white place about so long—" she spread out her two arms to measure the distance "—would make it look a great sight nicer; and I think you might lend me just that much. I can handle a brush; I ain't a mite afraid. I'm strong; I can tote around great heavy things. I carry a whole big basket full of beans from the store, and I can lift Mrs. Perkins's baby that weighs lots and lots of pounds. A hundred white-wash brushes couldn't weigh as much as that baby does."

"You're a smart little girl," said Nero, nodding his head approvingly, "I believe you are. It's a dreadful pity you're Jim Bruce's girl. Why don't you get your pa to whitewash the wall?"

"He can't," said Vira briefly; "he don't work."

Nero chuckled. "No more he don't," he said. "Just the laziest person I ever knew in my life is Jim Bruce. But it's all the whiskey that makes it, I s'pose. If he would get rid of the whiskey he could whitewash, and do lots oh things."

"Yes," said Vira gravely, "that is what mother says; but he don't get rid of it. Say, Nero, will you lend me your brush just a little while? It won't take but a few minutes."

"I tell you what I'll do," said Nero; "I'll stop there on my way home and see about it. I'd like to see the picture, too. I'm mighty fond of pictures: and maybe we can manage it somehow—anyway we will talk it over. Will, that do?"

"Yes," said Vira, hopping down from her window-seat, "that will do first-rate. When you see the picture, you will see that there has got to be some white around it, and I almost know you'll let me have your brush. Good-bye."

The child was alone to receive her caller that evening. The father had not yet reached home, and her mother had departed before Vira came back from her errand to Nero. Mrs. Bruce had heard from her neighbor, Mrs. Blake, that someone was wanted to scrub the piazzas of the hotel, and she hoped to earn enough to get her family some supper. Vira was standing in the doorway watching for her friend, when he turned the corner and rolled along the street toward her.

"Here I am be," he said, "according to promise. Now let's see the picture, little girl." And placing his whitewash pail on the doorstep, he strode into the dirty room, and gazed at the motto on the wall.

"That's a beauty, and that's a fact," he said, after a moment's silent survey. "No mistake about it's being a first-class pretty thing. And you want a kind of a tablet to put it on, don't you? That is what they calls them kind of things—great big white slabs that they cut letters on to, and hang them up in church sometimes. I've seen 'em. What do those letters say, do you s'pose, now?"

"Can't you *read?*" asked Vira, turning her great wondering eyes upon him. Both her mother and father could read; so could all the neighbors around. Vira had not realized that there were men and women among them who did not know how to read.

Nero shook his head and dropped his eyes, and the look of importance which he generally wore faded from his face. "No, little girl, Nero can't, and that's a fact. I'm mighty sorry for it, too. If I could read enough to read a little in the Good Book, I'd feel mighty glad."

"The Good Book?" repeated Vira. "That's the Bible, ain't it?"

"Yes, Missy, it's the Bible; that's the Good Book. Old Nero loves it, if I can't read it, and I'm going to Heaven by it straight; I reckon I'll know how to read it there. I suspect they'll put an angel to work to teach me, soon as ever I get inside the golden gates."

Vira did not laugh; her ignorance upon all these subjects was dense. She knew almost nothing about the golden gates or angels. As for the Bible, they had none in their home.

"These words are from the Bible," she said, pointing to the motto on the wall.

Nero looked even more interested than before. "Is that so?" he asked, a slight incredulity mingled with admiration. "From the Bible? Now, ain't that great! Then they're bound to be good words. I would like a picture from the Bible, that I would. What are the words, Missy? You can read, I s'pose?"

"Yes," said Vira, with proper dignity, "I can read. The words say, 'Blessed are the pure in heart, for they shall see God.'"

"Is that so!" said Nero, with emphasis. "That's Bible, sure enough. Ain't them lovely words, now? Yes, that's what I live for; I'm going to see God one of these days, just as sure as you live."

"What do the words mean?" asked Vira, a new idea flashing into her mind. It had not before occurred to her that Nero could possibly know more about the words than she did herself.

"Oh they means just what they say," said Nero, running his fingers through his hair. "Blessed are the pure in heart. You know what 'blessed' means, little girl? It means just to be all tickled to death, almost."

"Mother says it means to be clean inside," said Vira. Nero nodded his head emphatically.

"That's just it: she couldn't explain it better if she was the preacher himself. You believe your mother, Missy, every time. Clean inside: don't do no good to wash outside if you ain't clean inside."

"How do you get clean?" asked Vira.

"Well, now, that is more than I understand; but He does it somehow, the blessed Jesus does, you know. I don't know how he makes folks clean, but he has promised to do it, and I am bound to believe it. You just ask Him about it, you know, and He does the rest. But it is a great thing to know how to read them words. Old Nero would give about five dollars if he could read words like that. Look here, now, Missy—what did you tell me your name was?"

"Vira," said Alvira Miranda. "That isn't the whole of my name, but it's enough."

"Just so," said Nero. "It's a very nice-sounding name. Well, Vira, I'll tell you what it is; you can't no more whitewash this wall than nothing in the world. It's a dreadful black wall, this is; but I'll tell you what I will do. I will make a bargain with you. I have got two little children down in my cabin—my grand-children, they are; my daughter died and left them to me—and my wife and I, we take the best care of them we know how: and they are nice clean little children. They keep their hair combed all nice, and keep theirselves clean as soap; but they don't know how to read, and I want them to grow up good and smart. Now s'pose I whitewash your wall for you, all along this side, as big a place as you want—it will take two or three coats to make it all white like chalk—and you teach my children to read words like that?"

Vira's at all times large eyes had seemed to grow larger as she listened. What a thing it would be to get a great big white place for her picture, done by Nero himself, and then to pay for it with her own work! Moreover, the idea of teaching anybody anything sounded very pleasant to her. She had never been to school in her life. For one reason, it was but a short time since a district school had been opened in the ward to which she belonged, and during that time she had not had respectable clothing; but the great ambition of her life was to be counted among the scholars. To make a great bound over all the preparatory course and become a teacher was a wonderful thing to think of. But even while her cheeks glowed with the thought her face clouded.

"I ain't got no slates and pencils, nor books, nor nothing, such as they use in schools," she said.

"You can use that," said Nero, pointing to the picture on the wall. "It's full of letters and words; it will take a mighty long time for the children to read all that. And, then you can take a piece of nice board and some chalk, and make letters on the board; that will do beautiful for a slate. I've seen 'em do it. My boss, he has a slate and pencil hanging up against the wall. But another man in our shop just uses a plain board, all made smooth, and a piece of black chalk—just charcoal. He writes figures, and words, and everything, just as well as the boss on the slate."

Vira stared at the picture, and thought. "Well," she said at last, "there is lots of letters in those words; maybe most all the letters are there; I'll pick them out and see. Well, Nero, I will teach your little children all the reading I know, if you will make a nice big white place for this picture."

"I will that!" said Nero, nodding his head with great satisfaction. "You will see that it will be just as white as milk. I will give it the first coat now, this minute: and I'll send the children 'round tomorrow to get their lesson. I will so!" Saying which, Nero rolled out to the door, and brought in the pail with its white mixture, while Vira, with trembling fingers, took the pins out of the motto and laid it very carefully on the table. Then, oh, wonderful transforming power of whitewash! Even the first coat was marvelous—a great square of shining white where before was blackness. How fast he did it! How wonderful it was that it stuck to the wall, instead of rolling off in drops! Vira watched him, breathless with astonishment and delight. He was doing a nice big place. All around the motto would be purity; what a wonderful change it would make in the room.

"There," said Nero at last, after the long smooth strokes were finished, "that is a tablet worth having. Now you must let it dry before you hang the picture up again, and tomorrow morning, when I am going back to my work, I will stop in and give it another coat. And I will bring the children along with me to get their first lesson."

"What a young one you are!" said Mrs. Bruce, as she studied the wall. "Alvira, you do beat all the children that I ever heard of for having your own way. How did you make Nero do it? I never heard that the old man was very anxious to do things for nothing."

"He didn't do it for nothing," said Vira gravely; I hired him to do it, and I am going to pay for it."

"For the land's sake! With what, child?"

"I am going to teach," said Vira. "He is going to bring his grandchildren along with him tomorrow, and I am going to teach them to read, to pay him for his work: and he is going to stop tomorrow and give it another brushing. He calls it another *coat*."

"Well, I never in all my life!" said Mrs. Bruce. "So you are going to set up and teach school, are you?"

"Yes," said Vira, "I am going to teach them all the letters on the picture; I don't know how many are there. There's A and B, anyway. But I don't know as there is a C. What will I do for a C, mother?"

"You might make it," said Mrs. Bruce, getting interested in spite of herself, "if you had a pencil, or a piece of chalk."

"Yes," said Vira, "so I can. I am going to have a piece of chalk, and a nice pine board: Nero is going to get them for me. That is to be my slate. They have slates in school, you know, mother. Well, that is my slate; and a piece of chalk, he said, or a piece of coal."

"Yes," said Mrs. Bruce, "that would do, I suppose. Well, Vira, it is just as I said, you are a queer young one, and no mistake. I suppose you might better be doing that than running the streets, though I don't know what the neighbors will say: but that streak of white on the wall does look nice, that's a fact."

"Yes," said Vira thoughtfully; "it looks nice; but it makes the rest of the wall look dirtier, doesn't it, mother?"

"I suppose it does," said Mrs. Bruce. "It would be a nice thing if we could have the whole room done."

"I didn't say a word about the whole room," said Vira. "I was only thinking of a place for the picture. It will be nice to have it white about that, anyhow."

CHAPTER 9

How It Became a Teacher

THE next morning, two trim little children, looking as fresh as soap and water could make them, presented themselves at the door of the Bruce home, while their grandfather produced in triumph from under his arm a smooth pine board, and several bits of charcoal from his pocket, and school life began in earnest. Vira, never having been to school, knew nothing about methods of any sort, and therefore was obliged to get up some of her own. She started out on what may certainly be called an original plan. The fact that she had a single verse on the wall for her text-book obliged her to discover at once how many letters there were in it. She was much interested to find that it took so many different letters to make the verse: and in the course of her instructions found that the letter was repeated nine times. She looked to see if any other letter was equally honored, and finding that there was a vast difference between this and all the others, came to an important conclusion.

"It has the most to do of any of them. It ought to be the first one learned: I will teach it to them this very morning."

Her first address to her scholars was after this fashion: "There's a lot of letters to learn. There are twenty-six of them in all—I counted them. And there is one that I am going to give you first of all. I will make a picture of it on this board," and she made with most careful and painstaking effort an exact copy of the *e* in the motto. "There!" she said, holding it up in triumph, the name of that is *e*."

The two children, who had watched her with round-eyed wonder, now solemnly repeated the magic word after her.

"Did you see how it was made?" asked Vira. "Look at it; see just how it curls in under, and everything; then you must say its name over ever so many times, because it has lots to do, that letter has. I am going to find it for you on that picture on the wall pretty soon—just as soon as you have learned its name."

The picture had been removed far away from the white tablet which had been prepared for it, and was now gracing the blackest portion of the wall on the other side of the room. The two pupils were presently allowed to cross to it, and put their clean black fingers on its lovely raised surface, the teacher calling their attention to the fact that its *e* was made just like hers on the board. Then the masterpiece of her educational theory exhibited itself.

"Now, Martha—Did you say your name was Martha?—Well, ever so many of those, *e*'s are on this little picture on the wall; I want you and George to count them. See which will be the first to pick them all out."

The most intense excitement prevailed. The two heads bent close together, the two forefingers traced the delicate outline of Nettie's work, the two wide-awake brains considered, argued, counted, disagreed and counted again, Vira herself growing so much interested as almost to forget the supreme object which she had in mind. It was a work of time; the teacher had to go over and over the motto with them, and point out their mistakes, and re-arrange their results. When at last it was accomplished, so also was another thing: George and Martha were from this time forth acquainted with the letter *e*. They knew every little curve in its queer body, and their sharp eyes might be trusted for detecting it upon any sign or advertisement, as they passed. Vira put this thought into their minds, like the rapidly developing teacher that she was.

"Now you can go home, you two. I am just as tired as though I had toted the baby all day; and I reckon you have had lesson enough for one day, only you must keep practicing on it, you know. There are lots of signs as you go along the street; there's the circus bills, and the horse-race bills, and two or three others. They've got lots and lots of *e*'s in them; see if you can pick them all out. I'll go down the street by and by and look at them myself, then tomorrow I'll see which of you got it right. I guess that letter *e* does about half of the work in all the reading."

While the teaching had been going on, Vira had done some vigorous thinking outside of the lesson for the day. It became increasingly plain to her that as there were twenty-six letters of the alphabet, and it took so long to be absolutely certain of the form and name of one of them, it was a much longer process to teach two children to read than it was to whitewash a square of the kitchen wall. Moreover, the longer she looked at the white tablet, and the whiter it grew under the touch of the sun and air, the more disappointed was she over the general effect on the surrounding blackness.

"It makes everything look ten times blacker," she murmured discontentedly, "and it didn't take him but just a little while to do it; not half so long as it has taken me to show them that *e; and that they can keep learning from all the time. I am just* going to talk to Nero this very night."

So Nero was watched for with unusual interest, not to say anxiety. Vira dashed down the street as she saw him turn the corner, and kept him company, talking eagerly.

"Nero, I have begun to teach your children to read; they know the letter *e*, and I don't believe they will ever forget it; but it's real hard work; harder than whitewashing, I'm sure. You see, there are twenty-six letters; and after you know them, you have got to learn how to put them together and make words; and I'll tell you what I think. If I teach a whole lot of letters, you ought to do the whole of that side. It looks awful black, as black again as it did before you touched it. You just come in and see. The other keeps growing whiter, you know, and this is—oh, too black for anything! I don't think we can stand it, Nero, and it's real hard work to teach; I did not think it was so hard."

"It is pretty black, that's a fact." said Nero, examining with the eye of a professional the ugly wall. "You see my whitewash is of a superior kind, and that white spot is so very white that it makes the surrounding blackness visible."

Vira started at him; those were larger words than she was in the habit of using; she had a good deal of respect for Nero, if he couldn't read, and a suspicion that he used better language than most of the people by whom she was surrounded. Still she was bent on carrying her point.

"It wouldn't do to leave it so," she said anxiously. "Don't you think you could make that whole side white, if I teach a whole lot of letters?"

"Well," said Nero, scratching his head thoughtfully, "I don't know about it; I don't have much time out of work hours. I have to work mighty hard and steady to get food for my family; there's my wife and my boy, and my three grandchildren, all dependent on me. My boy is sick; he can't do no work, and I have to support him, too. And then, you know, I have to put three coats on the wall."

"Well," said Vira, "I have to teach a great deal more than three letters; and it takes a great deal of time, Nero, to learn one letter; you wouldn't believe that it would take such a lot of work and time."

Yes, he would. Nero kept his own counsel, but the truth was he had gone home to dinner instead of taking it with him, as the house where he was at work happened to be not far from his cabin, and he had reason to know what hard work it was to learn *e*. Martha and George had pounced upon him as soon as he appeared in sight, and from that time until he seized his hat and went back to work in self-defense five minutes before the hour was up, he had been obliged to make *e* over and over and over again on the pine board, and had utterly failed in making the great sprawling characters that he produced look like the delicate outline which grew under the skillful hands of Martha and George.

"Those children are geniuses, sure enough!" he said, as he tramped back to his work. "They'll be knowing how to read, and reading off the signs along the road before I know it! Who knows but they'll learn how to read in the Good Book? And Nero can't do it; it's too hard work. That queer curly thing they made so easy—I couldn't do it like they do at all: and I've forgotten its name already, though they said it over to me so many times. I always knew those children were smart!"

But the memory of his lesson kept him from making any reply when Vira assured him that teaching was hard work. He said at last, remembering the "geniuses" and the good time they had had that morning, "We'll call it a bargain then; I'll do the whole of the wall on that side, but I must do it at odd spells, you know, child; just little squares, like I did for the picture; can't get no time to do it all at once. Just when I'm going back and forth; and the children can come every morning and have another letter. By the time I get the whole side of that wall done I reckon they'll about know them all."

"I don't know," said Vira; "there are twenty-six of them, and it is very hard work to learn letters—a great deal harder than it is to whitewash—and besides, it lasts, Nero, and whitewash has to be done over again. My mother says when she was a girl her mother used to have her kitchen whitewashed every single year. But you don't have to learn letters over again after you have learned them once."

"That's true," said Nero, gazing upon her with admiration; "whitewash don't last, that's a fact. You have to keep going over it to have it white and clean; but they don't go and make new letters that you have to learn, do they? It's the same old letters year after year: they don't wear out, and they don't get out of fashion, like clothes. I never thought of that before; I guess you are pretty smart yourself."

Vira saw her advantage, and followed it up with eagerness. "There is something I have been thinking about since you came in. You see how dreadful this room looks with that white patch in it, and when we get the whole of that side done, the other side and the two ends will look dreadfuller."

"Shouldn't wonder if they would," said Nero reflectively, "and the top of the wall, and all; it's a great big job."

"Yes," said Vira firmly, "I know it is; but so is reading. It took me weeks and weeks to learn how to read, and I thought sometimes I never would know how. There's two letters, p and y, that you get mixed up in spite of yourself. One turns one way, and one the other, and you never know which way they turn: and it's just so about b and d; they are the awfulest things. A little bit of a curl this side or that" twisting her head by way of gesture—"is all the difference there is to them two letters; and you have to work with all your might to remember them."

Nero sighed; he had visions of having to work hard on the pine board, trying to satisfy the "geniuses" making b's and d's, and telling the difference between them; however, he was an honest man, and an aspiring one. He had promised to white-wash the wall, and he had set out to have his grandchildren learn how to read; he did not mean to draw back from either position.

"I'll tell you what it is," he said, as the greatness of the work grew upon him, "you and me are in for it. You teach the children to read, so that they can read from the Good Book itself, and I will whitewash the whole wall, top and all, see if I don't. Just as sure as my name's Nero Jackson. You can ask any of the folks I work for, and they'll tell you I am to be depended on; I don't go back on my word."

"Neither do I," said Vira resolutely. "If you will do the whole wall, I'll make George and Martha read before spring, see if I don't. Mrs. Perkins, the baby's mother, has got a book, and I can borrow it. I am going to school, anyhow, as soon as I can get some clothes; then I can learn more things to teach them. And I do want this whole wall white worse than anything."

"It is a bargain," said Nero, bringing his fist down on the table.

From that time work progressed steadily in the Bruce home. Nero came morning and evening on his way to his work, sometimes five, ten, fifteen minutes ahead of time, and in the evenings, after his day's work was done, and the walls grew steadily white under his skillful hand, while George and Martha gained steadily upon the letters. *A* was the next one chosen, then *r* followed, chiefly because they seemed to have the most work to do in the motto, which was the text book. It was not until all were learned that Vira herself discovered that the three formed one of the words of the wall picture. Great was the delight of Martha and George when she pointed it out to them; great was their surprise when they found that the combination was pronounced as though it were a single letter.

"Why couldn't they just have *r* standing all alone?" speculated George, "as well as to put a letter before and a letter behind it, and then call it *r?*"

"'Cause," said Vira, "that isn't the way, that's why. The word is just named after the letter, don't you see? Didn't you ever know a boy or girl that was named like his father or mother?"

"Yes," said George promptly, "I am; my father's name was George."

"Well, then, you ought to understand: this word *are* is named for the letter *r*. That's the reason, and that's reason enough."

George accepted this new theory in philology, and looked with respect upon the word; and his grandfather bought a newspaper that very day, over which George and Martha studied until their grandmother grew desperate and sent them to bed. They were hunting out the word "are," and putting a mark on their pine board for every time they found it. Their respect for the word grew with every column of the paper that they hunted through; a very important word it was, surely.

"Here's another, grandfather," would Martha pipe out in her shrill voice to Nero, as he sat in the little kitchen smoking his pipe.

"You don't say so?" he would reply, taking out his pipe and looking upon the students with delighted eyes. "Another? Well, I declare! Appears like that word would get tired; it has a lot to do in the world.'

"Ha!" said George. "Here's a line that's got two of them in; just one line, grandfather."

In this way the education of the "geniuses" went on. Meantime much thinking was done by the teacher; she had one day which she could devote exclusively to thinking, being obliged to dismiss her school that morning because she had stood too near the lime, and got a spatter of it in her eye. Great was the distress for awhile, though Nero, being fortunately at hand, knew just what remedies to apply. Then Vira sat all the morning with a rag tied around her eyes, rocking to and fro in the chair which Mrs. Perkins had brought in, and thinking industriously.

CHAPTER 10

How It Managed the Floor

A GREAT problem was before this little girl. Nero was putting on the last coat this morning; the walls were white; a wonderful change had been made in the home. Even Mrs. Bruce, who had been used once to white walls, declared that she had forgotten that they made such a "dreadful difference," and had spent many minutes with her hands on her sides, watching the effect. But Vira, if she had supposed that she was going to be satisfied when the walls about her were white and pure, was woefully disappointed. No sooner had the first coat given her an idea of how it would look in its purity, when a feeling of doubt and dismay knocked at her heart, and entering, sat down there. It had to do with the floor. Of course the floor was no blacker, no more stained or worn than it had been before; but it struck Vira as a strange thing that she had never in her life thought of it until the walls grew whiter; neither had she thought of the walls until the motto gleamed on them. Now they were all so white, and matched the picture so well, and behold, there was the floor.

"They don't whitewash floors," said Vira, rocking back and forth; "they clean them. I've seen Mrs. Perkins scrub her floor many a time; why don't we never scrub ours? We will have to, now that the wall is white; there is no other way." She had appealed to her mother, only to be disappointed.

"They have to have soap, child, to scrub floors, and a scrub-cloth, and a brush, and hot water; we can have the hot water, and that is about all. I ain't got no clothes to use for a scrub-cloth. I suppose any of yours or mine would do better for scrub-cloths than for anything else, but then we couldn't spare them, you know; we have just got to wear them. And now, Vira, I tell you what it is, you are trying to brush up, and be clean, like other folks, and it ain't no kind of use; I've tried it again and again. Your father, he don't care for nothing but whisky. If we had so much as a cake of soap—and I haven't seen the money that I could spare to buy one this many a day —but if we had as much as that he would take it whisky, so what's the use?"

Said Vira, speaking in slow, determined tones, "The floor has got to be cleaned, mother; it don't match. We had to have the walls made white to match with the picture, and now the floor will have to be got clean somehow, so that it will match. Things have got to fit. Father can't take the white walls off and change them for whisky, and he couldn't take the clean floor off, neither; we've got to have it."

"I don't know how," said Mrs. Bruce, with a sigh. "Land knows, I work every chance I can get, for the sake of keeping him and you and me from starving, but when it comes to scrubbing such a floor as this without any scrub-cloth, or brush, and no soap to do it with, I am free to confess I don't know how to manage it. You are dreadful set in your way, Vira, and you always was ever since you was a little mite of a baby, but I don't know how you are going to bring that about."

So Vira rocked and thought all day, peeping out from under her bandage every once in awhile at the floor to reassure herself as to its size, that she might calculate just how much soap and scrub-cloth would be required. Suddenly she stopped rocking, and clasped her hands together, making a curious little sound with her lips, which always meant in Vira's mind-language, that she had an idea. It had been a great source of satisfaction to her that she had earned the white-washed walls, "and no begging about it," she told herself complacently. "I taught school and earned it, like other folks." It is true that her pupils were such bright little creatures, and were making such rapid progress, that it had been a great pleasure to her, rather than otherwise, to teach them. A looker-on wiser than herself might have discovered that Vira was quite a skillful teacher; but nevertheless it was work, and she had thereby earned white walls. The question was, could she not earn some soap, and even a scrub-cloth, by her own industry? The thought was a very large one. Up to this time it had never occurred to Vira that there was work for her to do in the world for which she could actually get a return.

The carrying out of her new idea found her in Mrs. Perkins' neat kitchen the next evening. Her eyes had recovered, and she had come to bring the chair home, and to look at Mrs. Perkins' clean floor; for it was scrubbing day in this little house, and everything was as neat and clean as soap and water could make it. Mrs. Perkins, the baby's mother, was a great source of comfort to Vira Bruce; she was very unlike any of the other neighbors, who were as a rule the same discouraged women as her mother; women who had lost heart in the world, and given up the hope of life having anything better for them than that to which whisky had reduced them. But Mrs. Perkins was different; she had lived in the neighborhood but a few weeks. They had come to the little cabin because it was cheap, and they were poor. Very poor they were; her husband had been ill for long weeks and months, and this had used up the few earnings which had been laid aside "for a rainy day." Then the baby had been sick, and even the mother, for awhile, so that troubles gathered fast upon them. When the house-rent of their little cottage at the other end of the town became due it could not be paid, and the owner had given them warning to go. Then they had hunted for and found this little two-roomed affair, down in the worst part of the city, where the drunkards, and their wives and mothers and daughters huddled together.

"It is a horrid place," said Mrs. Perkins cheerily, in explaining to her young husband what she and Baby had found while he was at his work. "There isn't a pleasant thing about it anywhere; but then it's shelter; and soap and water and whitewash, and a good deal of hard work, will make it clean. I think it will do nicely; the rent is very low. The building is so tumbled down they couldn't in conscience ask any more. We can stay there until we get the doctor's bill and one or two other bills paid, then when we get ahead a little again we can move into a better place. I took the house, John; I knew you would want me to, because we have to go somewhere, and it is the only one I felt sure we could pay for."

That is the way they came to the Bruce neighborhood. And the baby? Oh, that baby! There was never a sweeter one, so at least thought the mother and father. In truth, she was sweet enough, with her pretty ways and "coos" to win the heart of almost anyone.

As for Vira, she had almost worshipped the Perkins baby from the first. Mrs. Perkins had looked on amused, and had said to her husband laughingly, "The child is a perfect little heathen, and Baby is her idol." But Vira had succeeded in making herself very useful to the young mother; it was something to be able to step out of the house on an errand, leaving in charge one whom she knew would not desert Baby, nor be careless about her, nor permit her in any way to injure herself.

"I have not been in the habit of trusting her out of my sight," said Mrs. Perkins to a neighbor; "but that little Vira Bruce is a born nurse, and she loves my baby so that I feel as safe with her as I should if she were a grown woman."

Vira had overheard some such remark one day, and it made her cheeks glow, and her eyes sparkle with pleasure. She thought of it when she was planning about the kitchen floor; in fact, it had to do with her new idea, and now in her straight-forward way she said, "Mrs. Perkins, do you ever hire folks to do any work for you?"

"Dear me, no," said that lady, laughing. "I never have any money to pay folks for working for me; I have to do all my work myself. Oh, I had to hire quite a little when I was sick, and Baby was sick," she added, her face growing grave over the memory of her troubles, "and I have not got it all paid up yet; but we are going to pay it; things are looking a good deal brighter than they did. Oh, no! I do all my own work. Why did you want to know?"

"I was thinking," said Vira, "suppose you didn't have to pay in money?"

"Why, child, what have I to pay in *but* money?" asked Mrs. Perkins curiously.

"Things," said Vira vaguely.

"I have not too many things, child," and Mrs. Perkins laughed. "I never did suppose I could get along with so few things keeping house as I do now. What my mother would think I don't know, I'm sure; and as for my sister Mary, she would be sure that she couldn't do it. There are ever so many things we can do without, if we try, that we never thought we could, and I get along real well. John says he is astonished every night to think of what I have managed to do, with the little I have to do with. I shouldn't wonder if you would be that kind of a woman, Vira; you have managed beautifully about white-washing the walls, I am sure."

"Yes," said Vira, with a long-drawn sigh, "but it is the floor, you see; I don't know how to manage that. I thought maybe, Mrs. Perkins, you would want to go down to the fair, one day—most everyone goes, and there is lots of nice things to see, they say—and I thought maybe you would let me keep Baby all day; I could feed her her milk, and her porridge, and everything, and I'd take just the best care of her; and then I thought maybe you would pay me by lending me some things."

"Lending you some things?" Mrs. Perkins was bewildered. "Why, child, what possible things have I that I could lend you that would do you any good?"

"A scrub-brush, and a scrub-cloth, and a bar of yellow soap," said Vira, with startling promptness. "They are the things I want. The floor has got to be cleaned, and mother says it can't be cleaned without a scrub-brush and cloth and soap, and we ain't got no scrub-brush, nor cloth, nor nothing at all that will do to make one; and as for soap, why, we ain't got a cake of soap in the world."

Mrs. Perkins was bustling about her neat little kitchen getting supper. She was going to have flap-jacks for supper, for John was uncommonly fond of such as she could make, and they had had only "a cold bite" for dinner; she was very busy, and in some hurry, but she stopped mid- way between the table and the stove, and turned to give to Vira an astonished and pitying look.

"Poor little thing," she said at last, and her voice trembled. "So you want to earn a scrub-cloth and a bar of soap? Why, child, I can lend them to you just as well as not. It doesn't take but a very little soap."

"No," said Vira firmly, "we won't do that; mother won't. She says she is low-down poor, and that we have to be ragged, and dirty, and all that, but she is going to be honest; she won't borrow, not from anybody, because she hasn't got anything to pay it with, and she doesn't expect to have; and we haven't begged yet, though mother says she doesn't know but we are coming to that; so I couldn't borrow the things, Mrs. Perkins, but if I could work and earn them somehow, earn the use of them, you know, I could bring them back."

"Of course," said Mrs. Perkins. "Why, that is easily managed, Vira; you have worked for me often already; you have paid for the use of my scrub-brush and cloth over and over again. See how I leave my baby with you and run to the store for yeast, or run to the well for water; I couldn't leave her a minute if you were not here to look after her. Oh, you have paid for the use of the scrub-cloth many a time, and the soap, too; but then I am willing to make a bargain with you," she made haste to add, as she saw the look of determination on Vira's face. "I don't want to go to the fair, because I have no twenty-five cents to pay to get in, and no time to spend if I had; but I do want to get some pretty sprigged calico to make some slips for Baby, the worst kind; I have been planning how to manage it for some time. It seems a good while to be gone and leave a baby with such a little girl as you, Vira, but I thought it all over, and I thought of asking yon to take care of her maybe tomorrow, while I went down to the store. I believe I could trust you better than I could some older one, Baby loves you so much; in fact, I just know I can depend upon you; and if you can come in tomorrow and stay an hour with her, while I clip to the store and get my calico and back again, why, it will pay for all the soap you can use on your floor with one scrubbing, and the loan of the bucket, and cloth, and brush in the bargain. You are a good little girl for trying to help your mother get things cleaned up; I don't think she ought to be downright dis-couraged, with such a little girl as you to help along."

"I have never helped along," said Vira gravely. "I never thought about it until I got the picture. I never thought that the floor was dirty, nor the walls, nor nothing; it was the picture, you know, Mrs. Perkins, about having a 'clean heart'; but that is inside of you, and you can't manage it; all I can do is to have things clean around it. Maybe that is doing something; it's nicer, anyhow. I like your floor—it looks nice—and I like our walls. Mother says she had forgot it did make such a difference, and father said this morning that it was as good as a picture to look at them. And the walls make me think of the floor. But I wish I could find out about the picture; you said you didn't understand how to explain it. Haven't you got any folks that you could ask about it, just how they do it?"

"No," said Mrs. Perkins, with a very flushed face; "I don't know that I have. I tell you what it is, Vira, you ought to go to Sunday-school; they explain such things as that there."

"I am going," said Vira quietly, "just as soon as I get clothes and things fit to go in. I haven't got only these, you know. Mother washes them out after I go to bed at night, but she has had to do it this long while without any soap, and she says they don't look nice like they used to; besides they are all ragged, anyway, and there is nothing to patch them with; but I am going to have clothes one of these days, when mother gets regular work; then I am going to Sunday-school. But it seems a long time to wait. Every time I see a funeral go by I think maybe I might die before I learned what it meant; then I couldn't see Him, you know, because I am not clean inside." And she shook her head sadly. "It means thoughts, mother says, and I have lots of bad thoughts. Sometimes I am mad at father. I think if I was a man I wouldn't sit on a barrel and whittle, and drink whisky, and not get my little girl any clothes to wear to Sunday-school. And then I feel wicked; feel as though I should like to kick him, or something. And I am mad at girls, sometimes, that go by all dressed up. Once I felt mad at Martha, because she had a nice clean apron on. It was starched, and it shone, and she had a ribbon on her hair. I am very ugly, I suppose, and I don't know how to help it. If you will let me earn the soap, and brush, and things, Mrs. Perkins, I will be just too glad for anything, because I am going to make it clean outside, anyhow, and see how it will look."

CHAPTER 11

How It Cleaned House

SHE is the queerest creature you ever saw in your life," said Mrs. Perkins to her husband, when he was eating flap-jacks as fast as he could, and throwing kisses meantime at the baby, who sat in her high-chair close at hand. "I wish you could have heard her go on this afternoon, like a little old woman. In some things she doesn't seem more than five years old, and in some things she is fifty, at least. Oh, dear, they are so poor! I declare I thought we were poor, but I believe I will call myself rich after this. My sister Mary doesn't know how I manage with the few things I have to keep house with; I wonder what she would think if she could see that poor Mrs. Bruce's house. But then she doesn't 'keep house,' poor woman, she just manages to live. I wish there were some way to contrive to get that little thing some clothes; she wants to go to Sunday-school. She asks the queerest questions about that 'picture' she has got, as she calls it; it is a Bible verse, and she asks questions that the minister himself couldn't answer. She is afraid she will die, don't you think, before she finds out what the words mean!"

"Oh," said John, in a very sympathetic tone. "What are the words, Nannie?"

Mrs. Perkins repeated them with a tremble in her voice, and a little touch of embarrassment.

"Blessed are the pure in heart, for they shall see God."

"Humph!" said John. "Pretty big verse for her to deal with, that's a fact; pretty big for any of us, Nannie. According to the way I look at the world, there ain't many to claim that blessing."

"I wish I knew how to explain it to her," said Mrs. Perkins gravely. But for this John had no answer.

Promptly at two o'clock the next afternoon Vira presented herself ready to be nursemaid, and the "sprigged" dresses for the baby were bought; delicate little white and blue calico, in which both mother and nurse agreed that baby would look "too sweet for anything," and the scrubbing-cloth and bar of soap were borrowed, ready for the next day's work.

"Mother thinks I can't do it," said Vira with gravity, "and I am going to show her. She has got work tomorrow; she will be gone all day long; she is going to wash at the hotel, and when she gets back I am going to have the room all clean."

"That is good," said Mrs. Perkins heartily. "I will come in and show you how to do it, if you like. There is just a little knack about it, you know, and then I guess you can do it quite nicely; but it is pretty hard work for such small bands as yours."

"My hands are strong," said Vira, looking at them gravely; "anyhow, they have got to scrub that floor. I can make it look better than it does now, I am most sure."

Perhaps you do not know what a little girl with willing hands, and plenty of hot water, and a good scrubbing-brush, and a bar of soap, and a kind neighbor to show her how to manage, can accomplish with a very dirty floor? Vira Bruce does; she had never worked so hard in all her life, but by five o'clock in the afternoon she sat in triumph on the front door-step. Every bone in her body ached as if it had the toothache; every nerve tingled with weariness; but the floor—Oh, you should have seen the floor! It was stained with mysterious daubs of something which refused to yield to soap and hot water, or even to a little bit of ashes which Mrs. Perkins resorted to, and it was burned in two or three places around the stove; but compared with the complexion it had worn in the morning, when Mrs. Bruce left; it was white; and Vira, tired but triumphant, sat where she could command a full view both of the clean floor and the street, watching for her mother, eager to catch the first glimpse of her astonished face when she should see the change. Perhaps you think Vira was happy? She had expected to be, and was a good deal dismayed when she discovered that no sooner had the floor dried enough to show how much improved it was, than straightway the window, and the stove, and the ugly black table, as if in revenge for her efforts, looked dirtier and more hopelessly disagreeable than ever before. In fact, Vira told the window, looking very solemnly at it, that it was a perfect disgrace to the floor, and if she were the floor she couldn't stay in the same room with it all night; she knew she couldn't. As for the gray old stove, and the black old table, the wall and the floor must hate them both.

"It never ends," she said, sighing heavily. "It is worse than the twenty-six letters; we have got to z now, and Martha knows them all, and George does almost, though he will get mixed up on b and d; but we have got to the end of them. But there is no end to this; first it was the wall, then the floor, and now it's the table and stove, and each thing makes the other look worse."

For about one minute she looked at them disheartened, then her face brightened; she doubled up her own brown little fist and shook it at the window. "I'll wash you," she said, "to-morrow, see if I don't; I'll find a rag somewhere that will do for you, and you shan't look so hateful and cobwebby another day, and I will scrub the table, too. Oh, I know how to scrub now, anyhow! I say it shall be clean outside, everywhere."

"Well, well, well!" said Mrs. Bruce. "Who would have thought that you could have done it? I declare for it, Alvira Miranda, I don't know what you will stop at; you are just the oddest child that was ever born, now that's a fact. But I do say for it, this clean floor does me good. I like clean things as well as the next one. Why, I was used to them, child. My sakes! I was thinking of it today: I met a young one coming along with her hands full of wild flowers, and it made me think how I used to go away out in the country after berries, and flowers, and things for mother. I used to wear a pretty blue and white gingham dress with short sleeves, and a white apron, and white stockings; and Carrie—that's my little sister that died—would be all dressed up in white. We used to bring our aprons full of things for mother; and when we got home she would be sitting there waiting for us, with a pretty dress on, and the room so clean that you could have eaten your supper off the floor. Talk about clean things! I've had 'em; I know all about 'em: Why, mother's stove used to shine so you could see your face in it!"

Vira looked thoughtfully over at the stove, as her mother said this, and Mrs. Bruce continued her remembrances.

"You remind me of myself, child, in some things. I used to like to muss around and make things clean when I was of your age. There were three of us girls, my sister Anna, and our Cousin Mary and I, and we liked nothing better than to wash the dishes and clean up the kitchen. We used to fly around and try to get everything done while mother was outdoors tending to something, and surprise her. But land! We had things to do with—soap, and towels, and everything, and nice long aprons to cover our dresses and keep them clean. Oh, I tell you I wasn't used to the kind of life that you are! Why, if I could get you one rig for Sunday as nice as we used to wear every day of our lives, I would be a happy woman. But there wasn't any whisky in our house; that made the difference. If we could go to a world where they haven't any whisky, we could have things like other folks. There isn't a better man living than your father, if he could let that stuff alone. Then we could have a shining stove, and bread and butter for supper, and a cloth on the table, and a great big pitcher of milk. Oh, dear me!

"Well, child, you have done wonders; it is nice to see the floor clean, anyhow. Your father can't take that and swap it off for whisky; and maybe he will like the looks of it."

"Mother," said Vira, intense earnestness in her voice, "isn't there anything that can be done to get father to give up whisky?"

Mrs. Bruce shook her head. "I don't know of a living thing, child; I gave that up long ago. He just can't let it alone. He means to; I believe in my heart he wants to, but it has got such a hold of him, somehow, he can't: he ain't ugly, though, and je don't kick us around like foot-balls, as some of them do; we've got something yet to be thankful for, Vira."

It was an interesting thing to watch that house change. Little by little the motto on the wall worked its wonders, over the wall, over the floor, over the window, over the ugly table, and the gray stove, and the rickety chairs, until Mrs. Bruce, looking about her one evening in satisfaction, said:

"There isn't a dirty thing in it, Vira, except us: and if you will go straight to bed I will make every dud you have as clean as hot water and this bit of soap that is left will do it. I haven't had any soap to wash them with in a good while, and it will make a difference. I am going to buy a bar of soap the very next time I go to the store. I might set it down as one of the necessary things again; I used to, but I got a spell of thinking I didn't care, and I would let things go, I might as well be dirty as clean. I thought there wasn't anything worth living for, any way, but it was all a mistake, Vira; it makes a great difference to have a clean floor and a clean table, if you haven't got anything to put on it. I declare, I had forgotten how it felt to be clean; but it feels good."

"Yes," said Vira, with satisfaction, "it does. I wish we could wash these bedclothes, mother; I think they are horrid."

"They are that," said Mrs. Bruce, surveying them with disgust. "I would like to own a pair of tongs, and then take them duds one by one and put them in the stove and set fire to them.

One of these days, Vira, when we get hold of some better things, we'll do it, though they would make good scrub-cloths, some of them. Now you just duck into bed, child, and I will scrub out your clothes and dry them around the fire, and mend them a little bit maybe, in spite of my saying they would never hold together to be mended anymore: we have got to do something to them to make them match this room better."

"It is all outside," said Vira softly to herself, as she closed her eyes, and the words which were almost constantly present now in her mind, said themselves over and over in her thoughts: "Blessed are the pure in heart." She thought of Nero's version of it: "Them that have clean hearts are tickled to death." How was she to get one? She had managed the floor, and the table, and all the little furniture in the room, and it had made a great difference; how was she to manage the inside of things? How was she to find out how to do it? If she could only go to Sunday-school. If she could only meet again the ladies who had given her the picture. She had looked for them often and often on the street, running after people who she imagined might be them, staring eagerly into strangers' faces, only to meet with cold rebuke, sometimes with angry reprimand. "I will find out, sometime, see if I don't," was the determined little girl's last thought before she went to sleep.

The wind sometimes blows hard even in the sunshiny country where Vira lived; the next was a very blowy day, for that part of the world, and Vira, with a big basket on her arm, filled with sweet potatoes which had been given her mother in payment for a few hours' work, was having much ado to keep her scant clothing in order. Suddenly she forgot all about the

wind, and the heavy basket, and the fun that it was to watch
other girls struggling. along like herself, for there in the distance
she was sure she recognized the form of the pretty lady who
had given her the picture. She knew Miss Southey and Mrs.
Carpenter only as "the pretty lady "and the other one." This,
she felt sure, was "the pretty lady." And in spite of the wind,
and the weight of her basket, she set off on the run to try to
overtake her. After having watched and waited so long, she felt
as though it would never do to lose sight of her again; it was
very hard work; what with the wind and the heavy potatoes,
Vira was well-nigh breathless when at last she plunged across
the street and stopped directly in front of her.

Some time before this she had made up her mind that she
was not mistaken in the person. Her keen eyes had carefully
studied the face and form of the lady with a kind voice and
pleasant smile, and she had a good memory.

"What in the world!" exclaimed Miss Southey, as Vira
landed directly in front of where she expected to step next. Vira
had not yet gotten her breath, and she spoke in quick little
gasps:

"Oh, ma'am! If you please—what does that thing mean?"

"What thing?" asked Miss Southey, very much startled.
"What are you talking about, my child? Where did you come
from, and what is it you want? Set down your basket, child; it is
too heavy for you to carry, anyway. What is the matter?"

"Why, nothing," said Vira, speaking more carefully, "only
the wind blew me and whirled me, and I kind of lost my breath.
I was in such a hurry for fear you would get out of sight before

I got to you; and I've been hunting and hunting you ever since, and I want to know what it means."

"My dear little girl, there must be some mistake; I cannot be the one you are looking for; I never saw you before. What is it you are talking about? What do you want to know?"

"The picture," said Vira. "You have seen me before; you and the other one was down to the big room where the tree growed right inside the room, and had things on it. And you gave me the picture, and I want to know what it means. Mother says it means 'clean inside,' but I don't see how it can; you can make things clean outside, because you can wash 'em, and scrub 'em, and whitewash 'em, and if they are stoves you can black 'em and make 'em clean. But you can't take the inside of you out and wash it, nor clean it anyhow, and I don't see what it can mean, nor how to get it."

"You poor little child," said Miss Southey, and the tones of her voice made Vira think of the music which she sometimes heard as she passed the church at the corner. "So you are Vira? You do not look the same, some way. And you have been looking for me? I am so sorry you did not know where to find me. I have been intending to go in search of you ever since the Christmas-tree. Why didn't you come to Sunday-school?"

"I couldn't," said Vira. "I ain't got no clothes yet that can go to Sunday-school. These is clean," and she surveyed them complacently, "and mother mended them again, though she said she couldn't; but she did, real nice; still, they ain't Sunday-school clothes, and never will be. I couldn't wear 'em there, you know, but I hunted the streets all over. Now can't you tell me what it means, real quick? 'Cause I've got to get these potatoes home.

Mrs. Perkins is going to have some of them, too, and she is going to let mother have a loaf of bread in place of them, that she baked herself."

"Which way do you go?" said Miss Southey. "I will turn and walk with you. Let me help carry the basket, Vira."

But this offer Vira stoutly refused. "The handle is all kind of dirty," she said; "you would get your pretty gloves dirty, and they are beautiful clean now; this basket ain't for such as you. I like clean things myself; we have been having them all clean up to our house this week, and they do look nice, that's a fact. But I don't know what the verse can mean."

CHAPTER 12

How It Puzzled Vira

HAVE you learned the verse, Vira?" asked Miss Southey.

"I should think I had!" said Vira. "So has George and Martha. I guess there is one verse they will never forget; no more will I. Don't you know which one it is?" and she said the words slowly and reverently, closing with the usual question: "Do you say that 'pure' means clean, and 'heart' means the inside of you? And if it does, how do you get it clean?"

"Do you know the difference between right and wrong, Vira?" asked Miss Southey.

"Of course," said Vira, turning grave eyes upon her questioner. "Everybody knows that it is wrong to steal, and tell lies, and such things."

"Yes; but perhaps you will understand better if I tell you that a 'pure heart' means a right heart—a heart that wants to find out what is right, then wants to do it and think it, and be right all the while. There is a sense in which you could call that being clean, you know." Vira nodded and looked grave; she did not fully understand it, but she knew enough about her own feelings to realize that it was not an easy lesson. "Then, as to the heart," said Miss Southey, "your mother's explanation was very good; it is that which we think with, and love with, and hate with, you know, and that helps us to be sorry or be glad over anything. It is the part which goes away when we say of people that they are 'dead.' The body is here just the same, you know, after people are dead. The eyes, the hands, the feet—in every way the body is just the same, but something has gone away; that is the part which does not die, and it is the part which the verse means when it says, 'Blessed are the right in heart.' Do you know what 'blessed' means, Vira?"

"Nero said it meant 'tickled to death,'" said the child, with deepest gravity.

"Who is Nero?"

Vira explained.

"Well," said Miss Southey, "his definition is not a bad one; it means very glad and happy."

"But I don't see how they get 'em," said Vira. "Do folks that don't lie, nor steal, nor swear, nor do any of them things, have 'em?"

"No," said Miss Southey; "there are other wrong things besides those. People who have right hearts speak gentle words, even when they are spoken to roughly; they forgive people who have hurt them in any way; they try to help everybody; in short, they try in all ways to please Jesus. Do you know Jesus, little girl?"

"Yes," said Vira, "I know who he is, if you mean that; mother told me something about him. I know that he is God's son, and that he knows everything that's going on, and sees people all the time. Sometimes I wish he didn't; I don't want anybody to see me all the time."

"Do you know about how He came to earth, and lived here for years in order to show us how to live? And how He helped people—cured the sick and lame and suffering ones every-where, and fed hungry people? And do you know about how He was treated?"

They had turned a street corner, where the wind had less power; so they moved slowly, and as they walked Miss Southey told that story which you all know so well, but which to Vira was very new, about the suffering, and finally the death of Jesus on the cross, and how he prayed for his enemies, even for those who mocked at and spit on him.

"What made them treat Him hateful like that?" burst forth Vira. "What did they hate Him for?" Then, suddenly nodding her head, as if she had discovered her answer before Miss Southey could speak, "I s'pose they was rum-sellers," she said fiercely. "Rum-sellers can do anything; I hate 'em!"

"Oh, Vira did not I just tell you how Jesus on the cross prayed for his enemies? Asked God to forgive them, although they had treated him so cruelly?"

"I couldn't," said Vira; "I should have hated 'em. I couldn't have prayed for them at all. I wouldn't want them to be forgiven."

"Then you wouldn't be like Jesus, wouldn't be trying to be like him; and I told you, you know, that that was one reason why he came to earth, to make a pattern for us. Do you know what a pattern is? Did you ever see a person lay down a paper pattern and cut something by it?"

Vira nodded her head. "Lots of times. Mrs. Perkins does that for the baby; she cut her blue-and-white dress out that way—the cunningest little pattern for a sleeve that you ever saw. And she has got a pattern for her cap, and, oh, lots of patterns."

"Very well; suppose Mrs. Perkins, having been given a pattern to cut her baby's sleeve by, had left it lying on the shelf, or rolled up in her basket, and had said, 'I don't care about that pattern, I will cut the sleeve as I like,' and then had cut it so that it was an ugly shape, and did not fit Baby at all; then she would be like the people who say, 'I cannot pattern my life after Jesus; I don't know anything about it; I'll pattern my life as I like,' and had gone on making their lives ugly and ill-shaped?"

Vira had no reply to make to this; she understood the illustration in part, but there were things about it which puzzled her. "How did He come to do it?" she asked presently. "What made Him let them kill Him, when He was so strong, and could do anything? Why didn't He tell them they shouldn't nail Him to that cross, and just go away and leave them?"

"Because, Vira, one of the things for which He came on earth was to die for us; it was necessary in order to save us. You cannot understand now, perhaps, why it was so. Men and women who have studied this question for years do not understand it fully, only they know the facts. All the world was full of people who had broken God's law, and who therefore could not go to Heaven unless some other way was made for them to go; they had spoiled the way by not obeying God, and they had to be punished; but Jesus came and offered to be punished in their place, and all who will accept of him as their Saviour he will take care of, and see that they get safely home to Heaven, to live with him there. But the people who accept him as their Saviour promise to obey him."

Vira drew a long, quivering breath. "And does he say that we have got to forgive folks, and not hate them when they have been ugly to us? Would I have to forgive Jim Bryan when he throws sand at me, and calls me a drunkard's girl? And will I have to forgive Pete Knowles, who sells rum to my father, and takes all the things he can get hold of to pay for it, so that mother ain't got no dishes to cook with, nor nothing?"

"Yes," said Miss Southey, firmly, "you will have to forgive them all, and try to help them, if you belong to Jesus."

"Then, I can't," said Vira. "There's no use in talking; if that is what it means to have it clean inside, I can't never have it."

"Yes, you can," said Miss Southey. "I haven't told you the whole of the story. This Jesus—who knows all about us, you remember, because he is God, and made us—knew that we couldn't do these things ourselves; couldn't make our hearts right—so he promised to do it for us. He said our part was to come to him and ask for clean hearts. If he saw that we really wanted them he would give them to us; then he would help us every day to keep them clean; to keep our thoughts and our words and our actions right; he wouldn't leave us for a single minute to ourselves, but all the things which we could not do he would do for us; that was part of his work."

"Oh, my!" said Vira. "How does he get it out and put a clean one in?"

"He doesn't do it in that way; he just changes it. When you have soiled hands, Vira, and want to have clean hands, you don't have to have a new pair of hands; you plunge those into the water, and take the soap and rub hard, and wash until they are clean. And Jesus, whom we cannot see, does something to our hearts; does it by his power—changes them as much as the hands are changed after we have made them clean. We do not understand how he does it, and we do not need to understand; that is his part. Our part is to ask him for the clean hearts, and then to obey everything which he tells us to do."

Vira came to a sudden stop at another turn in the road. "You better not go down Swamp Lane," she said. "It ain't a nice place. You've got such a pretty dress on, and you can't keep it clean going through the lane. I've got to go home now. I understand about the verse better than I did, anyhow."

"You must come to Sunday-school," said Miss Southey, "then you will understand it better. I am so sorry that I lost sight of you all these days. Which is your house, Vira? I am coming to see your mother. Is she at home now?"

Vira shook her head. "She has gone to the hotel to scrub; she won't be home in a good while, and I am going to get the dinner myself. We are going to have sweet potatoes, and Mrs. Perkins is going to let us have a loaf of bread, and we have got a little molasses in a cup, and some salt, and we are going to have a splendid dinner. There is only one thing that I wish about it. Mrs. Perkins spreads a cloth on the table every time she has any dinner, and it looks just as nice—almost as pretty as a picture.

And we ain't got no cloth; mother says it will be a good while before we have one, even if she gets work steady, because there is a thousand things to have first."

"Do you think your mother will be at home this evening?" said Miss Southey. "I want to have a talk with her."

"I guess she will," said Vira; "she is mostly home evenings. She used to go out after father, but she don't anymore; she says there is no use. Pete Knowles gets hold of him, and gives him whisky in spite of us. Maybe it is a good thing that we haven't got a cloth for the table; I s'pose Pete Knowles would want it for his table if we had."

There was intense bitterness in the little girl's voice. It was clearly going to be a very hard thing for her to forgive Pete Knowles, on whom she laid all the blame of their desolate home. Miss Southey looked at her pitifully; she had never known so forlorn and ragged a little girl, nor one who talked in this way. Certainly the child must be gotten into Sunday-school, and that without delay. She resolved to go that very afternoon, and see Mrs. Carpenter and one or two other ladies who had children, and see if a package of clothing could not be made up to fit Vira out respectably. So with a promise to come in the evening without fail, they separated. It was a very grave-faced little girl who went about the clean room, started the fire in the clean stove with pine chips, got out the useful tin pail and put some water in it, with a view to boiling three sweet potatoes. Even sweet potatoes, in that land where they grew plentifully, were not very common in this family. To have a good-sized one apiece at a meal was a luxury. Vira had expected to be full of happiness as well as importance over the getting of this midday meal, but some things which Miss Southey had said had filled her heart with unrest. As she moved about she tried to keep her eyes away from the "picture" on the wall. But despite her efforts the familiar words would stare at her: "Blessed are the pure in heart."

They might well be 'tickled to death,'" she told herself gloomily. "Folks who can be as good as that, ought to be happy, I s'pose; but I never can, never in this world. I dunno as there is any use in trying."

For nearly fifteen minutes poor Vira was in despair. Then her face began to clear; she had decided that there might possibly be some mistake. There was no use thinking about forgiving Pete Knowles; that, of course, was out of the question. Miss Southey didn't know "them kind of folks," she assured herself, and could not, of course, be expected to understand how impossible it would be to forgive them; but He knew all about it, if He knew as much as Miss Southey said He did. He would not expect her to do what she couldn't. Miss Southey's promise of a wonderful Helper had been but dimly understood. Vira could not comprehend how anybody could make her do what she couldn't do, and she declared to herself that she never could and never would forgive old Pete Knowles, and nobody needn't ask her to. But there must be some way of getting around it; at any rate she wouldn't give up yet.

CHAPTER 13

An Eventful Sunday Morning

VIRA BRUCE stood before her bit of glass and looked at herself with an astonishment which was too great for words. By the way, that bit of glass has a history. It was not more than six inches square—in fact, it was not square at all, but was an irregular triangle. One morning down at the corner store an accident had happened. A man hurrying through the room with a heavy sack on his shoulder had run against what seemed to Vira to be an elegant mirror, and knocked it from its place on a shelf; it broke in many pieces. Vira, who was waiting for a quart of meal out of the very sack which had done the mischief, uttered an exclamation of dismay over the ruins.

The head clerk, who was looking on at the wreck, turned and looked at her in apparent astonishment. He must have been used to young people who went through the world with careless eyes, and thoughts indifferent to the amount of damage which things suffered, provided they did not belong to them. Suddenly the man stooped, and selecting the largest piece from the wreck said:

"Here, little girl, do you want to look at yourself?"

This was excitement enough, but when it was actually made plain to her that she might take the treasure home and keep it always, she grew positively pale. What a wonderful thing to happen to her.

Taking Mrs. Perkins into her confidence and displaying her treasure, that good lady had suggested that the edges be bound with a bit of bright paper for a frame, and had herself furnished the bit of paper and the paste, Vira doing the work under her direction. The result was a thing of beauty, at which Vira gazed many times a day.

It will seem strange to the young people who live in houses where toilet mirrors are part of the furnishings of all the chambers, but it is a fact that Vira had never looked into a glass before, except when she stood on tiptoe and peeped at herself occasionally when one of the little mirrors in the store was placed low enough for her to do so. To have a glass of her very own was a possession which she had thought too improbable to even dream about.

It must be confessed that the image which was always shown her had been very unsatisfactory indeed, but on this particular morning a change had come. It is hardly a wonder that she stood silent before the vision, and felt that it could not be the reflection of Alvira Miranda Bruce. It had her hair and eyes, it is true, but the hair was neatly combed, and the eyes sparkled as Vira had not imagined hers could. It had on a white dress sprinkled over with tiny reddish-brown leaves; very small leaves, and so natural that it seemed to Vira she ought to be able to pick them. It is true that the material was only calico, and the dress had been laundered many times, but it was by far the prettiest one that Vira had ever worn. Moreover, she knew that underneath it was a clean white skirt, and underclothing whole and clean; and her feet were dressed in neat stockings and low shoes, which fitted her as well as though they had been made on purpose for her feet, instead of having been worn one summer by Alice Wilson, one of Miss Southey's friends. On the chair beside Vira lay a hat. It was one of those which had traveled southward for the Christmas-tree, and it had been made in Nettie Beldon's own room, while she worked steadily at her motto, and watched with deepest interest the hat grow before her eyes. It was intended by Mrs. Carpenter and Miss Southey for a little girl who was ill on the night of the Christmas festival, so it had been laid aside until Minnie should get well enough to claim it; but time proved that Minnie needed no more hats, or clothing of any sort such as we use here. She went away one morning to the bright country where all needs are supplied, and the hat, lying on the upper corner of Mrs. Carpenter's store-room shelf, had been forgotten until Miss Southey stopped there on her mission, and said:

"Now I have everything but a hat; I think I must go home and see if I can manufacture one for the child."

Then Mrs. Carpenter said, "Why, I wonder if Minnie's hat wouldn't be just the thing?" She got it down from her shelf, and it was "just the thing." How interested Vira would have been could she have known that the hat and the motto grew side by side.

"She looks just as nice as the best of them," said Mrs. Bruce, standing in the doorway watching Vira until she became a speck in the distance.

"Why shouldn't she?" asked Vira's father, who for a wonder was at home, and was sober. He had looked with a good deal of interest upon Vira as she passed out of the door; it astonished him not a little that a girl so well-dressed and so pretty should be his daughter.

"Why shouldn't she look as well as the rest of them? Better, for that matter; she is a prettier girl than any of them around here; I'm sure I didn't know she was so pretty."

Mrs. Bruce drew a long sigh. "She's pretty enough," she said wearily, "too pretty; I've often wished she wasn't so good looking. It is harder to get along, being good looking, and live the life she has got to live."

For some reason this sentence made old Joe, the drunkard, feel cross at his wife. "You are always complaining," he said snarlingly. "What's to hinder her living as good a life as any of them? She's smart, and she's pretty, and she will make her way in the world, like enough."

"No, she won't," said Mrs. Bruce, with not a touch of anger in her voice, just a dull discouraged tone. "The things that will hinder her you know just as well as I do. Her father is 'Old Joe, the drunkard,' and she lives in an old hut that is not fit for even low-down pigs that respect themselves; and she hasn't got a rag to her back except what is given to her in charity. She has got a hard life to live, as her mother had before her, and the quicker her good looks go, the better it will be for her; and I don't know as her smartness will do her any good; she can't go to school, because she hasn't got clothes to wear. The lady that brought her her things said that the hat she has on was to belong to a little girl that died; and I said to myself while she was telling it, that maybe I ought to wish that Alvira Miranda would die now, while she is a little girl, and pretty, and trying to be somebody, and not wait until she grew up and lost all heart, and lived like the pigs, and didn't see any way out."

"That's always the way," said Old Joe, in an injured tone; "never any peace; always flinging at me because I ain't rich, and can't dress you in silk and satin. 'Tain't any wonder I spend my days at the saloon, I'm sure; no peace to be had at home."

"Home!" said Mrs. Bruce bitterly. "A charming home you have provided for your wife and child to stay in, now ain't it? I don't wonder you stay at saloons, either; you show good taste. I suppose they have got comfortable chairs to sit down on, and wood to make a fire with when it is cold, and blinds to shut the sun out when it is hot. There is no use in talking, Joe, you have ruined yourself, and your wife, and now you are going to ruin the child; there ain't nothing for her to live for, more than there is for me. But there! I don't know why I go all over it; I may just as well keep still, as I made up my mind to long ago. Seeing her go off fixed up to Sunday-school, as I used to when I was a little girl, set me to thinking, that's all."

"Maybe you think I didn't use to go to Sunday-school," said Joe, laying down the pipe he had been smoking. "I was dressed up nicer than you ever saw me, and went off Sunday mornings to Sunday-school and to church as regularly as the day came. You ain't the only one that was brought up."

"More shame to you, then," said Mrs. Bruce. "I know you were brought up nice, and know how things ought to be, and how your father had them for his wife and children; if you didn't there would be more excuse for you."

It wasn't a pleasant Sunday morning at all. All this talk didn't do Joe, the drunkard, a bit of good, and more than that, his wife knew it wouldn't. She realized dimly that it would be a great deal better if she could keep her tongue from saying any of those sharp, uncomfortable words; but the morning was warm, and she had worked hard the day before, and had not had sufficient breakfast, and she felt tired out, and more discouraged than usual. She did not want to hurt her husband; the probability is that if anyone else had been giving him a lecture, she would have stood up for him bravely, and have said that there were worse men a good deal than he was; that if he could be coaxed to let whisky alone she wouldn't want a better man. But to his face she could not bring herself to say an encouraging word. She went away from the room at last, and out to the back door and sat down in a cluttered-up little stoop, because she wanted to get a breath of air, and get away from the man whose presence irritated her. Poor father and mother. What ruined lives; I hope somebody will come soon with a helping hand, or there will be two utter wrecks in that home.

Meantime Vira, who was full of wonder over all she saw and heard, was seated in a bright Sunday-school room, in one corner of which stood the very same Christmas-tree that had astonished and delighted her eyes a few weeks before. There were mottoes on the walls, or "pictures," as Vira called them— Bible verses in illuminated text. She read them each carefully, but assured herself that there were none so pretty as her own. She listened attentively to the lesson. It was a surprising story, the like of which she had never heard before, about a blind man being cured with a touch of clay upon his sightless eyes; she wondered over it in her own mind a great deal, but felt very shy of asking questions. Six well-dressed little girls about her had the effect of hushing her into silence; the questions which on her way to school she had resolved to ask Miss Southey, remained unspoken. She felt as though it would be impossible to form a question, with all those bright eyes leveled at her, and all those keen ears listening to every word she said. It was as much as she could do to reply in the briefest of monosyllables to Miss Southey's questions directed to her personally. For the rest, she sat in the utmost silence, losing not a word that was said, and watching with the deepest eagerness, that if possible some word might be uttered which would throw light on the problem which interested her.

Each little girl had a Bible verse to recite, which seemed in some way to fit the story of the lesson, though as each was allowed to make her own selection, sometimes the connecting link between them and the story was hard to see. For instance, one little girl repeated, "We shall all stand before the judgment seat of Christ."

When Miss Southey asked how she fitted that to the lesson, she answered promptly that she was thinking she would like to have seen Jesus when he was here on earth; she would like to have stood there and watched him open the blind man's eyes, so she tried to find a verse which said she would see him one day.

Vira looked curiously from one to the other. Who was this "Christ" that the little girl talked about? Miss Southey seemed to understand the puzzled look in her eyes.

"He has two names, Vira. People called him Jesus when he lived on earth, and call him so now a great deal, but another name he has is Christ."

"He has lots of names," volunteered one little girl.

"Yes," said Miss Southey, "we know Him by many beautiful names. Can you give another one for Him?"

"He is God," said the little girl gravely. And now Vira Bruce looked startled indeed. "Jesus" and "Christ" and "God" one and the same. How could that be? Then the little girl who had given the verse about the judgment made a statement which puzzled Vira still more.

"Gertie Nolin says that my verse isn't true; she says we couldn't all stand before Him; there wouldn't be room. She says that there are thousands and millions of people, besides thousands and thousands that have died, and there wouldn't be room for them; there can't only just a few stand before one person."

Miss Southey smiled gravely. "Nevertheless, Nannie, the Bible is right, and Gertie Nolin is mistaken. We shall all stand before him; he will make room for us in some way, and each of us will be seen just as plainly as if there were no other there."

Vira went out of the class bewildered. If all people were going to stand before Christ, and another name for Christ was "God," then what did her verse mean, "Blessed are the pure in heart, for they shall see God"?

CHAPTER 14

Perplexity

MISS SOUTHEY had meant to have a little talk with her, but she slipped away, and was walking slowly, with her head down, thinking over her bewilderment. One of the boys rushed past, jostling against her in his haste, knocking from her hand the card which had been given her.

"Halloo!" he said, stooping to pick it up. "If it isn't Alvira Miranda. Were you in Sunday-school—*our* school? I didn't see you."

"Oh, Sandy!" said Vira, with animation, glad to see someone she had ever met before. "I didn't see you, either. Say, Sandy, I want you to tell me something."

"All right," said Sandy, moving along beside her, "what do you want to know? Pitch in, and let's have it, quick, for I promised mother I'd hurry home to take care of Delia and let her go to meeting."

Sandy may be said to be Vira Bruce's one acquaintance of about her own age. He lived only a square away from her home, but on a better looking street, where the houses were comparatively neat, and the people who issued from them were all clean, and their clothes whole and in order. Sandy was a red-haired, freckled-faced boy, with turned-up nose, and not a single pretty feature; yet he had a good-natured smile, and seemed always so merry and happy, that I think most of his acquaintances would have been astonished if they had heard strangers call him homely. He had distinguished himself in Vira's eyes by three times pumping her pail full of water for her, before he filled his own, and asking her cheerily how she was getting along, and when she would begin going to school. This was the extent of her acquaintance with him; but it was a great deal for Vira; not another boy had she ever met who would take the trouble to fill her pail for her, or even make way and give her a chance to do it for herself, before they were supplied. More than that, the most of them made remarks about her bare feet, and ragged clothes and tangled hair, loud enough for her to hear, and disagreeable enough for her to resent with angry eyes. Sandy had never appeared to notice that she was not as well-dressed as himself; but on this Sunday morning he let his twinkling gray eyes look her over from head to foot before he said:

"You look tip-top this morning, Alvira; got on your Sunday best, I guess? That is the reason I did not know you at first—makes a lot of difference. I did see a new scholar over in Miss Southey's class, and wondered who it was; but didn't think it was anybody I knew. I say, Alvira, you've got a tip-top teacher, the best in the school, we boys think."

"Yes," said Vira gravely. "Sandy, I want you to tell me something."

"All right," said Sandy, "I told you to go ahead."

"There's a verse out of the Bible that I have got hanging up at home—it is made into a picture, you know and I want to know what the words on it mean: 'Blessed are the pure in heart, for they shall see God.' Those are the words. I know what the first part of it means, some, but what does 'and they shall see God' mean?"

"Why," said Sandy, his speckled face blushing red, "just what it says, Alvira." He had not expected a question of this sort. "When folks, die, you know, they will see Him then."

"It can't," said Vira positively. "Or—I mean it must mean more than that, or different, somehow; everyone dies—drunkards, and rum-sellers, and all sorts of folks. Very awful bad people, as well as good people; I know enough for that. I have seen lots and lots of funerals go by, and I have known about all sorts of folks dying."

"Of course," said Sandy, "everyone dies."

"Well, that is what I say; the verse can't mean just that, because everybody sees God; my teacher said so this morning. There was a little girl said a verse about it—about standing before Christ—and the teacher said that was what it meant; and that everybody would, and that there would be room for them all, and that he could see each one as plain as if there wasn't anybody else there. Now how can my verse mean that? Did you ever hear it before?"

"Yes," said Sandy gravely; "it is one of the Beatitudes."

"One of the *what?*"

Sandy laughed. "The Beatitudes; I know them all; we have them in Sunday-school every month—to recite in concert, you know. 'Blessed are the pure in heart, for they shall see God.' That's the sixth Beatitude."

"The sixth!" repeated Vira, in astonishment. "Are there more verses like it, Sandy?"

"Not exactly like it," said Sandy, "only they all begin with 'blessed.'"

"And does 'blessed' mean 'tickled to death?'" questioned Vira.

Sandy laughed uproariously. Vira, her face flushing and her eyes looking troubled, said, "That is what Nero said it meant; he talked as though he knew about the Bible, and verses."

"Well," said Sandy, trying to sober his merry face, "I don't know but it is a good definition; I never thought of tacking it on to a Bible verse. I suppose it means folks that are very happy; I don't know but that it will do first-rate to help you understand it."

"But I don't understand it," said Vira. "What would they be tickled about? And if everybody is going to do it, anyway, what difference would it make whether they had things clean inside or not?"

Sandy's round face grew grave, and his gray eyes took a look of determination, almost of awe, over what he was about to try to do.

"I know what you mean," he said; "but there are two kinds of ways to see Him, Vira. When all the folks stand there that time, there is a lot of them that will be scared; they won't want to see Him. They will feel just as you do when you have done something bad and mean, that you know you ought not to do, and you don't want your mother to look at you. That is the way they will feel, a lot of them—scared, and creepy. But there's another kind of folks; they will be tickled about it. They want to see Him, and stand right up before Him and talk to Him. My grandma was one of that kind. She said she wanted to go and live up there, and see Him every day."

"And if you are clean inside is that the way you feel?" asked Vira eagerly. "Is that honestly what it means?"

Sandy nodded. "I guess that is what it means, Vira."

"Oh, but, Sandy, aren't you sure—no matter how bad you have been, or how little you know, or anything?"

"Of course," said Sandy, confidently now. "No matter how bad you have been; it don't make any difference how dirty a thing was, you know, if you only get it clean."

"That's so," said Vira, thinking of the wall and the window-seat at home; "it does make an awful difference with things to have 'em clean; and you can make things clean that were so awful dirty you thought you couldn't. I should think folks would be tickled! You are sure about it, aren't you, Sandy?"

"I reckon I am," said Sandy, with the gravity of a minister. "Grandmother used to talk a lot about such things—it is only a few months since she died and I don't know but that word 'tickled' just describes it. She was tickled about it, and wanted to go as bad as ever a fellow wanted to go to a show, or a fair. She had all the places about living there marked in her Bible, and she used to get me to read them over and over again, till I knew them by heart. I could read them as well with my eyes shut as with them open."

"And did she feel so way up to the time she died?" asked Vira, her great eyes taking on an earnest, solemn look.

Sandy nodded his head several times, then spoke in subdued tones, "Yes, she did; she talked to mother about it up to the last minute, and told her to be sure to come, and all of us; and she said she saw the angels waiting for her, and they were going to take her straight to Jesus. Oh, she was just glad!"

"Well," said Vira, her anxiety taking a new form, "but maybe she had never done anything bad; maybe she had felt so all her life?"

But now Sandy's head shook vigorously. "No," he said, "I told her that one day. I told her she did not know anything about how boys felt, that grandmothers were good, of course, and she was always good. She told me that she used to be very ugly and bad; she said she was worse than she would like to tell me anything about. She was bad until she got to be a grown-up woman, she said, and she kept growing worse and worse till she found this out—this that your verse tells about, you know—and got it; and that made her different all the rest of her life."

Vira drew a long breath of suppressed excitement. "It is just the same story Miss Southey tells," she said eagerly. "Now how did she get it? That is what I want to know."

"I don't know," said Sandy. "I don't know that part."

"Oh, Sandy, don't you? Can't you find out? I want somebody to tell me that I can understand. I want to do it, Sandy Smith; I just feel as though I had got to do it; I have been cleaning up—Oh, weeks!—ever since I got my picture. I made the wall clean—or I got Nero to—and I made the floor clean, and the stove, and the window, and everything; and mother washed my clothes and made them clean; but it was all outside all the time, and I want it clean inside. Can't you find out for me how to do it? Miss Southey tried to tell me, but she talks large words, you know, that I don't understand; if you could find out, you could explain it to me."

"Well," said Sandy, clearing his throat, "I know about how it is done, of course; they pray."

"Who do?"

"Why, the people who want clean hearts. They ask for them, and then they get them."

"Who do they ask?"

"Why, Alvira, they ask God, of course. You aren't a little heathen, are you? Don't you know that folks pray to God? Didn't you hear the superintendent pray today in Sunday-school? They shut their eyes and speak, and God hears them, and gives them what they ask for."

"Does he give them everything they ask for?"

"Well, no," said Sandy; "I don't suppose He does. No, of course He doesn't, or else folks would have all sorts of things that they do without. I don't know just how it is, Vira; you better ask Miss Southey about it. There are some things I know He gives them; grandmother was just sure of some things, and she wasn't of others. Yes, I know how that came, too; she said there were some things He had promised her, and she was sure of them."

"Of course," said Vira, "if He had really promised, she would be sure."

"Well," said Sandy, "there's a promise in your own verse, don't you see?"

"But it doesn't tell you how."

"Well, the how is to ask for it, I know that. Here, bless me! I know a verse that promises it plain enough: 'A new heart will I give them, and a right spirit will I put within them, saith the Lord.' That's the verse I recited last Sunday."

"Give who?"

But Sandy looked perplexed. "I don't know," he said, "folks that want them, I suppose."

"Doesn't everybody want them?"

"I reckon not." Sandy was beginning to get uneasy. The conversation was becoming very close and personal. "I tell you what it is, Vira," he said again, "you better ask Miss Southey; she knows all about such things, and I don't. And I have got to hurry right home to take care of Delia, you know."

CHAPTER 15

The "Big Book"

W ELL, but," said Vira, detaining Sandy by a hand on his jacket sleeve, "Miss Southey has gone home, and I can't see her again until next Sunday; and I don't want to wait, not another day. I can't wait, Sandy," she added, with increasing earnestness. "I have just made up my mind that I want it dreadfully. Do you know, Sandy Smith, that if I ask for it I will get it?"

"I suppose you will," said Sandy; "that's the way to do it, I know. Miss Wheeler says so in the class often enough for me to know so much. You see, you just make up your mind to do the things He wants you to do, and you ask Him, and somehow or other He does it; I don't know anything about how."

"How would you ask?" said Vira, awe-stricken. "What would you say?"

"Why, I suppose you would ask just as you ask anybody for anything. You know enough to ask for a thing if you want it, don't you? Especially if you are talking to somebody that has promised to give it to you for the asking, I should think."

"That's so," said Vira. "Well, Sandy, I am going to try it, and I will tell you how it turns out. Only there is one thing— you said you had got to make up your mind to do what He said. How will He tell you what to do?"

"Why, there's the Bible, you know. Haven't you got a Bible, Vira?"

She shook her head, "I never had a Bible," she said gravely. "Mother used to have one, but father sold it, and I never had any. It is a great big book, besides. Isn't it that big book on the table in Sunday-school?"

"Yes; but that is a large-print book; there are smaller ones. We have got two or three small enough to carry around, though I always forget mine and don't take it to Sunday-school. You ought to have a Bible, Alvira."

"But it is such a big book," said Vira; "there is so much to find out. What will I do till I find out?"

"Why, you have to do just as you do about other things as fast as you find out a thing you do it; things you don't know about have to wait till you do, I suppose."

"Oh!" said Vira. "Well, that isn't very hard. After I have found out a thing I could do it, of course, only—"

At this point she made a full stop. A vivid remembrance of Miss Southey's directions about "forgiving" came to her at the moment. Everything else was beginning to seem easy, but not that. It seemed to her that about that one condition there must be some mistake, because, of course, if God knew everything, as Miss Southey said he did, he knew that she simply could not forgive the man who not only furnished her father's whiskey, but actually coaxed him to buy some whenever he had a few pennies in his pocket. It was silly to talk to her about forgiving such a man. But these thoughts she kept quite to herself.

"Humph!" said Sandy, in response to her last remark; it was evidently not his view of the question. But at this point they had reached the corner where he turned, and with the announcement that he must go and look after Delia right straight off, for there was no end of mischief that she could get into while your back was turned, the freckle-faced boy skipped around the corner, leaving Vira to walk slowly toward home with a face very thoughtful, and a look of resolution slowly settling upon it.

A very decided little girl had Alvira Bruce always been; what she made up her sturdy little will to, she had at least tried hard to do, all her life. Here was the largest task she had ever undertaken. There were things about it that she did not in the least understand; she comprehended that it might lead her toward things that she did not in the least want to do. Nevertheless, during the days in which she had studied that fair blue and brown picture on the wall, there had grown in her heart the desire to be among those who are accounted "Blessed"—to be clean inside.

"I want to be," she said; "I want it, I want it! I don't care what I have to do, or where I have to go; I want it, and I have got to have it. I am going to ask for it this very day, so there!"

The house was deserted. Mr. Bruce, finding it dreary to be left alone, although the kitchen was clean and looked more inviting than it had for many a day, had wandered off to the saloon, where he was always sure of finding what he called good company. And Mrs. Bruce, after sitting on the dreary little stoop until she was tired, had put on her sunbonnet and gone to a neighbor's to inquire about a sick child.

Vira walked directly to the motto on the wall. Perhaps she could not have put her thought into words, but the thought was that the closer she got to that motto, the nearer she would be to God. She knew nothing about praying, save for her experience that day in Sunday-school. Never in her short life had she seen anybody kneel to pray, therefore she stood before the motto and folded her hands as the superintendent had done, and closed her eyes, and said, in low, slow tones, full of awe, "God, up in Heaven, I want to be clean inside." Then, after a moment of silence, she repeated her call, substituting the exact words of the motto: "I want to be pure in heart. Did the promise you made about it mean me? I am Vira Bruce."

A strange little prayer, certainly. There were boys and girls in the Sunday-school from which she had just come who would have laughed immoderately could they have heard her, and who would have repeated the prayer to other boys and girls as a joke, because they understood so well how to use words and forms of prayer that hers to them would have been only a fit subject for ridicule, yet none of them had as honestly prayed as Vira Bruce had that morning. It was a strange day to Vira. She stayed away from the neighbors' all day, not even going in to see Baby Perkins. In her mind was a vague feeling that the day ought to be different, somehow, from any other of her life. Had she not stood before the motto and asked for a wonderful thing?

"To be sure," she said to herself, "I didn't get it; I am not any different from what I was in the morning. I wonder how many times you have to ask? Maybe a great many, it is such a great big thing."

She had taken off her nice clothes and folded them away; they were to be kept for Sunday wear. She had put them in an old box, which she covered over with paper before she fastened the cover tight to it, then set it outside the door among the rubbish which her father seldom disturbed. She was haunted all the while by a fear that the pretty clothes would be exchanged for whiskey.

"I ought to wear them day and night," she muttered. "It is the only way of keeping them safe. If I had them on I would like to see him get them. I'd fight him like a tiger, I would! But I'll keep watch of them; there shan't anybody change those clothes for whiskey."

Dressed in her every-day suit, which was really very clean, and as neatly mended as her mother could compass without patches, she went about the room trying to contrive how, out of very few resources, she could make something nice for a Sunday dinner. From time to time she looked at the motto with a respectful air; it had become even more to her than it was before. Several times during the course of the long slow morning she went over toward it, and folded her hands, closed her eyes, and repeated those same words, growing each time more awe-stricken, if possible. She vaguely realized that she was speaking to an unseen being, who surely heard her, and understood just what she wanted, and who had certainly promised some people, at least, that He would give the thing she asked. The solemn question was, did the promise belong to her? Sandy Smith thought it did; but then, he had confessed that he knew very little about it. There was nothing for her, she thought, but to wait until she could talk with somebody who really understood. Meantime, it could do no harm to speak those words of prayer, because God, if He heard her, would understand that she didn't know any better, and was simply trying to find out whether He meant her or not.

Toward the middle of the afternoon a new idea came to Vira. Sandy had said that almost everybody had a Bible; perhaps Mrs. Perkins had. She had never seen one in her room, but she might keep it packed away somewhere in a box or drawer. Mrs. Perkins had several drawers. She meant to call upon her and inquire about it.

"Because," said Vira to herself, "it is a very big book, and if I am to do the things that are in it, I ought to begin. I wonder if you begin at the beginning?"

Mrs. Perkins was alone with Baby, and was engaged at the moment of Vira's entrance, in comforting her because of a prick which her fat little finger had gotten from a pin. She was stooping down, and had her arms around her, with a loving look upon her face. Vira, watching her earnestly, wondered in her hungry little heart if her mother used to love her so much when she was a baby, and why mothers stopped loving their children when they grew older.

"Sit down," said Mrs. Perkins briskly. "We are glad to see you, Baby and I. She is lonesome; she is used to having her papa on Sundays, you know, and she misses him. Mr. Perkins has gone up to a young men's meeting up at the Mission building. A real nice young man asked him to go, and I am as pleased as can be. I like to have him go to meeting; it looks respectable, and it is the way we were brought up. What have you done with your nice clothes, Vira? You looked so pretty this morning I hardly knew you."

"Packed them away," said Vira. "Couldn't afford to wear them all day at home. I put them out in the back yard in a box; but if it rains I am afraid they will get wet. The box has a crack in the side."

"Dear me!" said Mrs. Perkins. "I am afraid they will, and the dews are very heavy—almost like rain. What made you put them out-of-doors?"

"To have them safe," said Vira. "I am afraid they would go off on the sly and change themselves for whiskey, if I didn't."

"Oh, dear me!" said Mrs. Perkins. Then, after a moment's thought: "Vira, wouldn't you better let me take care of them? I will keep them in my upper bureau drawer with my husband's best shirt; then they will be safe from rain and dew and everything."

"That will be nice," said Vira gratefully. "I shall like it very much. Father is home now, taking a nap, and when he goes down the street again I will go and get the box and bring it in here. Mrs. Perkins, have you got a Bible?"

This sudden change of subject astonished Mrs. Perkins. Her face flushed a little as she answered, "Why, yes, child; you don't think we are heathen, do you?"

"Are folks that don't have Bibles, heathens?" asked Vira, still very grave. "We are heathens, then; we haven't got any. Mother used to have one, but it went long ago, like the other things. Mrs. Perkins, couldn't you let me look at your Bible just a minute?"

"Why, surely, child; I would be glad to. It is a very handsome one—so handsome that I can't keep it around every day; it was given to us when we were married. A great big beautiful one; it has pictures in. I keep it wrapped in a flannel cloth, and laid in the bottom of my trunk; but I will get it for you with pleasure. You will like to look at the pictures."

Vira surveyed the handsome volume, which was brought out and unbound from its flannel cloth, and displayed with great pride. It was beautiful. Mrs. Perkins placed it on the little table in the corner and summoned Vira to a seat beside it, so that she could have a good chance to look at the pictures; but it was not the pictures of which Vira was thinking.

"It is very big," she said, with the air of gravity which had been upon her all day.

"Yes," said Mrs. Perkins; "it is large—too large to handle without having a table to lay it on. I used to have a small one, but it got shabby; some of the leaves were loose, and two of them were even torn. When we moved, it disappeared somehow. I didn't care so much, you know, because I had this large handsome one; still this wouldn't be convenient to take to church, would it?" She laughed, and turned over the beautiful leaves with pride.

It is hard to find out all the things that are in such a big book," said Vira. "I should think it would take anybody's lifetime."

"It does," said Mrs. Perkins complacently. "People read the Bible all their lives, you know; they never get through. I had a grandfather who read it over and over, I don't know how many times; it seemed to me he would know it by heart; but he never got tired of it. It is a book that lasts for a lifetime."

"I wonder where they begin?" said Vira. "Do they begin at the beginning?"

"Who? The people who read the Bible through? Why, I suppose so, of course. I never read it through; I never have time for so much reading. I like to find the stories and read them; but some of it is pretty hard reading; I don't understand it."

"What is the very beginning?"

"Why, the beginning is 'In the beginning,'" said Mrs. Perkins, and she laughed pleasantly. "Take care, Baby. Don't you put your fingers on that big book; it is too precious a book for you. My grandfather and grandmother and two aunts and an uncle gave me that Bible. We are going to keep it forever. One of these days, Baby, it shall be your very own, but you mustn't touch it yet." And she made prisoners of Baby's little fingers, which were after the leaves, while Vira turned slowly and reverently to the first page, and read the words:

"In the beginning God created the heavens and the earth," then she drew a long sigh of relief.

CHAPTER 16

A Troublesome Verse

"THERE is nothing to do in that verse, anyway," said Vira.

"Nothing to do?" repeated Mrs. Perkins wonderingly. "What do you mean, Vira?"

"Why, there's things to be done. Sandy Smith—Do you know Sandy Smith? He's a freckle-faced boy with curly red hair; he goes by here every once in a while. He lives on the other street, but he goes down to the wharf this way sometimes. He is the only boy in this town that is fit to look at. He stopped and played with the baby one day, Mrs. Perkins; don't you remember him?"

"Oh, yes!" said Mrs. Perkins. "I know; he is a very neat-looking little boy; I like his face. What about him?"

"Well, he said that the Bible was full of things that we had to do, and that if you wanted to be one of the people that my picture tells about, you know, you had to have a Bible, and do the things it said; but it seems as if it would take forever to find them out."

Mrs. Perkins looked with thoughtful eyes at the strange little girl before her. "You are a curious child," she said at last, with a faint smile on her face, and a tremble in her voice. "I don't know that I ever saw one just like you; but it is true enough, I suppose. There are a good many things in the Bible."

"Then where do they begin?" asked Vira almost impatiently. "That is what I want to know. How am I to find out? I want to begin to do the things, if He meant me, and whether He meant me or not, I don't suppose He would mind my trying to do the things."

Mrs. Perkins was turning the leaves of the large Bible with one hand, and holding Baby away from it with the other. "There's a card in here," she said, "which has a Bible verse on it that tells what we are to do. I don't know as it would help you any—you haven't any enemies; but it is one of the things from the Bible that are put on cards, for people to live by; I used to have them given to me when I was a girl. I had a box of them once, but they have got scattered and lost; I don't really know what has become of them, but I know there is one in here somewhere; I thought I would keep it for the sake of old times … Oh, here it is!" And she drew forth an illuminated text card, about two or three inches wide, and handed it to Vira.

The coloring was pretty, and the letters were large and plain. Vira carefully spelled out the last word, then read it aloud: "'Love your enemies.' Mrs. Perkins, is that a Bible verse?"

"Why, yes," said Mrs. Perkins; "don't you see it tells where it is to be found?" And she pointed with her finger to the chapter and verse, then turned the leaves of the Bible and found the place for Vira to read it in the big Book itself.

"That's a fact," said Vira gravely; "but, Mrs. Perkins, don't enemies mean ugly people—people that you hate?"

"It means anybody that hasn't been good to you, I suppose; folks who treat you as if they didn't like you."

"And it tells you to love them! Well, all there is about it, I can't do it," said Vira. She closed the Bible almost with a bang, and flung rather than laid the card down on the table. "How could anybody do it, I should like to know?" she said, with her eyes flashing. "Think of my loving Pete Knowles, will you, as he stands in the door watching for my father when he goes by? Just as sure as he knows of his having done a speck of work, and having a bit of money, he watches for him. Mother says he did from the time father began to drink. Time and again, mother says, father stopped drinking and promised her he would not touch another drop, and meant it, too; but on his way from work Pete Knowles called him in to see something, and coaxed and wheedled him along, and offered him some whiskey, telling him that it shouldn't cost him anything, and managed till he got every cent from him. Think of my loving such a man as that. I can't and I won't; and I think it is mean."

"Oh, hush!" said Mrs. Perkins. "You mustn't talk that way, Vira. Who ever heard a little girl go on so? Why, those are God's own words, child; I am just afraid to have you speak that way."

"I ain't," said Vira, her cheeks burning with indignation. "I don't see any sense to it; it can't mean that. I know what 'love' is just as well as anybody; don't I love my mother? And I love the baby, and Miss Southey; and I could love even Nero—he whitewashed the wall for me; I have liked him ever since—and

Sandy Smith, and lots of other folks; but when it comes to Pete Knowles, that's another thing. There needn't anybody ever expect me to love him, because I just can't do it; I couldn't if I wanted to, and I don't want to."

"People do," said Mrs. Perkins with great gravity/ "People who study the Bible a great deal love their enemies. They don't love them as we love our own folks, you know, not in the same kind of way; but they love them enough to be kind to them, and help them when they can. There was a man once who was just as mean to my grandfather as he could be; he stole his money, and he told lies about him, and he treated him just awfully; but Grandfather forgave him, and when he was sick went to see him, and helped him, and did everything he could for him."

"I wouldn't have done it," said Vira. "I wouldn't help Pete Knowles—no, nor any of his folks, not if he was starving to death, and I had something to give him. I hate him, that's what I do."

"Well," said Mrs. Perkins with emphasis, "I don't know much about these things, Vira; I am not good—not in that way, as Grandfather was, and as my own mother was, but I know this much: you can't have those feelings, and follow the Bible. Why, there is a good deal more about it; that was only a piece of the verse; you want to read the whole of it, Vira, then you will see how people have to feel who are going to take the Bible for their guide. Just you turn to the verse, and see what it says. Here, I will read it for you." She turned the leaves again, then read in a slow and impressive voice, "But I say unto you which hear, Love your enemies, do good to them which hate you; bless them that curse you, and pray for them which despitefully use you. And unto him that smiteth thee on the one cheek, offer also the other; and him that taketh away thy cloak forbid not to take thy coat also. Give to every man that asketh of thee; and of him that taketh away thy goods ask them not again. And as ye would that men should do to you, do ye also to them likewise. For if ye love them which love you, what thank have ye? For sinners also love those that love them. And if ye do good to them which do good to you, what thank have ye? for sinners also do even the same. And if ye lend to them of whom ye hope to receive, what thank have ye? for sinners also lend to sinners, to receive as much again. But love ye your enemies, and do good, and lend, hoping for nothing again; and your reward shall be great, and ye shall be the children of the Highest: for he is kind unto the unthankful and to the evil."

It would be impossible to describe the changing look upon Vira's expressive face, as she listened to these words. Resentment, anxiety, astonishment, bewilderment, and despair chased themselves rapidly over it; and when Mrs. Perkins, who had read with slow and careful emphasis, closed the book, Vira turned her great brown and hungry eyes upon her face, saying:

"Then I may as well give up first as last. Mrs. Perkins, I never heard anything like it in my life; that just means Pete Knowles from beginning to end—using me spitefully, and using mother spitefully. That is what mother calls, it, persecution; she says she doesn't wonder that father can't reform; it has just been persecution from those who wanted to ruin him. Pete Knowles has been the worst of all; and me to do good to him, and pray for him! Why, I never could do it in the living world, and I may as well stop first as last; that's the reason that everybody don't try, I suppose. I told Sandy this morning that I thought it would be easy enough to do things if you could only find them out; but it ain't easy at all. Nobody can do it; at least I can't."

"My grandfather did," said Mrs. Perkins firmly, "in that great trouble; I couldn't have done it; but then I wasn't a Christian, you know. Grandfather was, and that made all the difference in the world. He used to pray for this man when he was treating him the worst; I have heard him pray for him when I was a little girl; I heard him ask God to forgive him, and make him a good man. And he did, too, before he died. There never was a better man than my grandfather, Vira, and he understood the Bible, I tell you; he studied it every day of his life. If there were more men like him it would be a better world." And Mrs. Perkins, who was astonished at herself for the kind of talk in which she was indulging, turned away to hide a tear starting in her eyes at the thought of her grandfather. He had been father to her as well, and had tried to bring her up to love the Bible, as he had done. "If I had followed his teachings all my life I would have been a better woman," she said, "and I would know better how to bring up my baby; I mean to teach her to study the Bible."

But Vira scarcely heard her. Mrs. Perkins's grandfather was nothing to her; she was busy with her own thoughts; she had come face to face with an awful problem. Here, at the very beginning of her determination to find out what God wanted her to do, and do it as fast as she could, was a thing at which all the soul within her rebelled; she was willing to accept anybody and everybody but Pete Knowles; but to love him, do good to him, pray for him—it seemed as impossible as it did to fly. Must she then give it all up, that dear hope of being made clean inside which had taken such possession of her? It did not seem as though she could do that either; but if Sandy Smith was right, and the way to heart-purity led through such a road as this, with Pete Knowles in the very middle of it, what was to be done?

"I can't even *want* to do it," she told herself mournfully, as she went back home and sat on the doorstep, the card in her hand which Mrs. Perkins had lent her, with "Love your enemies" staring her in the face.

That night, before she crept into her miserable little bed, she stood once more in front of the "picture," and whispered softly the words, lest her mother should hear her:

"God in Heaven, I want to be clean inside; I want to have a pure heart, but I can't love Pete Knowles; what will I do?" She was almost frightened over the words. What if she had no right to speak them? If she could hear Him speak, would he tell her that since she would not do as she was told He wanted to have nothing to do with her? Would He forbid her saying those words over to him? Her poor little dark mind was all in a whirl, and it was not till long after her father came staggering home from Pete Knowles's, so intoxicated that he did not know his own doorstep, but tried to open the window as though it were a door, and make his entrance there, that his little girl, with her heart full of anger against his enemy and hers, finally dropped to sleep.

There had been times when this poor little girl felt as though she almost hated her father; but on this evening she said sorrowfully that if the words had only been about her father she could have obeyed them.

"He has been a real and truly enemy sometimes, too," she told herself. "Hasn't he taken away all the nice things mother and I ever had, and made us live like pigs, and be half-starved most of the time? But I can love him, and do good to him, and pray for him; if God would only leave Pete Knowles out, and let me take father instead. He has used me mean enough, but I can forgive him, and love him, and everything; but as for Pete Knowles—Oh, dear me, what shall I do?" And at last she cried herself to sleep.

Such a woebegone little girl as Vira was all the next day. Your heart would have ached for her I am sure, if you could have seen her poor distressed face and disappointed air. Her mother watched her anxiously, and asked more than once what had "come over the child"? Even her father asked if she was "ailin'," she seemed so different from her usual energetic self. Toward the middle of the afternoon the little girl went out and sat down on the doorstep, her mind still absorbed with its perplexity. Ought she to pray that prayer anymore? She was quite unwilling to give it up, yet she was still sure that she could never, never love, or help, or pray for Pete Knowles.

"What is the need of my doing it anyhow?" she asked herself bitterly. "Pete Knowles don't want me to love him, and there is nothing in life I could do to help him if I wanted to ever so much; and as for praying for him, what good would my praying do anybody, I should like to know? Why can't I just let him alone, and not think about him at all? Miss Southey needn't have told me that part; I think it was mean in her. I wish I hadn't gone to Mrs. Perkins and asked to see her big Bible. I have a mind to tear up her old card. There are hundreds and hundreds of verses in the Bible; why need she give me just that one? But I don't know what good it would do to tear the card up. The words will be in the Bible all the same; I saw them there with my own eyes. They are in all the Bibles in the world, I suppose. Oh, it does seem too everlasting bad, just as I was beginning to understand!"

Around the corner came Sandy Smith, and in his hand a cluster of lovely rosebuds. Vira exclaimed over them. She lived in the land of flowers, where roses, such as in the North belong to hothouses only, flourished and bloomed all winter long in people's door-yards; yet none bloomed around Vira's door. Truth to tell, although they would bloom royally if the ground were carefully fed, they did not like to grow on soil which was not fertilized, and Vira did not know how to fertilize it, and had no flowers to experiment with.

"You like flowers, I guess," said Sandy, noting the look in her eyes.

"I guess I do! They are almost the prettiest ones I ever saw. We don't have no flowers. I had a geranium once, and it grew real splendid; but father stumbled over it one night when he was drunk, and broke it clear off, and I never had another. Do they grow in your yard?"

"No," said Sandy, shaking his head; "not this kind. We've got flowers, sights of 'em; they grow for mother; anything does that she sets out; but these are a new kind that my aunt brought from the North. My aunt lives five miles away; but she has brought mother a slip, and we'll have them, I expect, after this. I'm going to take these up to Mrs. Bennett; mother sent 'em.

Would you like one? You can have it just as well as not; mother won't care."

CHAPTER 17

A Puzzled Theologian

VIRA held out her hand eagerly; she could not remember when she had had a lovely white rose all her own. "Mother will like to see it," she said. "I guess it is like the roses that grew in her yard when she was a little girl. Mother used to have lots of things, Sandy; she wasn't much like me. Her father didn't drink whiskey, you see. She used to be dressed up real nice every Sunday, and she went to church and to Sunday-school. Oh, Sandy, don't you think I can't do it, after all!"

"Can't do what?" asked Sandy. Vira jumped from one subject to another so suddenly that he found it hard to understand her. To tell the truth, he was somewhat uneasy; he was sorry for this forlorn little girl, and was quite willing to give her a rose; but the last thing he wanted was to get caught in such a conversation as had embarrassed him but the day before. He felt that he had given Vira all the knowledge he possessed on the subject which had interested her then, and if she was going back to it, what he wanted was to get away without hurting her feelings.

"Why, that," said Vira, "that I told you about yesterday. Don't you know I said it was easy enough to do things when you found out what they were? Well, it isn't."

"H'm!" said Sandy. That meant, "I thought you would find out that things were not so easy as you had imagined."

"No," said Vira, "it isn't. It's so awful outrageous hard that I can't do it! What do you think of that?"

"What have you struck?" asked Sandy curiously. He thought things of this kind were generally hard, but Vira spoke with such intensity that he could not help wanting to know just what was the matter.

"The worst thing there could be, for me; the very worst. Sandy, how much do you know about the Bible, anyhow?"

"Not very much," said Sandy, growing uneasy, "and I must trot along home or I shall be late to school."

"Just wait a minute; it isn't school time yet by a whole hour; look at the sun. Sandy, I've *got* to have somebody to talk to. It kind of makes mother feel bad, I guess, for me to talk to her, because she knows I haven't got chances like she had; and Mrs. Perkins—well, she has a great big Bible, but she keeps it wrapped up, and I guess she doesn't know much about it. Sandy, you have been to Sunday-school ever and ever so long, haven't you?"

Sandy nodded. "Always," he said emphatically. "I began before I could talk plain. I don't remember when I didn't go."

"Well, and you learn out of the Bible in Sunday-school always, don't you? Then I should think you ought to know a great deal. I should, I know, if I had had a chance. Sandy, are all the things in it God's words?"

"Of course," said Sandy, shocked by such dense ignorance. "What do you suppose? When He hasn't given folks but one book it isn't likely He would let it go and get mixed up with other folks' words, would He?"

"I don't know. Other folks wrote it; He didn't come down out of the sky and write the Bible Himself, did He? They might have got some of their own words in by mistake, or because they wanted to be big and have their words mixed up with His. Where did the first Bible come from, anyway, Sandy? Who had it?"

"I don't know," said Sandy; and he added, "You beat all for asking questions that I ever heard! Why don't you go and ask them of Miss Southey ? She could tell you no end of things, I suppose."

"Because," said Vira, "it's no use beginning—that's just it; there's no end to the things I want to know about. But this that I was telling you is the queerest. Mrs. Perkins gave me a card with a verse on; I wouldn't have believed it was in the Bible, only she found the place and showed it to me, and I read it with my own eyes: 'Love your enemies.' Did you know there was such a verse in the Bible as that?"

"Of course," said Sandy, looking wise. "It was in our Sunday-school lesson only a few months ago. I learned the whole verse, and the one which comes before it and after it." Whereupon he rattled them off as fast as his tongue could do work. "Ye have heard that it was said, 'Thou shalt love thy neighbor and hate thine enemy;' but I say unto you love your enemies, and pray for them that persecute you; that ye may be the sons of your Father which is in heaven."

"There!" said Vira, "that is the very verse—about praying for them, and all. It is in your Bible, too; and in all the Bibles, isn't it?"

"Why, of course."

"Well, then you know what I mean. I say it can't be done. Look here, Sandy, do you do it?"

"Do what?"

"Why, what it says. Do you love your enemies?"

"I haven't got any enemies, I guess; I never heard of them."

"Why, yes, you have. Don't you remember when I told you about Jim Bryan, how he threw sand at me, and called me a drunkard's young one,' you said he was the hatefulest boy in town; that he was as mean to you as he could be, and you meant to pay him off some day? That isn't loving him, anyhow."

"Oh, well," said Sandy, wriggling uneasily, and remembering once more that he ought to go; "it doesn't mean that kind of loving; there are different kinds, you see."

He did not expect Vira to accept this bit of logic, and only said it to gain time; but she answered thoughtfully:

"That's so. I know there are different kinds. I love the little Perkins baby. I'd do anything for her that I could; but I don't love her like I do mother. But then, I don't call it any kind of loving to talk about Jim Bryan as you did. I don't believe you love him a bit more than I do—and I know I hate him, and Pete Knowles, too; there it is, you see. Think of me praying for Pete Knowles, will you? And as for loving him, there isn't anything mean I wouldn't like to see come to him. Now, how can I help it, and how can I do what the Bible says?"

"I don't know," said Sandy. "I told you I didn't know about such things; and I say you ought to talk to Miss Southey instead of me. There is a way, and she can explain it; but there is no use in asking me to, for I don't know how; and besides, I must go this minute."

"Oh, but, Sandy! Just wait a second. Why don't you learn how? Then you could tell me. There's lots of folks you might ask, you know; and I don't go nowhere to ask things—and I shan't see Miss Southey till Sunday, and it's a long time till then. Don't you want to know for yourself?"

"No, I don't," said Sandy, who was growing cross. "I don't care anything about it."

"Then I don't understand it at all," declared Vira, looking not only perplexed, but indignant. "If it says so in the Bible, and people can't have clean hearts without doing it, and they can't see God in the way you said your Grandmother did, unless they have them, why, I should think you would need to know for yourself."

"There is time enough," said Sandy, and he bent down and tried to fit the toe of his neat shoe into the sand in a way that would leave an impression; but Vira was simply astonished at this answer.

"Sandy Smith!" she said impressively. "I should like to know how you can tell that? Folks die when they are a great deal younger than you are, and you said it would have to be done before they died. Anyhow, I should think you might find out for me; maybe I'll die right off today, for all you know, and then you'd be sorry you hadn't helped me."

"I told you all there was to tell yesterday," said Sandy. "Folks pray about such things, and God tells them all they need to know."

"Then why hasn't He told you? Don't you pray, Sandy?"

But at that moment Sandy determined that at all hazards he would get away; and moreover, he would see to it that he did not come by the Bruce cabin again until Vira had forgotten her perplexities, or gotten over them in some way. He declared emphatically that he could not stay another second, and enforced the statement by starting at a brisk run down the street. Vira looking anxiously after him the while, and calling out something which he did not understand.

"She beats all the folks to ask questions that I ever heard of!" he said to himself as, once at a safe distance, he dropped into a comfortable walk. "And somebody ought to help her out of her muddle. It's the funniest thing to hear her talk about loving Jim Bryan and Pete Knowles; of course she can't. And of course the verse doesn't mean that; but I don't know what it does mean, and she ought to have sense enough to ask somebody else."

Nevertheless he went on his way feeling conscience-smitten. It was a strange thing, after all, that a boy who had been brought up, as one might say, on the Bible, who had heard a great many sermons, and learned a great many Sabbath-school lessons, and had earned a splendid new Bible only last year by repeating five hundred Bible verses without a mistake, should not know how to direct one as ignorant as Vira Bruce in the very first step of her new way.

Sandy was an honest boy, and he admitted thoughtfully that if she had asked him some geography questions that he had been over, and had got a prize for learning, he should have been ashamed not to be able to answer her. There were evidently some things for him to find out; if not to practise on, then to explain, for the benefit of others.

Vira, left standing at the gate, her lovely white rose in her hand, was the victim of many conflicting feelings. Sandy Smith had failed her; either he did not know, or he was not willing to explain to her what the Bible verse meant, or what step one was to take who had settled it in her own heart that she could not do as it seemed to say. She wondered if she would really have to give it all up. Perhaps there were people who could not do the things which were necessary, and that was why there were bad folks and good folks. Here was her father, for instance; he couldn't help drinking whiskey, so her mother said, and probably Sandy could not help the way he felt toward Jim Bryan; but then, of course, Pete Knowles could help selling whiskey if he chose, and Jim Bryan needn't throw sand.

"There is a difference between feelings and doings," said this poor bewildered little girl, "and God wouldn't treat us all alike; some of us for the bad things we couldn't help, and some for the bad things they could help—that wouldn't be honest. Oh, dear, I don't know anything about it. Sandy says ask Miss Southey, but she doesn't make it plain."

Then Vira went over in her mind all the words she could remember that Miss Southey had spoken to her on that windy day. Did not she say distinctly that people who went to Jesus and asked for clean hearts would get them, and that he would see to His part of it all, if they did theirs? But then, didn't she say He came to be a pattern for folks to copy, and didn't He pray for his enemies after they had nailed Him to a piece of wood? And didn't she know she couldn't have done it? What was the use? Hadn't she prayed about it all day?

Suddenly Vira's thoughts were arrested. Down the street with slow and solemn tread came a funeral procession. There was the minister walking ahead, then six boys carried a little coffin, and one of the boys was Jim Bryan. Following close to the coffin, with bowed head, and oh, such a sorrowful face, was, of all persons in the world, Pete Knowles himself. It was his baby, then, who was dead. Vira had seen the little laughing creature many a time, dressed in its pretty white suits, being rolled through the streets by a little servant girl whose sole duty in life seemed to be to take care of it; and Vira had scowled on the baby and hoped—Oh, yes, she had; she was a fierce-hearted, untaught little girl!—hoped it would have a horrid, ugly life, such as Pete Knowles with his whiskey was making for her. Now it seemed God had taken the baby away. And she had scowled at it! A great lump came in her throat as she told herself, if she could only take that scowl back and smile at the little baby once, she would be so glad.

They were directly opposite the door now with the pretty white casket. In an instant Vira's resolution was taken. There were no flowers on the casket; the baby should have her white rose to take to Heaven with her. "Maybe she will know up there that I am sorry I scowled," thought the child. Out she rushed and dropped the beautiful, fragrant rose on the casket. Pete Knowles started, looked down at Vira, and actually there were tears in his eyes; yes, one was rolling clown his cheek, and his voice trembled as he said, "Thank you, little girl; she loved flowers."

Very slowly Vira went back, thinking about that tear. "Poor father!" she said. "I am sorry for him."

"What!" It seemed to her that her own heart spoke that startled word. Was she? Was she really sorry for him? Why, he was Pete Knowles!

"I don't care," she said stoutly, as one trying to defend herself; "I don't care if he is Pete Knowles. I say I am sorry that he hasn't got any little baby now, and I'm sorry I scowled at her, and I'd like to help her have a nice time, so there!"

Then had she forgiven Pete Knowles? She was not sure; that might not be forgiving—It certainly could not be "loving" —yet she was equally certain that she felt different toward him from what she ever had before.

CHAPTER 18

Ready for Work

MRS. PERKINS' kitchen was in perfect order, and she sat by the south window making a dress for Baby. Baby Perkins was sleeping sweetly. It was just the time for Vira to have a long talk. When her shadow darkened the doorway, Mrs. Perkins looked up.

"Good-afternoon," she said cheerily. "I was just wondering what had become of you. How very nice you look; and those are not your best clothes either."

"They are clothes that I earned," said Vira, surveying them with great satisfaction. "Mother washes for Mrs. Hunt at the hotel, and when she was there the other day Mrs. Hunt asked her if she knew of any little girl to wear the clothes that her Annie had outgrown. Mother said she thought of me in a minute, but she isn't used to begging, so she said she supposed there were lots of little girls who would be grateful for them; then she asked Mrs. Hunt if she knew of anything a little girl could do to earn some clothes. That begun it, and they talked it over; and Mrs. Hunt said she liked people who had self-respect, though I don't know what she meant by that; we haven't anything hardly, and so it isn't likely we have any of that; but she told mother that if I would get her a great big magnolia blossom and some of the gray moss, and some of those pretty velvety green things that grow in the hammock land, she would sell me the clothes. She was afraid to have Annie go to the hammock, or to go herself, on account of snakes; but I'm not afraid of snakes, and I never heard of clothes being earned so easy, and mother hasn't either; because, you see, we liked the fun of it. Mother went along, and we got a basket full of the prettiest things; and mother said it was great fun to think that we were earning clothes all the while. Mother never has any fun, you know, and it was real nice."

"I should think it would have been," said Mrs. Perkins with hearty sympathy. "So that is where you were yesterday? I missed you. And how nice the clothes look; they fit as well as though they were made for you."

"Yes," said Vira, looking down at herself with grave pleasure; "but I didn't come to talk about clothes, Mrs. Perkins; there are other things. I've got a lot to say, and I don't know how to begin."

"Is that so? Why, begin right in the middle. When I have a great many things to say to John, as I do almost every evening—they gather through the day, you know, and I pack them away in my mind; then when he is nicely going with his supper I start in on the first thought that comes to me, and they all work in after a while."

"Well," said Vira, "then to begin, do you know Jim Bryan?"

"What, the boy who throws sand at you and calls you names? Why, you told me about him, you remember; that is all I know of him, and from what I have heard, I don't care to make his acquaintance. Has he been troubling you again?"

"No," said Vira slowly, "he hasn't, because I haven't seen him; if he could get a chance at me, I suppose he would. But I have been thinking about him all the morning, and I can't tell what to do."

"About what?"

"About him. You know the verse you gave me—'Love your enemies.' Well, he is my enemy, and if I've got to love him, why, I ought to be trying to do something for him, and I don't know what. There was a lot more to the verse, you know, about doing good to them that hate you.' He hates me, I s'pose; anyway he acts like it, and I don't know any good to do."

Mrs. Perkins was silent from very astonishment. It seemed to her that Vira had taken great strides since she saw her last.

"I thought you couldn't forgive him," she said almost timidly, wondering how she ought to talk to this little girl who had come to her for help.

"Well, I have," Vira answered, speaking very gravely. "I almost know I have, I feel so different. I've done worse than that; I've forgiven Pete Knowles."

"How came you to do it?"

"That's the queer part of it," Vira said, a little flush rising on her face. "I don't know I didn't do it, it did itself. One minute I thought I never could, and the next I was willing. He had a funeral, you know. Did you know his baby was dead? Well, it is; it went by, he walking after it, and he had tears in his eyes. I gave it a flower; it was a lovely pinky white rose like what used to grow in mother's garden at home, and I was going to give it to her; but I gave it to the dead baby, and he thanked me and said the baby loved flowers, and I felt sorry for him; I couldn't help it."

Vira spoke the words almost as though they were something to be ashamed of.

"I don't wonder," said Mrs. Perkins, her lip quivering a little, and she looked over toward her darling to see if she was safe and happy. "Poor man! What a dreadful thing it must be to go back to his house and have no baby there. I don't wonder you were sorry for him."

"It is more than that," said Vira, shaking her head. "I felt sorry for Jim Bryan when his mother died; I said I didn't, but down in my heart I knew I did, a little; but it didn't last. The next day I hated him as hard as ever; but this lasts, and is different. "I ..." She hesitated, dropped her eyes to the floor, and spoke lower, "I prayed to God to help him this morning, and to help Jim Bryan, too; and I feel like I wanted to do something for them both; that is the way I know it is different."

Mrs. Perkins was startled. Here was an ignorant little girl who had not even a Bible, yet who had been mysteriously changed.

"I guess you have been converted," she said softly; using the phrase with which she used to be familiar when a girl.

Vira raised her head and looked at her with curious interest. "What is that?" she asked quickly.

Mrs. Perkins was very much embarrassed; she did not know how to explain, and she wished she had not spoken.

"Why, it is what they used to say of people up North, where I lived years ago; when they felt different, you know, from what they used to, and tried to do things different, and to be good, they said they had been converted."

"What does it mean?"

"I never knew exactly. It always meant something good, and people used to respect them. It made the greatest difference in some of them. There was a man who used to drink—Oh, he was a dreadful drunkard! He used to whip his wife, and he almost killed his little girl; but he was converted, and after that he never drank another drop, and was as fond of his wife and babies as anybody."

Vira drew a long breath. "Oh, my!" she said. "Father ought to get it; what a thing it would be if he could! Where do they get it, Mrs. Perkins, and what did you mean by saying I had it?"

"Why, you know—it isn't a thing that they get, exactly; it is something that God does for them, I believe," said Mrs. Perkins, feeling her way timidly, and speaking in an awe-stricken tone. "He changes their feelings and makes them want to be different; I don't know how, but I know they call it being converted."

"Perhaps it is a new heart," said Vira, thinking of Miss Southey's talk, and Sandy's verse. "There is a verse in the Bible about that; Sandy Smith said it to me. I don't remember quite the words, but it is about getting a new heart, I know."

Mrs. Perkins looked relieved. "That is what mean," she said. "It is the same thing; sometimes they used to call it a 'change of heart.' I used to hear them talk about such things, but I don't pretend to understand them."

Vira's face was actually pale now, with excitement. "Mrs. Perkins," she said, drawing her breath hard, and speaking almost in a whisper, "do you truly mean that you think I have got it? I asked Him for it, oh, a hundred times, I should think; and I told Him if it was for such as me I'd be so glad, and I'd do anything; but I didn't really think—but there is a different feeling, just as you said. I don't exactly love Pete Knowles, but I don't wish all sorts of evil things to come to him, and I am sorry he feels lonesome without his baby, and I'd like to do something to help him, and Jim Bryan too; but then ..."

"Then," said Mrs. Perkins, gathering courage and resolving to be as much of a helper as she knew how, "I believe you have got the changed heart they tell about, and I'm sure I'm glad of it; for they were dreadful nice folks, those that I knew who got it."

"And you say they were different about all kinds of things?"

"Well, everything that there was a chance for. Of course, they kept on doing the good things that they had before, but they left off the bad ones, and that made an awful change in some of them."

"Of course," said Vira, "I can understand that; but there wouldn't be much of any change in you, or in your husband, would there? Because you are both good now."

"Oh, dear me!" said Mrs. Perkins. in a tone of dismay. "That will do to say of John, maybe, but I know lots of things in me that need changing. I'm not half so good a woman as I wish I were, for Baby's sake; I often think of it."

But Vira's thoughts had already traveled away from Mrs. Perkins.

"There is one thing I wish," she said earnestly, "and that is that I could earn a Bible as easy as I earned these clothes. Sandy Smith says Miss Southey would give me one, but I don't like to beg Bibles any better than anything else. I wonder if they cost a lot of money?"

"They have them all prices, I guess. We used to have some real cheap ones in our Sunday-school at home. One Christmas the superintendent made every boy and girl who had learned the eighth chapter of Romans a present of a Bible; and I heard him say he got them very cheap."

"Oh, my!" said Vira. "I wish he was the superintendent at our school. I would learn the eighth chapter of Romans for one in a minute, if I could. What is it?"

"I don't remember," said Mrs. Perkins, laughing. "I used to know some of it; I caught it hearing my older sister recite it to mother, but it went out of my mind years ago. It is a chapter in the Bible, you know. I declare for it, you ought to have a Bible of your own if you want one; it isn't often that girls of your age care for such things. I'll tell you what you would like, a New Testament; they are bound by themselves, you know, and they are awfully cheap up North."

"The New Testament?" repeated Vira. "What is that?"

"Why, it is the last half of the Bible; the part that tells all about Jesus, when He came to earth and lived—what He did, and all. There are some splendid stories in it; I used to like to read them myself."

"Mrs. Perkins," said Vira, "would you mind my reading a little while in your Bible? I'd like to look at this New Testament; I never heard of it. I've got my clean clothes on, and I scrubbed my hands, so there can't be a speck of dust on them; and I'll be awfully careful."

Mrs. Perkins declared herself to be perfectly willing; she should rather see it read in than not. She brought out the treasured book, established it on the little old-fashioned stand, found the place where the New Testament began, and further advised that the reading commence with the second chapter, because the first was only "a lot of hard names that nobody cared for."

People who have been used to reading the Bible, and hearing it read all their lives, and to whom the story of Jesus being born in Bethlehem, and worshipped by the wise men, and sought after by Herod, is as familiar as their own names, will hardly be able to understand what an intense interest it all had for Vira. She bent her head over the great book, entirely absorbed, reading through the account of the flight into Egypt; fairly holding her breath with suspense until the baby was safe. She exclaimed in dismay over the fact that the devil came to tempt Jesus to sin; she paused to ask Mrs. Perkins some bewildering questions which that good woman could not answer, as to why Jesus didn't make the stones into bread right away, and after a moment's reflection she said, "I s'pose it was because he was bound not to do what the devil told him to, anyhow. I won't, either, if I can help it." She read where Jesus walked by the sea and called the brothers to follow him; and there she stopped and gathered her new blue-and-white apron to her eyes and burst into sobs.

"For pity's sake!" said Mrs. Perkins in dismay. "Whatever is the matter?"

"I wish I had been there," wailed Vira. "If I only had, maybe He would have called me; and I'd have followed Him anywhere, I know I should; and I want to."

Poor Mrs. Perkins! If she only knew how to comfort this strange little girl who had stolen into her heart.

"I wouldn't cry," she said, in a sympathetic tone. "People do say it is pretty much the same thing now. He does call folks to follow Him, I know that; I have heard it time and again, in sermons and Sunday-school and everywhere. I guess you can do it if you want to; He listens, you know, when folks pray."

Vira dried her eyes suddenly, like one who had no time to spare for tears, and read on. Read how they brought to Him the sick, and the lame, and those possessed with devils, and He healed them all. She stopped to say to Mrs. Perkins that her mother believed the devil got hold of people who drank whiskey, and asked her why Jesus didn't cure such people nowadays, if He could see and hear what was going on just the same as He did then. And Mrs. Perkins not being able to answer, Vira further said, after several minutes of silence, speaking in an awe-struck tone, "Maybe He didn't cure anybody unless he wanted to be cured; and maybe He cures all such people now. What if father wanted it, Mrs. Perkins, and He would?"

But it was over her own "picture" verse and its surroundings that she stopped longest. That wonderful chain of "blesseds" in the fifth chapter of Matthew, which you and I know so well, and which Vira read for the first time.

She did not understand them all; she appealed to Mrs. Perkins to know what sort of people were "meek;" and she wondered much over "Blessed are they that mourn," and inquired whether Pete Knowles mourning for his dead baby could be meant. She was eager to know what "righteousness" meant, for she declared that she understood perfectly about "hunger" and "thirst;" she had felt them both. If it means that people want to do right as bad as they want something to eat when they are hungry," she said, "why, then you have to want it awfully, because that is a horrid feeling; and you think after a while that you must have something right away or you cannot live. I don't believe I want to do right as bad as that; I just feel willing to try. Oh, Mrs. Perkins, here is my picture, word for word!"

After that, there was silence in the kitchen for a long time. Vira, with her head bent over the book, read as though her very life depended on it, and Mrs. Perkins watched her with a strange feeling tugging at her heart.

Presently the little girl sat up and closed the book. "Mrs. Perkins," she said, "it is wonderful. What do you think I found? Why, He says people shall be blessed who have mean things said against them for His sake. So if I think of something to do for Jim Bryan, and he makes fun of it and says hateful things, and won't be helped, why, Jesus says He will bless me all the same. Ain't that wonderful, now? What could I do?"

"About what, child? You go so fast I can't keep track of you."

CHAPTER 19

The Baby Helped

S
HE is certainly a strange little girl," said Mrs. Perkins, when she was telling John all about the afternoon visit. "Sometimes she talks like a very baby, and at other times one would think she was fifteen at least. John, dear, she says there would not be much change in us, even if we were church members, because we are so good now."

At this the baby's father whistled in a way which showed he was astonished and amused, but also a little touched; his face grew grave almost immediately. Then Mrs. Perkins told him Vira's words about Jim Bryan, and added:

"She wants to help him, don't you think! After she had finished her Bible reading, she asked what she could do about it. 'About what?' I asked; and she said, 'Why, about everything.' But especially about Jim Bryan, because he wasn't such a great deal older than she, and she ought to be able to help him if she could anybody; and if she was going to forgive and pray for him, she must do something else or she couldn't stand it. Isn't that queer talk for a child like her? She says Jim hasn't any place to stay evenings, except in the bar-room. It seems he earns his board by tending that saloon at the corner of Orange Street; the man is away a good deal during the day, and Jim hangs around and smokes, and waits on customers when he is needed, and they give him something to eat to pay for it. Evenings the man himself is there, and doesn't want help. But Jim has nowhere to go, so be stays around. I don't wonder that he makes Vira's life miserable. A boy with such a bringing up couldn't be anything but bad."

"He is a pretty hard boy," said Mr. Perkins thoughtfully, "and as you say, it is no wonder. It is Pete Knowles's saloon that he is in, so the poor child's enemies are all together. It is really pitiful to think of her trying to do something for them. She is none too soon, either; if something isn't done for the boy before long, it will be too late. What is the little girl's plan?"

"Oh, she hasn't any plan; only she wants to match her praying,' she says, by doing something. She wanted me to ask you how to begin. She has great faith in you, John."

"We might ask him here once in a while," said Mr. Perkins, looking around the neat little room and contrasting it in his mind with the place where Jim Bryan spent his evenings, "provided we knew what to do with him when he came— supposing he would ever come, which is doubtful."

"Oh, dear me!" said Mrs. Perkins with a dismayed face. "I shouldn't know what in the world to do with a boy! If he were a girl, I could teach her a good many things and keep her interested; but a boy …" Here she stopped; seeming to think the subject too great for words.

"Boys are worse than girls, no doubt," said her husband, "and for that very reason I suppose they need help worse than girls do; there doesn't seem to be anybody trying to do a thing for Jim and his set. As nearly as I can see, this little Vira is the only one who has thought of them at all, in the way of help. It is a queer quarter for help to come from, I must say. But maybe—" and Mr. Perkins stopped; if he had been accustomed to the use of such language he would have said, "maybe the Lord put it into her mind." As it was, he asked after a moment, "What started her in such ideas?"

"Oh, it all came about through that motto I told you of. It is queer, I declare, to think how one Bible verse worked on a bit of cardboard could rouse her up so. Really, John, she has made a wonderful change in their room; you wouldn't know it for the same place. They keep it as clean and neat as wax; but it is dreary enough, of course, with so little furniture. That is the trouble with trying to do anything. We haven't much furniture ourselves, you know, John. Do you suppose a boy like Jim Bryan would care to come to our little house, even if we wanted him to?"

"He might if he thought we didn't want him to," said Mr. Perkins, laughing. "He is a boy who on general principles expects to do and likes to do the things that people don't want to have done."

"Well, but I don't see what good it would do him to come, then, and he might be hateful to Baby."

"Oh, no!" said the father, looking fondly at his sleeping darling. "He couldn't be that. Why, I suppose a glimpse of a clean room, especially if there was a cookie or something of that kind thrown in, would be a wonderful sight to Jim. He hasn't any home, you see—never had, I guess. I suppose he knows clean things when he sees them, but perhaps he doesn't. I know what kind of board he gets at that restaurant; they toss him the leavings, and he eats them leaning against a garbage barrel in the back yard, or seated on an old box by the pig-pen. I went there one day just at noon on an errand for our foreman, and the smells and sights matched the dinner Jim was putting down. Oh, I don't suppose we can do anything; we certainly won't try if you don't think best; but I had a notion that you wanted to help the little girl out in some way."

"I do," said Mrs. Perkins; but she spoke doubtfully, and had a troubled look on her face. After a moment she added, "If you really think that is the way to do it, I'm willing to try. I made some cookies today, and they're real good; but I shouldn't know what to say to him."

"I'd risk you, little woman, if he ever gave you a chance to say anything. We might have the little girl in to help entertain him; perhaps they would get into a pitch-battle, and scratch and bite each other! We'll think about it some more, before we decide. Would you mind staying alone for an hour this evening? Mr. Holmes asked me to drop in at the Mission and help them sing. I told him I couldn't do it because I didn't like to leave you alone; but that little girl's attempt to help along makes me feel kind of ashamed of myself, and as though I ought to be doing something."

Now, Mrs. Perkins did not like to stay alone evenings; but she did very much like to hear her husband talk about being asked to "drop in at the Mission to help." It sounded so respectable and manly. Therefore she made up her mind to say that she and Baby could manage nicely; and if she felt lonely she would have Vira in to sit with her. So both Mr. and Mrs. Perkins made their little sacrifice that evening for the good of others, being helped to do so by the thought of Vira. But she knew nothing about that.

On the following evening Mr. Perkins brought home with him a broad-shouldered, rough-looking boy in very shabby clothes and uncombed hair, and introduced him to his wife after this fashion:

"Nannie, I've brought some tools to fix that stand that you've been waiting for, so long. Jim Bryan says he knows how the little spring works that fastens up the leaf; he fixed one of them once, and he thinks he can do it again; so I brought him along for a bit of supper, and after that we can go to work. Is that all right?"

"Yes, indeed!" said the wise little woman with a smiling face, and a much troubled heart. "I shall be so glad to have that stand fixed; and we've got rice cakes for supper, John, and maple sugar on them, don't you think! Baby and I went around to Mrs. Wilder's this afternoon with the curtains I have been hemming, and she gave me a great cake of it; it came from her old home at the North."

"Then I've hit on the right minute for company," said Mr. Perkins gleefully. "I'll venture to say that Jim never tasted anything in his life any better than your rice cakes."

Now, Jim Bryan, although he could talk fast enough with his own set, had no words with which to answer Mr. Perkins, especially while sitting in his clean little kitchen waiting for supper to be served; so he stretched his wide mouth into a foolish-looking smile, and said nothing. At that moment came Baby, toddling in on uncertain feet from the bedroom. She stopped in the middle of the room and surveyed Jim with round astonished eyes. Why she was not afraid of the great shock-headed fellow in his soiled and ragged clothes I am sure I cannot tell. Who can ever tell what a baby thinks, or why he does or does not do certain things?

Why Baby Perkins, who was growing afraid of strangers, and always hid behind her mother's chair when the man came for his rent, or the boy from the grocery waited for his basket, should have decided to smile at Jim, and travel towards him and put up her small fat hands to be taken, is something which will never be known; but that was precisely what she did.

"Well, of all things in this world!" exclaimed Mrs. Perkins. "John, do look at Baby." For John was at that moment burying his head in a basin of water, taking what he called a "famous wash." "She isn't a bit afraid; and she wants to go to him. Isn't that strange?"

As for Jim, he looked down at the small sweet morsel in her pretty blue-and-white sprigged calico, and had the queerest feeling tugging at his heart. The baby's mother did not know anything about it; but Jim had had a little sister once, and had loved her, oh, so much. When she died, poor ignorant Jim was angry, and said he would never speak to nor look at another baby as long as he lived; and here was a fair little one smiling up at him, waiting to be taken. Suddenly he reached down, lifted the child to his arms and hid his homely face in her curls. And the mother, who kept her darling always fresh and clean and hated to have any soiled thing touch her, kept back the exclamation of dismay which was almost on her lips, and bravely smiled. For if they really meant to try to help Jim Bryan, and Baby was willing to do her share, the mother felt that she must not spoil it, but she did wish the boy had washed his face and hands.

The way Jim ate rice cakes and maple sugar showed that he thought them good. He behaved very well, too; it is true he tipped over his cup of tea, but Mrs. Perkins was so nice about it that he soon recovered from the horrible feeling which it gave him. While she was drying the tablecloth with a clean towel she told how John once tipped over a cup full of coffee in exactly the same way, and, in fact, she had done it herself, before now.

When the table was cleared, the little old-fashioned stand which had belonged to Mrs. Perkins's mother was brought in, and Jim handled it with the air of one who knew what he was about. Yes, he knew just how to fix the spring; there was a little catch to it, didn't Mr. Perkins see? The catch had got bent, and that was all that was the matter. If he had a pair of pincers, and the catch wouldn't break, he could fix it in a trice. And Mr. Perkins who saw at a glance what was the matter, and who had lacked only time to fix the stand long before, looked on and nodded appreciatively as Jim explained, and furnished the pincers and held the bit of brass, and expressed his thanks heartily when the work was done.

"He is a handy fellow with tools," said Mr. Perkins, when Jim was gone. "He ought to be at work with them; he hankers after such work, it seems. His father was a carpenter, and he used to handle a saw and plane when he was a little chap. He says if he could get a chance at such work he would quit the saloon; but nobody wants a boy. The trouble is nobody wants a boy with such habits as he has; and then, too, his clothes are against him. I could get him in at our shop if he had a decent suit, and I could recommend him; but there are two if's in the way. I tell you what it is, Nannie, there are worse fellows in the world, after all, than Jim Bryan; I really quite take to him. And didn't he like the rice cakes!"

"The baby took to him," said Mrs. Perkins. "That shows there is something to him; babies won't go to all sorts of people, and she is real timid, you know. She grows more afraid of the rent-man every time he comes. But I had to give her a bath tonight before I could put her to sleep. If Jim is coming here once in a while, couldn't you coax him to wash up?"

"All in good time, little woman," said Mr. Perkins, laughing. "I saw you wince when Baby went up to him; but you were real brave about it. A little outcry from you just then would have spoiled it all. Well, Nannie, what do you say? Shall we take up new work and see what we can do? I've got news for you. They put me into the next room today, and raised my wages; and the little cottage where we used to be, is vacant. We can go back to it when our month is up, if we want to; or we can stay here, and save a good bit on the rent each month, and have a little extra, for rice cakes and things, and have Jim here now and then, and try to help the little girl and her mother. You shall decide. The agent spoke to me about the cottage this afternoon; and I told him it was for you to say; that I reckoned you would want it, but there was no telling what notions women would take."

Mrs. Perkins's answer was somewhat mixed.

"Oh, John, have they raised your wages already? How nice! I knew they would as soon as they found out what a splendid worker you were, and faithful, and all that. Why, these little rooms aren't so bad, now we have them all cleaned and fixed up so nicely. It would cost a bit to move; and there is a great difference in the rent. It would be real pleasant to be down near to Mrs. Wilder's again; but then, poor Vira would miss us dreadfully; and I should really miss the child very much, and her mother, too. She is neighborly and good-hearted. John, it does seem so nice to think of your working in the Mission and helping other people. Let us stay right here and see what we can do."

"All right, little woman; I thought you would say just that. It is time we were helping somebody; we have had a good many comforts, when we compare our lives with lots of others. I've done a good deal of thinking about such things since I was sick; but after all, you can tell the little girl it was she who set us to work. And there is something else I have decided on; I'm going regularly to the Mission Sunday evenings, after this; and I'll keep Baby in the mornings so that you can go. Like enough you can manage so the little girl and her mother will go along. We meant to start out by going regularly to church, you know; but sickness and one thing and another have kept us from it; but we'll get back to it. It won't do to let people who have had no training, and children at that, get ahead of us. When I think of that little girl, with a drunken father and all sorts of hindrances making so much out of one Bible verse, it makes me ashamed of myself. I want to begin all over again. Can we manage it, little woman?"

There were happy tears in the "little woman's" eyes when she answered that she was sure they could. To herself she said that she would never forget Vira and what she had done for her.

To think of John being one of the regular workers in the Mission!

CHAPTER 20

Vira's "Enemy"

IT is surprising how soon people can get used to things which at first seemed to them very strange. In a little while Mrs. Perkins, who had been so startled over the thought of Jim Bryan being invited to tea, had grown so accustomed to hearing her husband say, "I shouldn't wonder if Jim would come home with me tonight," or, "Shall I ask Jim up if I see him?" that it seemed the most natural thing in the world. In fact, she was often the one who did the saying, running after her husband to the door, to call out, "I mean to have a little treat for supper; bring Jim with you."

As for Jim, it took him longer to get used to being invited out. He always accepted the invitation with a look on his face which can only be described as a grin; and each time wondered why it was given, and whether it ever would be again. There was no denying that he liked to go. In the first place, he was nearly always hungry. Getting his meals by snatches, and having them made up of scraps which were not needed in the restaurant, was a very unsatisfactory way of living. He had never realized it so much as since those suppers with the Perkins family. He was not a favorite with the cook nor with any of the waiters. He was not surprised at that; for he had done what he could to annoy them all at different times, merely from the habit he had of being disagreeable to people. For this reason, they never had any comfortable little bits laid aside for him, as they did for one or two little girls who came for left-overs. The merest refuse was generally tossed to him; some of the time there was not enough nourishment in them for a respectable mouse; but it was of no use to complain. Jim had an undertone feeling that he got as much as he earned, which kept him quiet. But he had ready a splendid appetite for the delicious rice cakes, and corn bread, and fried mush; for it was such dishes as these that were accounted dainties in the Perkins home.

But there was a second reason why Jim always accepted his invitations—he loved the Perkins baby. It seemed a surprising thing; nobody was more astonished than he to find that he could not resist her smiles. Had he not decided never to care for another baby? Had he not passed them on the streets by the dozen, tipped some over indeed, with his selfishly careless feet, and left them crying, while he called them "squalling brats"? Yet the fact remained that when Baby Perkins crossed the room to him, her face all in smiles, and put two soft hands on his knee and puckered her rosebud of a mouth for him to kiss, Jim Bryan surrendered, and knew that he was thenceforth that baby's slave. Nor did she forget her part of the programme. Her delight in Jim grew with each passing day, so that now the mother knew by her shouts of delight when he was coming down the walk. This opinion of the baby's went far toward making Mrs. Perkins first satisfied to see Jim frequently, and then deeply interested in him. He could not be so bad a boy as everybody had supposed, she told John earnestly, or baby would not be so charmed with him. Babies *knew*, however they found out, she was sure she could not tell; but she believed babies always knew who were to be trusted, and who were not.

Certainly, as the days went by, Jim Bryan improved. There was a certain afternoon, when Baby was dressed in her freshest white gown, that he stopped to give her some flowers he had found in the woods; and in caressing her, he left two great soiled spots on the whiteness of her dress from his own un-washed hands. His face grew very red, but he said not a word, nor did Baby's mother. She even managed to look the other way, and act as though she did not see the soil; but Jim knew she did. The next time he came to supper, his hands were as clean as soap and water could make them.

Within a month from the time of their first friendliness, Mr. Perkins contrived to get Jim a chance in the shop where he worked; and as it was in a room where work was going on which interested the boy, he took hold of it with such handiness that the foreman said he believed that fellow would make a workman after all, though he did not look very promising. After this, when Jim came to supper, he and Mr. Perkins arrived together; and as they came directly from the shop, it seemed the most natural thing in the world to offer him a chance to "wash and brush up." After the first grand wash, at which time Jim copied Mr. Perkins as well as he could, the boy seemed to like it, and the change which it made in his appearance fairly be-wildered Vira.

"I declare!" she said solemnly to Mrs. Perkins, "ain't it wonderful what a difference clean things make? I saw Jim Bryan yesterday when he went away, and his hair was combed and his face was as nice! Do you suppose it makes as much difference in hearts as that?"

"In hearts?" repeated Mrs. Perkins, bewildered. She often found it difficult to keep up with Vira's thoughts.

"Yes; to the angels, you know, or whoever the folks are that see hearts. Miss Southey thinks perhaps the angels can. I wonder if it makes as much difference to have them washed as it does to have faces and hands? If it does, the angels must have nice times watching folks."

During all this time Jim and Vira had not met. Again and again had Mrs. Perkins invited the little girl to come and have supper with them, but she always refused.

"I better not," she would say with decision. "You see, he is my enemy, and he wouldn't like to eat supper with me. He has never been anything but nice to you, and of course he wouldn't be; but he has never been anything but bad to me; he wouldn't know how to treat me any other way. I like him best when I don't see him at all; and I mean to keep away from him just as long as I can. I'm awful glad to have him come here, and get nice suppers, and learn things, and I'm not his enemy, you know. I hated him, but I don't now; but I want to keep away from him."

"I don't believe he is your enemy now," Mrs. Perkins would answer. "I think he is trying to be a real nice boy. The way Baby takes to him shows that. If you would come in and eat supper with him, I believe he would treat you real nice."

"Mrs. Perkins," asked Vira, breathless interest in her voice, "has Jim Bryan learned how to pray? Has he got a clean heart?"

"Oh, dear, no!" said Mrs. Perkins. "I don't believe the poor fellow ever thinks of such things; he has just begun to care anything about clean hands, you know; but for all that, he is quite a decent boy."

But Vira shook her head. It was clear she had little faith in any radical change that was not made by way of the heart. Jim Bryan looked and acted better, and of course he would behave himself a little with a grown-up man and woman, and of course he would not be bad to their baby when they were right there looking at him; but for herself, she had no desire to trust him.

"Wait till he gets a clean heart," she would say with a grave, business-like air, "then I shall want to see him and hear him talk."

Mrs. Perkins repeated these queer words to her husband and laughed over them, while she said if poor Vira did not talk with Jim until he had a clean heart, she was afraid she would have to wait a long time. But Mr. Perkins did not smile; instead, he looked very thoughtful, and after a moment said that he supposed Jim needed that more than he did anything else; he supposed they all did. He didn't know but it was a queer thing that they did not attend to it for themselves.

Over this sentence Mrs. Perkins spent a good deal of time. In her heart she did not believe that her John needed anything; he was as nearly perfect, she thought, as he could be. For herself, there was chance for great improvement; and of course for poor Jim. But why did John talk in that way?

Meantime, Jim's bewilderment over the way he was being treated was increasing. Why should the Perkins family have taken him up in this way, and keep inviting him home, and spend their money in making him have a good time? At last he decided to ask a plain question.

"Look here," he said to Mr. Perkins when they were on the way home, Jim having been invited to share in a treat of warm biscuits and honey, "I should just like to know what makes you do it. I've been thinking of it, off and on, since the first time, and trying to find out; and I own it beats me. What's it all for?"

"What are you talking about?" asked Mr. Perkins, laughing. He asked the question to gain time, for he thought he knew pretty well what Jim meant.

"Why, this going to suppers, and getting me a place where I can work, and putting me in the way to get some decent clothes, and all kinds of things that you've done. Nobody ever took the trouble before, or cared whether I had anything to eat or not."

By this time Mr. Perkins had decided what to say. "The fact is, Jim, though we ask you now because we like you, and because Baby likes to have you come, in the first place, we did it to please the little girl. I don't suppose I should have thought of such a thing even, if it had not been for her."

"What little girl? Not your baby?"

"No; she is too little to think of such things, bless her! She will be doing for other folks one of these days, I hope. No; it is the little Bruce girl. You know old Bruce, the poor fellow who staggers about carrying a lot of vile whiskey, don't you? Well, he has a little girl—Vira, they call her. Haven't you seen her often?"

"Lots of times," said Jim briefly.

"So I thought. Well, she is a friend of yours. She wanted something done to give you a good time. She would come in and talk with my wife about it, and try to plan ways to do it, and at last we thought maybe you would like some of our good things to eat, so we tried it, and Baby took a notion to you, you know, the first thing; so that settled it."

There never was a more astonished boy than Jim Bryan. He stared at Mr. Perkins for a few minutes too amazed to speak. At last he said, "You are all out. That there little girl is about as far from being a friend of mine as she could be. I reckon she just about hates me; she ain't had no reason to do anything. else. Whatever made you have such a notion as that?"

"I got it from the girl herself, Jim. She was all worked up about your having a better time; she said she couldn't stand it any way in the world if something wasn't done. She said she was praying for you, Jim, and that the praying and the doing ought to match."

"*She* praying!" said Jim Bryan. Two words could not have expressed more.

"Yes," said Mr. Perkins, "praying for you; every day of her life. That's a great little girl, Jim; she hasn't had any chance in the world. You know what her father is; and her mother is a poor, broken-down, discouraged woman, and has forgotten a great deal that she used to know, I suppose. The little girl doesn't seem to have any friends. The only nice thing she has got in the world is a motto that they gave her up at the Mission Sunday-school the time they had their Christmas doings; and that motto has seemed to make her all over some way. It is a

Bible verse; the only one she knew, and she has been living by it ever since she got it."

"Well, but," said Jim, "how do I come in? I tell you, Vira Bruce don't know anything about me but what is mean. I've plagued her a good deal, off and on. She is such a spiteful little thing that I liked to see her fire up; then she would throw sand or anything she happened to have in her hand at me, and that made me mad. Why, we've had awful times, she and I."

"Can't help it," said Mr. Perkins; "you were one of the first persons she thought of when she made up her mind to be different, you know; and she has kept at you steady ever since."

Jim could not get his thoughts away from this astonishing bit of news. He made up his mind to be on the watch for Vira, and find out for himself if she had really become a different being. Some extraordinary change must have come to her if the half that Mr. Perkins had told him was so.

In the course of the next week he had an unexpected chance to study Vira. Since he had begun regular work at the shop, and so was not to be seen at all hours lounging around street corners, Vira, who had long avoided the places where he might be, had grown less careful; and on this particular afternoon came upon him just as she was coming with Baby Perkins across the street near the grocery. That small lady had arrived at the dignity of taking walks on her own little feet, and was very proud of doing so; and nothing gave Vira a greater sense of importance than to be allowed to guide those same footsteps along the street. Truth to tell, Mrs. Perkins found it very hard to trust her baby to any care but her own. Still, Vira seemed so womanly, and Baby was so fond of her, and begged so hard to go with her when she went to the grocery where the family supplies were bought, that for a week or two Baby had been allowed to trot by her side.

The grocery was only a short distance from home, on a quiet enough street, and Vira went at a time of day when few teams were passing. It hardly seemed possible that any harm could come to them. The trip had been made in safety and comfort perhaps half a dozen times, when to Vira's great dismay she came upon Jim Bryan at the corner. Now, although she put Jim daily into her prayers, this little girl did not understand praying well enough to have the faintest expectation, or even hope, that he would be any different to her from what he had always been. It was all very well for him to be nice before Mr. Perkins; Vira could not imagine why anyone should be otherwise. And Mrs. Perkins was a lady who had a house of her own, and made rice cakes, and things that Jim liked; why shouldn't he be nice to her? But Vira Bruce, the drunkard's girl, was another matter. She expected trouble. Had she not once been walking down this very street with the little Simmons girl, who was only two years old; and had not Jim rushed at them, making an awful roaring noise which frightened the Simmons baby so that she screamed and clung to Vira? And didn't Jim seize her neat little bonnet from her head and toss it up for a ball, and throw Vira's sunbonnet into the vacant lot near at hand, or the lot that would have been vacant had not a pony been put in there to eat grass; and didn't that pony step on her sunbonnet and the Simmons baby's hat and ruin both of them? And didn't Jim Bryan laugh and call her names when she tried to tell him what a mean, ugly fellow he was? Oh, what if he should seize upon Baby Perkins's new lovely white cap that her mother finished for her only that day? Such trouble as they had been to about that cap! Vira herself had gone up and down the street three different times for the purpose of getting a nearer view of the little girls at the hotel that she might be able to tell Mrs. Perkins just exactly how the ribbon which held the cap was wound about its crown, and what sort of a knot it was fastened in behind. Then they had sat up until after nine o'clock tying knots of ribbon and twisting and contriving, until at last the cap had been made to look almost exactly like the one which the littlest little girl at the hotel wore. Vira's satisfaction in it had been complete; and Mrs. Perkins had not been far behind her in expressions of pleasure. They both agreed the next day that Baby looked "too sweet for anything" in the cap; and Vira had been allowed to take her for this first walk in its honor—and here was Jim.

Here, too, was the vacant lot. There was no pony in it now; it was really and truly vacant. If she could only get Baby over the high fence, then they two could run across the lot; no, she could run and carry Baby in her arms and reach Dr. Barton's door, surely, before Jim could catch them. Fairly on Dr. Barton's doorstep, bad boy though Jim was, surely he would not dare to do anything to Baby; for she would scream, Vira declared to herself, loud enough to scare the deaf woman who worked in the doctor's kitchen, if Jim but looked at them. Oh, to be over that fence! She could climb it like a cat; but to climb and hold on to Baby at the same time would be hard. And there was Jim fairly upon them! There was no hope of getting quietly over the high fence and hiding behind it so that he would not see them at all, which had been one of her plans. Jim was evidently at his worst; for instead of moving on down the street, as a decent boy would do, he was taking great strides in their direction—looking at Baby, too; and it was only last week that Vira had heard of her sitting on his knee and pulling his hair. How could he be ugly to her now?

"I will put her behind me," said Vira, with the energy of despair, "and I'll hold on to him like a giant, and I'll scream so her own father will hear me up at the shop. I'll keep him from touching her, even if he kills me!"

CHAPTER 21

Enemies and Friends

S HE clutched at Baby so fiercely as almost to frighten the little one, and struggled with the fence; but it was higher than she had thought. Easy enough to manage alone, but with Baby Perkins in her arms quite another matter; and Jim was gaining on them. He landed at last close to Vira, all but breathless with his sudden dash.

"I'll lift her over," he said, and suiting the action to the word, he seized upon Baby who was chuckling with delight at the sight of him and struggling to get to him, and lifted her over the fence as if she had been a feather before the astonished Vira could say a word. In truth, she did not stop for words. Seeing Baby safe on the other side of the fence, she went over to her like a cat, unhindered by Jim, who looked on quietly. Fairly over, Vira took time to think. How queer it had all been. Jim had handled Baby as tenderly as her own father could have done, and he had made not the slightest attempt to trouble her, with hands or tongue. She turned and looked at him.

"What did you want to get over there for?" he asked.

"To get away from you," said Vira promptly. Then, scarcely knowing why she did so, she laughed. Jim joined her in a long, loud burst; not a mocking laugh, but one which had real fun it.

"My eyes!" he said. "How you did go over there. What's the matter? Did you think I would hurt her, Vira Bruce? Look at her; she's about crazy to get to me. I wouldn't do anything to worry her, not for a whole boat-load of apples; and you ain't of much account if you think I would."

"How did I know?" asked Vira. "Did I ever see you that you wasn't worrying somebody?—Mostly me and the things I had to do with. I didn't know but her being with me, you kind of couldn't keep from it; and I wasn't going to have her scared if I could help it."

"I didn't come over here to worry neither of you," said Jim cheerfully. "You needn't go to suppose that folks always do things because they have done them once; folks change sometimes. I heard you had yourself. Have you given up being such a spitfire that a fellow couldn't help plaguing you just to see you sputter? I thought you wanted to get over into that lot to have a run on the grass or something, and I come over on purpose to help you. If you ain't got nothing in particular to call you there, I might help you back. Shall I? Come here, Sissy."

"Sissy" obeyed as fast as her little dumplings of feet could take her to him; he reached his long arms over and gathered her to them, and by the time Vira had climbed back, the baby was smothering Jim's face in kisses and love-pats.

"Now," said he, as he at last set her down, "if you've got over your scare, we might walk along together as far as the corner. I want to ask you something: Why did you want to have me invited to the Perkins', and to have a good time?"

"How do you know I did?"

"He told me so. He said you said a good deal about it, and wanted me to have a nice time; and I can't understand it at all. I never meant to bother you half so much as you thought I did. I wouldn't have downright hurt you, you know, but you always expected the worst that a fellow could do; kind of dared me, you know; and I own I've been mean; so what made you care how bad times I had?"

"Well," said Vira reflectively, "you see, you are my enemy."

"I'm your what?" from an astonished boy.

"My enemy. You know what an enemy is, don't you?, I think you have been mine; you don't act like one today, but you always have before; and you know that verse about 'love your enemies?' It is in the Bible."

"Can't say I ever read it there," said Jim dryly.

"Well, it's there; and I wanted to do it. I've made up my mind to try to do every single thing that is in the Bible, just as fast as I find it out; and I wanted to try that. I didn't feel like loving you."

"I should think not!" and Jim chuckled; but Vira's gravity was complete.

She continued, "But I made up my mind to try; and the first thing I thought of was your having a better time. I didn't see how anybody could be anything but mean, living all the while in Pete Knowles's saloon; and I talked with Mrs. Perkins about it; I haven't been able to do a thing myself, but she has. It has made a great change in you, hasn't it?" she added simply.

Jim roared. "You are a queer party!" he said when he could speak. "I never heard anybody go on like you. All the same I am obliged to you. I ought to stay your enemy, according to your ideas of things, so I could get some more nice times. But I don't feel like it, somehow. What will you do if I turn around and be your friend?"

Vira looked at him with her great thoughtful eyes. "Will you she asked. "Do you truly mean it?"

Jim nodded. There was a look in her eyes which kept him from wanting to laugh. "I reckon," he said; "you see, me and Baby is great friends already, and it wouldn't do to have one of her friends for your enemy."

"That's so," said Vira. Then she drew a long unchildlike sigh, and said gravely, "I shall like it first-rate; I never had no friends, only Sandy Smith, till I come to know the Perkinses. And I can come in to supper sometimes, now; I never would before, because I thought I better not. I've got an enemy, though. Pete Knowles is the worst enemy I ever had; worse than you, because, you see, you only plagued me; but Pete, he is after my father all the while. Three times father has tried to go all day without drinking whiskey; he promised me in the morning he would try, and he did; and he got some jobs to do, and Pete, he just watched out for him, and asked him to come in and drink; and father can't help it, you see. He says whiskey kind of masters him when he hears about it; and I believe it. If Pete had only let him alone that time, he would have got home all right. He got past four saloons, because they didn't watch out for him; but when Pete stood in the door and smiled, and said he looked tired, and wasn't he thirsty, it was too much for father. Isn't he an enemy, now?"

Jim nodded gravely. Then he brought forward an argument which must belong naturally to a certain type of mind; for, although one hears it often enough, certainly Jim had never before argued about this matter.

"But then, Vira, if it wasn't Pete Knowles's saloon it would be some other fellow's. There's lots of them here, you know. They will all coax fellows when they think they have any money in their pockets; that is what they are after."

"I know it; if Pete Knowles's saloon was out of the way, I s'pose I should pick out some other one to hate; but I hate his the worst just now. You don't have to love the saloons, Jim. I asked Miss Southey about it; and I'm glad of that; for if you did, I'm afraid I couldn't do it."

"And do you pretend to say you love Pete Knowles?"

Vira hesitated, and spoke slowly and carefully: "It isn't exactly loving, Jim; at least, it isn't the kind of loving that I should like to have people do for me; but it is feeling different to them from hating—oh, a great deal different. I hated him downright, once. I wished lots of ugly things to him; but you know when his baby died?" Jim nodded. "Well, it was after that that I began to feel different. I didn't suppose I could even be sorry for him, but I was. Not at first, but afterwards."

"All on account of the baby?" asked Jim, his voice choking a little.

"No, it wasn't all that. It was because I—Jim, do you know what praying is?"

"I've heard tell of it," said Jim dryly.

"Well, I prayed and prayed, until I felt different about even Pete Knowles. I can't explain it, because I don't understand it myself; I only know it's true."

"Know what's true? I can't keep track of you."

"Why, that you pray and pray, and a thing gets to feeling just as different! You don't do it, you know; but it gets done."

Said Jim, "Humph!" Then, after a moment, "I've got to turn off at this corner. I'm out on an errand for the boss. And don't you go to climbing no more fences on account of me; we'll go in for friends after this. I don't understand about the praying, but from what I've heard, I reckon it's a good thing. Now I'll give Sissy into your care."

During all this time they had been moving slowly down the street; Baby Perkins clinging to Jim's neck with one round arm, and chattering all her pretty little words into his ear. Vira received her again, almost like one in a dream. What wonderful things had happened! Here had she been moving through the street beside Jim Bryan, not only talking to him, but actually telling him some of the most important happenings of her life; and he had not laughed, nor sneered, nor been in any way like the Jim Bryan she had known before. She let her bewilderment come to the surface in a single question as he turned to leave her.

"Look here, Jim; wait just a minute. What has made you different?"

"Rice cakes and maple syrup and things," said Jim with a short laugh, just as he was moving away. But he glanced back to say, "Maybe the praying had a little something to do with it; shouldn't wonder."

So great had been Vira's interest and bewilderment that she had well-nigh forgotten the errand at the grocery which had started them out. It was for Mrs. Perkins, and was a whole quart of molasses. Vira knew there was to be molasses gingerbread of a certain soft, sweet kind which Mrs. Perkins knew how to make, and that Jim was to be asked to come to tea. "And if she asks me again," said the little girl, as she retraced her steps to the grocery, "I'll come."

Molasses, Baby, and Vira were moving peacefully down the street a very short time afterwards, when something happened which made even the surprising interview with Jim slip into the background. They had reached a building which was being repaired, and which had a tall scaffolding built around it. Vira looked up at it. Men were moving around on its top, as carelessly as though the flooring on which they stood was broad and secure. Dangerous-looking planks and beams stuck out all ways, and Vira shivered a little at the thought of, "What if one of them should fall on Baby?" It was characteristic of this little girl that she did not once think, what if one should fall on herself.

"We'll go across the street," she said, explaining matters carefully to Baby, after a fashion she had. "We won't go under those great ugly planks and tools; one of the men might drop his hammer down, or his saw. Ugh!" Or, "Wait, Baby ; there are. wagons in the road now, and there is a carriage with two horses that don't want to step on all their feet at once. We won't cross until they get by, because we promised your mother we would be very, very careful about wagons and horses and things. Oh, wait, Baby come back."

For Baby had suddenly broken away from her hand and
made a quick little run forward, not across the street, but under
the scaffolding. It was all done in a moment of time. Vira's call
and dash after the baby, the shout of workmen, the loud
cracking of planks and sticks, the screams of people on the
street who seemed to discover as if by magic that something
was happening, and ran together from all ways at once, the
screams of the poor frightened baby, and the falling of that
mass of scaffolding, right on her dear little yellow head! No, not
that; one other thing happened. From inside the building a boy
dashed just as the crackling began, giving a bound right into the
midst of danger, called back by a dozen voices inside, but
plunging on; a flash of him was seen for a second, then he
disappeared, and the crash came and was over; and two men
were holding Vira back, for she would have gone headlong into
certain death, and she was screaming wildly, "The baby, the
baby! Let me go!"

"What became of the boy?" shouted men who were
crowding out from inside the building. "Was he killed?"

"There was a child!" screamed a man from behind the
crowd. "Where is the child? She must be under the planks."

"The child is safe!" shouted a man from his carriage,
leaning out to join in the calls, while his driver had his hands full
with the frightened horses. "The boy saved her; he sprang like a
deer in great bounds, and snatched her in just the right direction
to escape. Look! There he is."

Sure enough; there was Baby Perkins, wide-eyed and trembling, but with her strong little right arm thrown about Jim
Bryan's neck; and Jim, his left ankle bruised a little by the end of

a timber as it fell, was yet quite himself and able to shout his own directions:

"Help the little girl over here; as soon as she sees the baby she will be all right. She doesn't sense the fact that she ain't killed."

"It was a very brave thing to do," explained the gentleman, as crowds of people surrounded him, seeming to feel that he was the only one present who knew exactly what had happened. "I thought no earthly power could save the child from being crushed to death; and the older girl was just saved by main force. Of course it all happened in a moment. The boy must have heard the first crackling of the timbers and guessed what was going to happen, and taken in at the same second the way to spring to escape the fall. I never saw anything done so quickly. If it hadn't been quick there would have been two victims instead of one. Bring them this way, gentlemen." For somebody was half-carrying Vira across the street, and Jim Bryan was following with baby, who resisted all attempts to take her out of his arm. "Bring them to my carriage; I will take them home. They are too much shaken up, all of them, to walk. Who are they? Does anybody know? Brother and sisters, I presume."

Yes, there were dozens who knew. No, they were not "brother and sisters" at all. One was old Bruce the drunkard's daughter, and the boy was Jim Bryan, a street loafer. As for the little thing, she belonged to a neighbor of the Bruces', they believed. She was nothing to either of the others.

"So much the more noble thing for the boy to do," said the gentleman firmly. "He must have known he was risking his life. If a corner of one of the planks had struck his head—and I don't see how it escaped—he would have been in all probability fatally injured. A street loafer with as much good in him as that, and as quick a brain, is worth looking after. Oh, yes, my boy! get in; I shall be glad to drive you home. This little one's mother will want to see you, I know. Jump right in. She objects to leaving you, and I don't wonder."

For by this time, they and the crowd had reached the carriage, and Jim was objecting to being helped in, and Baby Perkins was hugging his neck with both fat arms, and frowning at any attempt to remove them. As for Vira, she was still crying so bitterly that she was incapable of helping to win Baby to herself. Her poor little nerves had been so utterly shaken that she could not as yet control them. Somebody had lifted her into the handsome carriage, and she had sunk among the cushions a limp heap of sobs and tears. There seemed nothing for Jim to do but step in beside her. A dozen voices gave the driver the necessary directions; the gentleman took his seat inside, and they were off.

"I'd hold up now if I were you, Vira," said Jim, gently touching her arm with his disengaged hand. "The baby is all safe; not even a curl out of place; and nobody is hurt. You ought to laugh, instead of cry. You're scaring Baby; she is beginning to pucker her lip."

This hint did more to help Vira to self-control than anything which had preceded it. She sat up, with a mass of apron to her eyes, and subdued her sobs to long shudders, as she murmured "Oh, Jim, if you hadn't been right by the window and seen her …"

"Well, I was right by the window, and seen her as plain as day; and I seen which way the thing was coming, too. I knew I could get her, if I made a quick enough dash, and didn't stop to explain anything. And I did it, and it's all right, Vira; don't you cry no more."

CHAPTER 22

An Afternoon To Remember

SUCH an excitement as there was at Mrs. Perkins's house for the next two hours! In the first place, the carriage made a sensation. It was a quiet little back street, not over-clean, as I have told you, and carriages of any sort almost never came that way. The ash-cart and the garbage-wagon, and occasionally a milk-wagon, rolled through there, but no carriages. This was an unusually handsome one, and the horses still stepped as though they had an objection to using all four feet at once. As they pranced along, holding their heads high, from every door and window along the street, heads appeared, looking after them; their owners called out to one another, trying to get news:

"Whose carriage is that? I never see it before."

"Nor I. Wonder who they are looking for? I guess they've lost their way."

"My land, if they ain't drawing up before Miz' Perkins'! Appears to me Miz' Perkins is coming up in the world dreadful fast! Company to tea every other hitch, and now a grand carriage. And there's Viry Bruce getting out of it; and that great rough Jim Bryan, too! For pity's sake, he's got the Perkins baby in his arms! I shouldn't wonder a mite if she was killed. I said the other day that if Miz' Perkins let Viry Bruce tote her 'round she'd be sorry."

The news spread like wildfire through the neighborhood that Baby Perkins was killed, or, at the very least, dreadfully hurt. Mrs. Perkins, whom the sight of the carriage had drawn to the doorway with the rest, came out on the step looking white enough to drop, but she did not; instead, she reached out her arms for her baby. Something had happened; but here was the baby, alive at least. Jim Bryan hastened to explain, for Vira, who could not understand what was the matter with her, and felt very much ashamed that it should be so, was crying again.

"There isn't a scratch on her anywhere," said Jim eagerly. "Don't you be scared, Miz' Perkins; she didn't fall, nor nothing. And there ain't a single thing happened—not to any of us."

"Thanks to this boy," said the stranger, who was out of the carriage almost as quickly as Jim. "There was an accident, madam, which was in great danger of being serious. This little one was in eminent peril; a scaffolding fell, almost on her, one may say. It is hard to realize even now that she escaped; but this boy was inside the building, and he saw it coming, and was out there with the baby in his arms, on the other side of the timbers, before the rest of us had a chance to think whether there was anything that could be done."

"Oh, Jim!" said Mrs. Perkins, her face no longer white; the blood was rolling in waves to her very forehead. "Oh, Jim! What can I ever do for you?"

What she did at that moment was to bend over the astonished boy, and kiss his rough, tanned cheek. Then you should have seen his face. It had been red before, but now it seemed fairly to blaze.

"It wasn't nothing; nothing at all," he said. "I see her snatch away her hand from Vira, and give a little dash ahead, and at that second I heard the tremble, and thought most likely the thing was going to fall; and I see which way it would fall, and I made a dash and grabbed her, of course, just as anybody with a grain of sense would, and got out of the way. That's the whole of it, Miz' Perkins; and I must get off to the shop just as fast as my feet can take me. I was sent after a chisel, and I reckon the boss'll think I'm waiting to make it."

"He will excuse you," said the stranger, "as soon as he learns what detained you. Where is your shop? Quite a distance away. I'll set you down there, young man; I am going to drive in that direction. Jump into my carriage, and I'll have you there before you could make half the distance on your feet, spry as they are."

And although Jim hesitated and stammered, and declared he wasn't in any such terrible hurry as that, he was overruled; and Mrs. Perkins and Vira stood in the doorway, and watched him whirl away, Baby throwing kisses at him by the dozen as he went.

"And, oh, Jim," said Mrs. Perkins, her voice still trembling, "come back to supper, won't you? I'll get as nice a one as I know how."

"To think," said Vira, looking after the carriage with eyes that were still glistening with tears, "to think that I ran away from him this very day, for fear he would hurt Baby." Then the whole story of the eventful afternoon had to be gone over for Mrs. Perkins's benefit. How Vira had grown afraid lest Jim's fondness for being "mean" to her should be too much for him, even though he was supposed to like the baby; how he whirled baby over the fence for her, she springing after like a cat; and how he lifted baby back again, and walked on peacefully by their side, talking in a way that Jim Bryan never did before. "And oh!" she said, breaking off to shiver, "What if he hadn't walked with me, but had gone on fast, and got his chisel, and been gone before baby and I got there; and the boards had come down, and—"

"Don't!" said Mrs. Perkins, and she hugged Baby so closely that the little one puckered her lip. "It doesn't seem to me," she said tremulously, "that I can ever let her go out of my arms again. Not that I blame you the least in the world," she added, noting Vira's grave face. "I know you took as good care of her as I could myself. I know just how she suddenly jerks her hand away and gives a little dash forward—I can see her do it; and you did your very best, I am sure—but, oh, it was such a narrow escape! Oh, Baby, I must hold you tight always!"

But the next moment she put her into Vira's arms, and began bustling about to make her soft gingerbread, and get the very best supper that her resources could furnish. Of course Vira must stay tonight; she was needed to watch Baby. I have always thought that Mrs. Perkins showed more what a truly kind-hearted woman she was by letting Vira have the care of Baby that afternoon than by almost anything else she had done, because her inclination was to keep Baby in her arms, and let

Vira do the work; but her keen eyes saw that poor Vira, despite all that had been said to comfort her, still blamed herself for the afternoon's dangers. Perhaps you can think what it was to her to be trusted again so soon by the mother.

Jim Bryan, riding down the main street in the handsome carriage, felt very queer. His companion did not seem to have any such feeling. He said he was almost a stranger, having been in town but a day or two. He asked questions about several of the buildings which they passed, and showed so much interest in the information which he received, that Jim was encouraged to talk as well as he could. At last, as they neared the shop where the chisel was being waited for, the stranger said:

"I am glad to have met you, my boy; and to have seen you do a noble act. It makes me feel that you will try to grow into a noble man. I wonder if you know how very near the other world you were today? Did you see that plank which all but grazed your temple? Do you know that if it had struck you there, the probability is you would have been killed?"

"Yes, sir," said Jim gravely, "I see it, and I thought likely it might kill me; but I couldn't let the little baby be hurt, nohow, and me escape, because they are the only folks, they and the little girl, who ever cared what became of me, and I was bound to do my best for 'em; besides, I love the baby. It wouldn't have mattered if I had been killed."

"Wouldn't it? You mean you are all ready to live or to die; and that whichever way it was, it would have been all right with you?"

"Oh, no!" and Jim's face was crimson. "I don't mean nothing of that kind. I ain't of no 'count, living or dying. I never done nothing but mean things, and I don't belong to nobody, and nobody cares; that is what I meant."

"What a mistaken boy! You belong to the Lord Jesus Christ. He paid a big price for you, and keeps looking out to see if you are ready to own Him as your friend; and you did an act this afternoon worthy of the relationship which there is, or ought to be, between you and Him. My boy, don't you know He wants to be your brother? You wouldn't have disappointed the father and mother of the baby this afternoon, because they have been good to you; don't you disappoint Jesus Christ: it isn't fair, after all He has done for you."

Then they were at the shop; and the foreman, looking out with an annoyed expression on his face, was just saying, "That fellow has been gone long enough to have a chisel made!" when Mr. Perkins said, "Here he is, sir, getting out of a carriage. Something must have happened."

Whether they would have heard what had "happened" from Jim is doubtful; by this time he had a good many things to think about. But the owner of the carriage got out of it also, and with a polite bow to the foreman told the whole story, in a way which did honor to Jim.

"What about the child?" interrupted the foreman, with a hasty glance at Mr. Perkins. "Did it escape all harm?"

"Oh, yes, indeed! It was not even badly frightened; not so much so but that it clung to the boy and smiled at the horses as soon as we were seated in the carriage."

"There, Perkins," said the foreman, not unkindly, "listen to that, and spare your fainting for another time. You looked white enough to drop. I reckon it was your little girl, wasn't it?"

"Is that so?" asked the stranger, shaking him heartily by the hand. "Then I congratulate you. The child certainly had a narrow escape; but it was an entire one, thanks to the boy. Oh, yes; I am quite sure. I saw the whole thing; and, as I am a physician, I took care to assure myself that no harm would result to the child, even from the fright. The baby and the boy were both saved from what would have been almost certain death. The Lord has some special work for each of them in the world, perhaps. I hope the baby's father belongs to Him?"

Mr. Perkins hesitated. "I don't know," he said. "I have thought about such things a good deal of late. I don't know as I have any right to say I belong to Him, but I know I feel differently from what I used to, and I am trying to do what I think He would like as well as I know how; still, I don't suppose I am what you mean."

"What I mean," said the doctor earnestly, "is just this. Have you made up your mind to take Him for your Employer? He wants you, and He offers splendid wages. Of course He wants His work done, and He wants faithful service. I fancy you are the kind of man who can give that. If you like the Employer and like the wages, why, it is for you to decide whether or not you belong to Him. He engages men for life, you know. It is as simple as that. Have you accepted His offer?"

There was a new light in Mr. Perkins's face just then. "I never thought of it in that way," he said heartily. "I don't think I quite understand it; but you make it very plain. Yes, sir, if He will take me, I'll work for Him all my days."

"Amen," said the doctor. "Let us shake hands on that. He has given you great proof of His love and care today. I know you will see to it that you teach the little one early to love and serve Him."

Then the stranger physician, who was taking a few days' vacation in his busy life, but who never took a vacation in the service of Jesus Christ, entered his carriage and drove away, with a smile on his handsome face. He hoped there had been good work done for his Master that day.

As for Jim, in the hour that was left of the day, he did the work of two; despite the fact that all the men wanted to question him about the accident, and made a sort of hero out of him. Jim was good-natured, and answered their questions, but he did not feel like talking. A wonderful thing had happened to him; a good woman, Baby's mother, had kissed him. He seemed to feel the kiss still on his cheek. Once, a long time ago, when he was a very little boy, he remembered his mother had kissed him and said, "Good-bye, Jimmie; be a good boy." That was the last time he had seen her; he did not at the time understand very well why it was, but he knew long afterwards that she had died. He had not obeyed her and been "a good boy;" but he had never entirely forgotten her words, even though for years at a time they would seem to be out of mind. Nobody had ever talked to him as the stranger had that day. He knew something about Jesus Christ, but not much. It was astonishing news that Jesus Christ knew anything about Jim Bryan, and wanted him for a brother. That, and the narrow escape which he had had, and the memory of the kiss on his cheek, made it a memorable afternoon. Over and over again he said those last words of the stranger: "Don't you disappoint Jesus Christ; it isn't fair, after all He has done for you." And those other words: "Good-bye,

Jimmie; be a good boy," and some way they seemed to belong together. Could he really be a "good boy?" What a queer thing it would be if he should hear somebody saying, sometime, "Jim Bryan is a good, faithful fellow—one to be trusted." He had heard himself called a "nuisance," and "no good," and a "quick-witted scamp," and several other like names—but nobody ever had, for a single minute, called him good; yet that was what his mother wanted him to be. Perhaps she cared yet; perhaps he was "disappointing" her, as that strange man said he was Jesus Christ.

There was a jubilee at the Perkins home that night. Not only soft gingerbread, but fried sweet potatoes and rice cakes with Northern maple syrup were served; to say nothing of a glass of guava jelly, and a dish of handsome oranges. Mrs. Perkins did her best; nothing to be had in this world was quite good enough for Jim.

As for Vira, she expressed her feelings in flowers. It was only April, to be sure; and in some parts of the country there was snow still on the ground, some of it having fallen that very day, so the papers said; but Vira, knew so little about the great cold North that if she had seen the papers, which she didn't, she could hardly have believed the story, so sunny was her Southern world, and so full were the woods of flowers. The table looked like a bower of beauty.

Jim expressed his pleasure in broad smiles, and all of them tried to be very gay; but each one felt an undertone of gravity which it was impossible to put away. Mrs. Perkins could not, even for a moment, forget that her darling had been in great peril that day. She looked lovely in her best white dress which had been put on in honor of the occasion, and her sunny hair was in beautiful order, and her small chubby hands were never more full of mischief; but how still they might have been by this time! Even the white dress made her mother shiver; she could not help thinking that she would have been dressed in that if she had been gotten ready for the grave. Of course the mother could not be exactly merry with such thoughts as these in undertone.

Vira, too, felt the spell of gravity. She had been on the spot at the moment of danger; she could close her eyes and see again the great planks as they came crashing down; she could hear the awful noise, the breaking of timber, the shouts of men, the yells of women and children.

But I do not know that any of them realized the peril through which they had passed any more than did Mr. Perkins himself. He had thought of little else ever since he heard the news. Yes, he had thought of one other thing. The words of the doctor who had told him the story, and the solemn decision he had made: "Yes, sir; if He will take me, I'll work for Him all my days." He realized what the words meant; he was not his own anymore. He owed Jesus Christ a debt of gratitude which no service could ever pay, and as often as he looked at Baby he should be sure to think of it; nevertheless, he would do what he could to show his gratitude.

"Nannie will be glad," he said to himself, looking over at his wife. "Nannie will join me; in fact, she is ahead of me; I should never have gone to that Mission regularly, it isn't likely, but for her. We will both serve Him; and we will bring up Baby to love Him."

Jim and he had been very quiet during their walk home from the shop. At first they had tried to talk about common things, as usual, but they had not succeeded very well; commonplaces seemed absurdly out of place that day.

At last Mr. Perkins, after a few minutes of silence, had said, "I haven't any words to thank you with, Jim; words don't seem to do it, somehow; but I'm not likely to forget that you risked your life for my baby, and if there is anything I can ever do for you in any way, why, you know—"

"Sho!" said Jim, interrupting. "I don't want no words, nor nothing else. Do you suppose I would have let her get hurt?"

"All the same, Jim, some folks couldn't have done it. They wouldn't have thought quick enough. He said you had an awful narrow escape; that he thought a long, sharp stick was going to hit you in just the wrong place; and he is a doctor, and knows. He said maybe the Lord had some special work for both you and Baby to do in the world. That's worth thinking about, Jim."

After that they had been entirely silent. And at the tea-table neither of them could forget that there had been grave talk between them, and that life seemed different.

CHAPTER 23

An Agreement

IT was several weeks after the accident. Vira and Jim Bryan were visiting together in Mr. Perkins's doorway.

Jim had come up to go with Mr. Perkins to the singing-school at the Mission; and while he waited for him to make ready, he and Vira had one of their talks. This had already become a most natural thing for them to do. From Jim Bryan being her "enemy," Vira had grown to consider him her "next best friend."

"Of course Mrs. Perkins will always be first," she told herself gravely, "but Jim is certainly next."

With this exception, things were not very much changed from that eventful afternoon when she and Jim had taken their first ride in a carriage.

At least, they two knew of no other change. To Mr. and Mrs. Perkins it had been a time which marked one of the most important events of their lives. They had stood up together in the church, and given themselves publicly and forever to the service of Jesus Christ.

Vira was at the church that day; so also was her mother. The service made a deep impression on them both. To Vira it was an entirely new experience; not so Mrs. Bruce.

"I've been to such meetings before," she explained on the way home. "I've been lots of times in the old church at home; your grandpa and grandma belonged, and were as respectable as any of them. It seems almost like home to see such things."

Said Vira, speaking very gravely, almost gloomily, "I suppose it was a nice thing to do, but it won't make no difference. Mrs. Perkins was good before, and so was he; and they'll go on being good now, just the same. If it was father who had gone and stood up there and made them promises, and kept them, oh, my, what a difference it would make!"

Mrs. Bruce sighed. "I've given that up long ago," she said.

"I haven't," answered Vira firmly. "I don't mean to give it up, ever. Maybe it will come someday. People get changed sometimes; look at Jim Bryan!"

But despite her firmness, Vira was often down-hearted; she was this evening. It was only a day or two after the Sunday service which had impressed her, and her thoughts had been busy ever since over her father.

"It seems so kind of dreadful and disappointing," she said to Jim; "since Mr. Perkins stood up in the church and made those promises, you know, I thought about father; if he could make them it would make such a great big difference. He wouldn't drink any more, nor laze around and do nothing, and everybody would know about it; but Mr. Perkins was good before."

Jim chuckled a little. "You can't get over that," he said good-naturedly. "You wanted Mr. Perkins to be a horrid kind of a man just for the pleasure of seeing the change; I'm sorry for you, but he always was pretty nice, I guess, and so it can't be helped."

Vira did not laugh. "Jim," she asked earnestly, "do you really believe that father ever will be different?"

"Why, I don't know," said Jim, trying to be grave. "It takes a lot of imagination to think of him being sober; but men do give up drinking sometimes. There is a fellow at the shop who used to drink like a fish, the boys say; never could keep sober half a day to save his life; but he hasn't drank a drop in two years."

"What cured him?"

"Well," said Jim reluctantly, "the boys say he had a little girl that got drownded; she felt bad about him and wanted him to reform; and after she was drownded, he did."

Silence for several minutes; then Vira said with slow gravity, "I'd be willing to be drowned, Jim, I really think I would; I feel so awful about father; and he thinks a good deal of me. Maybe it would make him stop."

"But you can't go and drown yourself, you know," said Jim hastily; "that little girl had an accident."

"No," spoken in a slow, half-discouraged tone, "I s'pose I couldn't do it myself, because that would be wicked; and there don't anything happen to me. Jim, there is something that I don't understand. You know how Mr. Powell talked down at the Mission the other night? Miss Southey says the same thing; and the superintendent often says something like it in Sunday-school. Well, that shows that God can do anything, doesn't it? Then why doesn't he make folks good?"

"Whether they want to be or not?" questioned Jim.

"Yes. He could make father be a good, sober man, if He chose; why doesn't He do it?"

Jim reflected. "Maybe it wouldn't amount to much of anything if He did," he said, after a few minutes' thought. "It would be like tying me up, so I couldn't do no mischief. If I was tied up all the time I would be a no account sort of a fellow. Couldn't do good nor harm, and I'd have to be kept tied everlastingly, 'cause the minute I was let loose—Whoop!—wouldn't I go at it worse than ever? Folks wouldn't care anything for such goodness as that. You wouldn't like me if I had to have my arms tied up all the while to keep me from hitting you. It is my not wanting to do it that makes it worthwhile; don't you see?"

Vira admitted that there was truth in this, but could not get away from her sorrow and regret about her father.

"He really does want to be good, and means to be," she said sadly, "but that Pete Knowles won't let him. Only yesterday, Jim, he said he would come home sober, if he died for it; and he got a little work and had some money, and he was going to get something for dinner, and I was to have it ready and surprise mother when she got back from the hotel; and don't you believe that Pete Knowles watched for him as he was coming home and asked him in to take a drink! Wasn't that awful mean? How can I help hating Pete Knowles? That scares me, too; I just can't help feeling awful about him."

"I wouldn't try," said Jim emphatically. "He is meaner than dirt. He will do anything for money; they all will, them rum-sellers."

"Oh, but, Jim, I have tried! I pray every single day to Jesus to help me not hate Pete Knowles; and last night I almost felt as though I did hate him in spite of it all. If something would only happen to him I believe father could get home sober—part of the time, anyhow."

"It is a pity he couldn't get drowned," said Jim vindictively. But at this Vira looked fairly frightened, and shut her ears so she could not hear, and begged Jim not to say anything so bad as that; because if anything should happen to Pete Knowles, it would be awful to think they had wished for it. She confessed that she was praying for something to happen to him that would spoil his business. She did not see what it could be, but perhaps God could do it.

Jim laughed again. "His business will last as long as he does, I reckon," he said. "Pete Knowles likes money first-rate, and he knows there is money to be made by it. You won't catch him shutting up his shop, or letting your father get by, so long as there is any money in his pocket."

Yet these two were mistaken in their estimate of Pete Knowles. Not that he did not love money; and carry on his liquor saloon in order to get it. But he was not so bad a man as they supposed. How astonished would they have been, for instance, could they have known that in his stupid ignorance he had offered Vira's father a drink of whiskey the night before out of what he imagined was gratitude!

"Poor old hulk!" he said to himself, as "old Bruce" shambled along. "He looks all battered up! He ain't had his drink of whiskey this afternoon, I reckon; can't get trusted anywhere, I s'pose. And his little girl gave the only flower she had to my baby. I wouldn't mind letting him have a drink now and then, if he would be content with one glass, just for the sake of that rose. I'll do it tonight, anyhow." And then he had called out, "Halloo, old fellow! You look beat out. Come in and have a swallow to help you home."

Yes, actually meaning kindness! He was ignorant to the degree that he supposed that a little whiskey really meant kindness. Then "old Bruce," being unable to resist temptation a minute longer, had gone in, and swallowed his one glass, and showed his silver quarter, and "stood treat" to four or five comrades, who crowded around at sight of it; and an hour later Pete Knowles, utterly disgusted with his attempt at benevolence, gave him an angry push, and told him to "get out of there." When Vira's father came to himself the next morning, he told her the sorrowful story; and neither he nor she saw anything in Pete Knowles's act but a keen foreknowledge of that silver quarter. Is it any wonder that the little girl's heart was as heavy as lead, and that she had to "pray hard and fast," as she expressed it, to keep from hating Pete Knowles?

The next time she had a chance to talk to Jim was on Sunday morning. She was on her way to Sunday-school, and Jim was on his way to Mrs. Perkins, to take care of baby while her father and mother went to the Mission.

"Jim," said Vira, beginning the conversation at the point where they left it last, as though it had been only a few minutes since they had seen each other, when in reality it was several days, "something has got to happen to Pete Knowles. I've made up my mind that father won't try hard enough to amount to anything so long as Pete Knowles is in his way; and I kind of feel that God will do something to him."

"Ain't that pretty near wicked?" asked Jim, awed, and somewhat uncomfortable, because of the air of quiet determination with which Vira said this.

"Why, no," said Vira, "it isn't wicked, because God won't do anything wicked; and I've left it to him. I ain't going to do anything."

There seemed no answer to make to this; so Jim went his way. It happened that three busy weeks followed, during which night-work of one sort or another was asked of Jim, and he and Vira did not meet. Mr. Perkins, also, had been at work on the extra job, and had not been to the Mission for several weeks. On the first evening that they were at liberty, Mr. Perkins brought Jim home with him to tea, and invited him to the Mission. At ten o'clock they had not returned. Vira left her mother asleep, after her hard day's work at the hotel, and went in to stay with Mrs. Perkins. "I don't know what can keep them so," said Mrs. Perkins; "they generally get back by half-past nine."

But at half-past ten they had still not appeared. "Why, dear me!" said Mrs. Perkins. "I am afraid something has happened." And just then they heard footsteps on the walk; and Vira went to unfasten the door, while Mrs. Perkins bent over baby, who had just stirred. Mr. Perkins went in to his wife at once, but Jim lingered at the doorway.

"Vira," he said, and there was a curious look on his face, "something has happened. Did you pray it so?"

Said Vira, "Oh, Jim!" clasping her hands like one in an agony of suspense. "Is it about Pete Knowles? Oh, Jim, I don't want him to be dead; I didn't pray that—He isn't dead!"

"Not a bit!" said Jim heartily. "He is very much alive; but he has about killed the rest of us with astonishment. Vira, he stood up in the meeting tonight, and prayed; and he did worse than that. When the meeting was out, he invited a lot of us down to his place, and me in particular, because he said he had had me there to work, and done me harm; though I don't know as he ever did me more harm than lots of others did, but anyhow that was what he said; and when we got there, what do you think he did? Opened every old keg and cask about the place, and let the whiskey run out!"

Every word that Vira could gasp out was, "Oh, Jim!"

He seemed to consider it sufficient. "Yes," he said, "he did that! There wasn't a great lot. He hadn't a big place, you know, and never keeps a lot of it on hand; but there was a great many dollars' worth, after all; and he said he had sold his last drop. He owns the place, and he says it is going to be a shoe-shop, or something else that's decent, after this. And he asked the pardon of all the fellows that he had sold whiskey to, and said he hoped they'd forgive him, and not let him have the credit of ruining their lives. It is the biggest thing that ever happened in this town. You never saw such a time! The fellows cheered, even the drunkards that couldn't help groaning a little when they saw the whiskey running into the gutter; all the same they liked his pluck, and they cheered right on the top of the groans. I say, Vira, did you pray that thing all out?"

"I never did!" said Vira in intense excitement. "Never in the world! I never thought of anything half nor a quarter so nice as that. I couldn't have believed that it would ever happen. Jim Bryan, I told you I left it to God; He is the only one who could make such a thing as that happen."

For the next few days Vira was happy. That the wonderful thing, which she had not expected, had actually "happened" to Pete Knowles was plainly shown on the very next morning, when she went downtown on purpose to see with her own eyes. The shutters were up in the front of the corner saloon, the door was closed, and on it was tacked a placard, which said in large letters:

> This place will open as a
> Shoe Shop next Monday Morning.

The energy which Pete Knowles had seemed to lack as a saloon-keeper was coming to him apparently. He had given himself very little time in which to prepare for a new business. Jim reported that he used to run a shoe-shop up North, and that he knew how to mend shoes first-rate, folks said.

Vira exclaimed over this. It was her father's trade, or had been, away back in those days when he was known as one who had a trade. Her mother had a pair of shoes now which father had made; and when Vira was a baby, father had made her some cunning little red shoes; mother said he was called an excellent workman. What if Pete Knowles should give him work to do?

The idea fairly bewildered her with its greatness. It was such a curious thing to think that she really wanted him to work for Pete Knowles. For a day or two Jim was sceptical; he only half-believed in the reform. He looked to see the saloon open again, and to discover that the whole thing was some sharp scheme of Pete's; not so Vira. She believed in the sudden change.

"I understand all about it," she said to Jim. "God has got hold of Pete Knowles. I don't know, I'm sure, what made Pete want Him to; maybe it was his little baby dying; he was crying that morning when I gave her the rose; but whatever it is, He's done it. And when God puts that want into your heart, Jim Bryan, there isn't nothing else that will do; you know you have got to have it."

Vira's sentences were mixed, but Jim seemed to know what she meant.

But her happiness did not last. Before the week was out she realized, to her bitter sorrow, that it was not altogether Pete Knowles's saloon which had ruined her father; it was his hope-less love for whiskey. For three memorable days he went and came sober; and the wonderful happened—Pete offered him a place in the new shop, which was to open on Monday morning; and on Saturday night, in honor of such a piece of good for-tune, he walked around to Dan Crane's saloon and spent not only the thirty-eight cents he had earned that day, but got trusted for a dollar's worth of liquor, which he used in treating his friends. Then was Vira, for the space of half a day, utterly broken-hearted. Her mother was not; and she tried to comfort the child.

"I wouldn't take on so, Vira. I am surprised at you. I thought you had more sense than to expect that he would quit. He'll give up whiskey when he lies in his coffin, and he won't before; I've known that these dozen years. Yes, I know Pete Knowles has quit; but they are different. In the first place, Pete didn't drink so terrible much himself; he is one of them kind that can drink quite some, and not have it seem to hurt him: and in the next place, he is altogether different from your pa; he hasn't got what you might call spunk. If Pete Knowles did get drunk, he would tear around shamefully, and scare you out of your wits, and knock folks down, and such things; and your pa has never been ugly. Them kind of folks hasn't the heart to give up the drink, I s'pose; anyhow, they never do."

Vira had no answer to make to this bit of logic. She was not convinced, but she did not know how to argue her side. She was hopeless for half a day; but by evening, when Jim came around to have a bit of Sunday supper, and go to meeting with Mr. Perkins, her courage had returned, and her resolve had been taken. Jim knew the minute he saw her that some new plan was born.

"I tell you what it is, Jim Bryan," she began, "I've got where I want your help."

"All right," said Jim, heartily. He was very much pleased with her appearance; he knew in what state her father had come home the night before, and he had expected to see her utterly discouraged. "All right; I'm ready for anything. What is to be done now?"

"Jim, it ain't Pete Knowles's saloon; his was the worst, but they are all worst now. Father will have the whiskey, if he has got to go ever so far to get it. And there ain't any way just now to get rid of them all at once. Is there?"

She looked for her answer so anxiously that Jim, who wanted to laugh, had to control himself as he said, "I should think not! You might as well try to get rid of the river frogs, or the moss on the trees, or the gnats in the air."

"Well, then, something has got to happen to father!"

I wish I could describe to you the impressive manner in which these words were whispered. They had their effect upon Jim; he confessed afterwards to Mrs. Perkins, that they made him feel "kind of creepy-like."

"What are you going to do?" he asked anxiously. "And what do you want of me?"

"I ain't going to do a thing, more than I've been doing this good while; and what I want of you is to help me to do it. Look here, I've found a verse that beats anything." She drew him towards the lamplight, and drew from behind her dress a New Testament, which had been a gift to her from Miss Southey; opened it to Matthew's Gospel, and pointed to a verse. Jim slowly read the words: "If two of you shall agree on earth as touching anything that they shall ask, it shall be done for them of my Father which is in heaven."

"There!" she said, with a kind of subdued triumph in her voice, when she saw he had taken in the words. "What do you think of that? Jim, I want you to be the one to agree,' and then we'll ask; and He will have to do it. because He has promised. We won't say what it shall be, because I can't make up my mind. I'd rather leave it to Him; but we'll pray and pray for something to happen—something that will make father give up the whiskey for always."

Jim looked and felt utterly dumfounded.

"But, Vira," he said nervously, "I can't do it, you know; I don't know how."

"You can learn," said Vira confidently, "it's easy. I learned when there was only Nero to help me, and my picture on the wall. Jim, you must! I've made up my mind that you are to be the one who 'agrees.' You said you was ready for anything."

What was to be done? Nothing which Jim had met heretofore dismayed him like this. He had not forgotten the words of the stranger physician; nor the impression which his narrow escape had made; nor the memory of his mother's words, which these events had so vividly recalled. In various ways he had improved his life. He had resolved that he would not use any more tobacco, and he would not swear any more, and he would be industrious and honest and faithful. But to pray was another thing entirely. Yet he could not bear to disappoint Vira; she was having so much disappointment about her father, and it was true he had told her he was ready for anything.

CHAPTER 24

Something "Happened"

IT was really the hardest struggle that Jim Bryan had ever had with himself. As it was, he only half promised, so that Vira went away not feeling absolutely sure that she could trust him as the one who had "agreed." Still, he felt bound to her, and it haunted him all through the Mission service. Strangely enough the man who spoke there that evening talked about prayer—what a simple and altogether natural yet important thing it was. Jim had to own, by the time the service was over, that he had been shown how to pray.

The three other boys who slept in the attic room which he now shared were all sound asleep when Jim stole out of bed, dropped on his knees in the darkness, and whispered softly, "O, God! Let something happen to him as Vira wants it to, and as You promised if we asked."

The weeks went by, and the heat of early summer was upon the Southland. Miss Southey, together with all the Northern guests, had gone home.

With our friends, the Perkins family, and Vira and Jim, matters were moving on much as usual to all appearances; but there were changes. Jim, having made a promise, was the one to keep it. Every night now he got down on his knees after the attic was still for the night, or before the other boys came in, and prayed his prayer for something to happen; not only that, but he added a sentence about himself:

"Help me to do what mother wanted and what the doctor said."

Many people might have thought it a very small prayer, but Jim meant it; and it was wonderful what an effect it had upon his daily life. Jim was steadily improving. That which he had thought almost impossible had happened to him; he had overheard the boss of their shop tell a man that he was a "smart boy, and trustworthy."

There had also been a change in Vira's father; for the worse, I am sorry to say. Whether Dan Crane's whiskey was meaner than Pete Knowles's had been, or whatever was the reason, he was more under its influence than before. He seemed never to be sober enough in these days for Vira to say a word to him; but she prayed on. And whenever she felt utterly discouraged she got out her New Testament and read that verse, and thought of Jim, and trusted. She did not call it that, but that was just what she was doing.

And one evening the "something" happened. It was not in the least what she thought it would be. Perhaps our prayers are not often answered in the way we think they will be. Down at the mill where the poor old father hung around occasionally, under the impression that he was waiting to see if there would

be a chance for doing any odd jobs, there was an accident. He
had come into the machine-room, and somebody had asked
him a question which he did not hear, and he had gone nearer
to the great wheel, and whether his unsteady steps had made
him stagger, or whether he turned faint just then, or how it
happened, no one quite knew. He fell over, they knew, and his
head struck the wheel, and his clothes caught in the machinery,
and there were shouts and cries, and a sudden stoppage of the
great and small wheels, but not sudden enough for the poor old
man. They carried him home unconscious; and the doctor
came, and the neighbors, and Mrs. Perkins planned to stay all
night, and Vira, white-faced and miserable, got through the
night as best she could.

The next morning, when the doctor said he thought the
man would live, but his lower limbs were so injured that he
feared he could not walk for many months, a sudden light came
into the little girl's face.

"That's what it is," she said to Jim when he came in the
evening to see how her father was. "It is the something; I'm
sure of it. He isn't going to die, but he can't walk any more for
ever so long, and if he can't walk after whiskey, he won't get it;
don't you see? We are not to blame, Jim, because we only asked
for the 'something' and left the how to God. Of course, if He
saw there wasn't any other way, He had to do it this way,
because He had promised."

Then began an experience which would be likely to be
remembered in all their after lives. For the first time in Vira's
recollection there was comparative peace in her home. The one
room was clean—it had been carefully kept so ever since the

whitewashing; the bed was neatly made up; Vira, with her mother's and Miss Southey's help, had accomplished that; and now, with no father to come reeling home at night and spoil its purity, it could be kept in order. Mrs. Bruce had work somewhere almost every day. The guests had gone from the hotel, but it was being cleaned and gotten ready to close for the summer; so were several other houses, which for a few weeks would make work plenty. Vira did the work at home, and took care of her father. Mrs. Perkins was at hand with help and advice whenever needed; and Jim came every evening of his life, and helped lift the father, and brought often some little comfort or dainty. As for Vira, she was almost at rest. Jim, who had become her entire confidant, listened in silence to her hopes.

"You see, father never meant to be bad; it was the whiskey; he thought he couldn't let it alone. Now he can't get it, and he is getting over the crying for it and begging us to get him some; and by and by he won't want it any more he won't, Jim, because God is going to give him a clean heart. I feel almost sure of it; I think he is going to want it. I tell him about it every day, and show him the words on the picture; and he lies and looks at them, and I feel almost certain he begins to want it. Jim, you must pray for that now, you know. We 'agree' about it, don't we?"

Jim nodded his head. His terror of praying had passed away. He felt awed at the thought; but he was beginning to like it, and to feel that in some strange way which he could no more understand than can others, it was daily helping him. Yes, he would "agree" to pray for Vira's father that the "something" which had happened to him might help him to want the pure heart which Vira was so sure he might have for the wanting.

Earnest talks had the little girl with her father during those long days while the mother was away at work; or, rather, earnest talks to him. He said very little; but he seemed willing to listen, although the bewildered look which would often appear on his face would have shown one better skilled than Vira that she was getting beyond his understanding.

"You see, father, He puts the pure heart inside of you; you don't have to do it; you can't; so He does it for you. After that, you want to pray, and you like to read the Bible, and you love to think about Jesus, and you are just as different! And the 'seeing God' means that you'll be glad to see Him. People all have to see Him, father, when they die; did you know that? Well, they do. It says in the Bible, every eye shall see him; 'and some will be scared.'"

"I should think so!" interrupted the poor father; and he shivered.

"Well, the 'pure in heart' won't—that's what it means; it is a different kind of seeing. They will be in a hurry for it, and be so glad! You want to have that kind of a heart, don't you, father? Think of us all being in heaven, and being glad! There won't be any whiskey there, you know, nor anything hateful."

Among the frequent visitors was Pete Knowles. Vira was always glad to see him come. "He talks to father," she said to Jim, quiet satisfaction in her voice; "so does the minister when he comes, and Mr. Perkins too; but father seems to understand Mr. Knowles better than any of them. Jim, the minister called him Mr. Knowles today; and so does Mr. Perkins now, all the time. Isn't it queer? I suppose that is because he doesn't sell nor drink whiskey any more. Do you suppose they will ever say 'Mr. Bruce' to father? I mean to call Pete Knowles 'Mr.' too. I like it."

Strangely enough, it was little Martha, Nero's grandchild, who led Vira's father at last into the road that leads to heaven. Vira had taken great pains with her little pupils during all the winter and spring; both of them could read now quite as well as Vira could herself, and little Martha had caught that other more important lesson. She had learned of Vira to pray to Jesus, and to trust him as simply as a little child trusts. She was younger by several years than Vira, and she knew less about a good many things; but she knew how to talk of Jesus to the poor bruised body and stunted mind in a way that he could grasp. Slowly the light dawned, and the strange marvel of what the Bible calls "being born again" took place.

When Vira actually realized that her father was, as she called it, "all made over," her happiness was almost too great. She told Mrs. Perkins that Nero said that at their meeting they sometimes jumped up and down and yelled when they felt real happy, and she could understand why they did it. She should like to yell just as loud as she could.

"I wish I could thank Him so loud that everybody would have to hear," she said earnestly. "And to think, Mrs. Perkins, that it was little Martha who showed him how! He seemed to understand her better than he did me. What if I hadn't taught her to read last winter? She couldn't have read those verses to him in the Bible which he says helped. And what if I hadn't showed her how to pray? Nero knew how, but he said he never thought of showing her while she was such a little thing. I told her all I knew, though; and she understood. I wouldn't have known how myself if it hadn't been for my picture. Hasn't it been a wonderful picture, Mrs. Perkins?"

The lady answered with great heartiness that it certainly had; that she was sure she should always be grateful to it; it had done a great deal for their home; and as for Jim Bryan, it had made him over entirely. She should think he would want to have one like it made in letters of gold. Maybe he would someday; for Jim was smart, and her husband said he shouldn't wonder if he would be a rich man; he was bound to get on.

Soon after this, both Vira and Jim began to plan a rose-colored future for the injured man. He was gaining steadily, they thought; and before long would surely be able to walk about with crutches. These must be planned for, as he would probably have to use them for a long time. Mr. Knowles's shoe-shop was proving a success, and work was waiting for the reformed man. Everything was as it should be. Privately, however, Jim had some fears, which he ventured to mention one day to Vira.

"Don't you ever feel kind of afraid, Vira, to have your father get out again? There is such an awful lot of saloons and drinking-places for him to pass. There is one to be opened between here and Knowles's shoe-shop, don't you think!" Jim could not bring himself to say "Mr. Knowles," and he would not say "Pete," since all his friends had given it up, so he compromised the matter by saying "Knowles."

Over this question Vira thought for some seconds before she answered; then she spoke with slow gravity. "I don't think I'm afraid, because God has done it all, so far; we only asked

Him to let something happen, you know, and didn't say what; and I ought to know He could do the rest; but I don't see how He will. Father heard about that new saloon yesterday, and I b'lieve it worried him. He asked Mr. Knowles if there couldn't anything be done to get rid of it, and said it didn't appear to him that he ever wanted to pass it; and when Mr. Knowles tried to cheer him up, he shook his head and said he was an awful weak man. And mother is worried to pieces about it; she asked Mr. Perkins if he couldn't get up a petition, or something, like what she had heard of folks doing; but he said he didn't know of anything to be done; that at the Mission they had talked about it, and couldn't see any way to get it stopped, because we didn't any of us that wanted it away own any property. Isn't it dreadful, Jim, that such thing's have to be, and we can't help ourselves? Mother says she will get no peace day nor night with thinking about saloons; she says if father should go back now, it would kill her. I told her I knew he wouldn't go back; but she feels awful afraid, and she has had such a hard life, she ought to get some peace somehow." Poor little Vira! Old before her time, trying to help carry the burdens of both father and mother.

Many talks of this sort were held as the days passed, and many plans discussed and abandoned for getting rid of the dangerous saloon. The man who was about to open it had been cautious and keen. He had obeyed the law in every way, and had the legal right to spread this trap before the feeble feet of this weak man. Mrs. Bruce thought about it until she was ready for desperate measures.

"I almost wish your pa had had his feet cut off entirely, so's he could never walk a single step," she said to Vira in a whisper, one evening while the father slept; "then we'd a-had him safe. We could have supported him, you and me; think how nice we've got along since he's been sick. I've had more peace these last seven weeks than I've had in all the twenty years of life that's gone. We could have had real nice times here, taking care of him, and working for him. Then he'd a-been safe, and I don't see how he is to be now."

"Oh, but, mother! How dreadful it would be to always lie in bed, or sit up in bed, and not take a step, ever."

"Folks do it," said Mrs. Bruce firmly. "I knew a man who hadn't taken a step in twenty-three years, and he was chirk and happy all the while. It is better than taking whiskey, child; and how is he to be kept from it, and he passing by and smelling it three or four times a day? I've lived longer than you have, and I know what that means; I tell you I don't believe your pa can stand it."

But they need not any of them have worried; God had it all planned.

It was Mr. Bruce who told them about it. His wife had been away at work all day, and Vira, who had been to the store for supplies, was bustling about to get them a comfortable little supper, when he called to her.

"Sit down, my girl, a little while; never mind about supper just yet; father has got something to tell you. You come and sit down too, mother. The doctor has been here this afternoon while Vira was out, and he told me something which I guess you ought to know. I've kind-a guessed it for a day or two, by some things; but I got at him today, and he told me the truth. Mother, you know that new saloon that's opened? It begun today, the doctor says. Well, I've been worrying about it, and I can see that you have; but there ain't no need. I'm a-going where that saloon nor no other can't hurt me. I'm going to be took out of this world, where they don't keep whiskey, nor nothing to tempt a weak fellow like me to his ruin. Mother, don't you cry! My land! It beats all, that a woman that has suffered as she has all through me can cry about losing of me. There, there! I wouldn't cry. Why, I thought you'd be kind of glad to think that all the fussing and being afraid was over. Come, Vira, you chirk up and tell her that it will be enough sight better. Look here, I'll tell you how I think it is; He knows it ain't safe for me down here. There's those that can get the smell of the stuff and stand it, but I can't. I ain't one of them kind. Of course He knows all about me, and He is just going to take me out of it all."

It came upon them like a thunderbolt out of a clear sky. Mrs. Bruce had worried a good deal about the saloon; but nevertheless, as she said, she had had a great deal of peace during the past weeks, and the old love which she had borne her husband when he was young and merry-looking, and strong-armed and steady of limb, had been coming back into her heart. She, too, had had her day-dreams. There had been days together when in her imagination she had gotten him safely past that new saloon, at home, seated at their tea-table, which should have a real tablecloth on it, and such bread as she had learned lately how to make. Oh, there were good times in store, so she had thought, between the spasms of fear. Now what was there? Do you wonder that she bowed her head, which was gray before its time, on her hands, which were scarred and worn with hard work, and cried as if her heart was breaking?

They settled down to it after a while, as people will to things which they cannot help. In a few days it began to be understood and talked about among the neighbors that Vira's father was going to die. There were those who did not hesitate to say that the family would be better off; but they said it with grave faces, and showed their sympathy as well as they knew how. There were some who began to recall the fact that "poor old Bruce" had never been hateful and dangerous, even at his worst times; and that there were worse men in the world than he. Perhaps the man himself, whom all this talk was about, was the quietest of them all. He held to his first opinion, and repeated it frequently to the grave-faced Vira.

"It's a good deal better as it is, Vira. Your mother will get along first-rate when I'm away, and you will be a comfort and an honor to her; I can see that. It ain't as if I was brought home drunk, and died so; or as if I had died the day I was hurt, when folks knew I had been drinking. I'm dying decent-like, and I've got the clean heart you've talked to me so much about. That's queer, ain't it, that He should give it to me? But He has! I've got it. You can't make no mistake about it after you once get it, can you, Vira? And I'm going to heaven; think of that! I've got a mother there; but I never expected to see her. I lie here sometimes and think how, as soon as I set eyes on her, I'll say, 'Here I be, mother, sure enough; and nobody can be more surprised than I am! But it's all along of my little girl and her picture that I've got here!' I'll tell them all that, Vira; and I'll speak a word about little Martha, too."

He talked a good deal about it, this man who had wasted his years and shattered his life. He knew he had; and he wondered once what would have "happened" if he had let the drink alone. But most of the time he lived in the future, and planned what he would say to his mother, and to a young sister who went to heaven before he began to drink; and, above all, what he would say to "Him." He spoke the pronoun with such reverence and awe that people could not help knowing who he meant.

It was a beautiful summer day when they carried him to the grave. Mrs. Bruce and Vira followed close after the coffin, and Mr. Perkins and Mr. Knowles walked together as bearers, while Jim Bryan kept close behind Vira, and was on the alert to serve her and her mother in every possible way.

It was quite a long procession, not only the neighbors, but many from the Mission, who had heard of the family, came to show their sympathy. The room in which the funeral services were held had been crowded. Mrs. Perkins had prepared it for their coming, making it as neat and clean as even Vira could desire, and Jim had brought vines and palms and ferns which covered all defects. The minister from the Mission spoke on the words, "Blessed are the pure in heart, for they shall see God," telling briefly the story of the motto on the wall, so far as it referred to Vira's father, and assuring the listeners that he had by this time found what it was to "see God." Then the choir from the Mission sang, "Hallelujah, what a Saviour!"

Certainly poor Mrs. Bruce could not but feel that her Joe had had all possible respect and honor done to his memory. It was curious and pitiful to see how strangely she ignored her sad past, and thought of the dead man only as her Joe, the merry-faced, curly-haired young man she had married. She talked about him, even to Vira, as though there had been no cruel years of disappointment and misery between that time and this. And Vira, who seemed to have grown five years older during her father's illness, encouraged the talk, and said to Jim in undertone, "I am glad she can remember him as he was then; I like to think of him as he was a few weeks before he died, and just the day before, when he told me he knew God had given him a clean heart. And, Oh, Jim, I am sure father was right, and it is all better as it is! God has got him now, and he is safe."

Among those who came to the funeral services, and heard a piece of the story of the motto, was Mrs. Carpenter, who, you will remember, had thought it "such a queer thing to send to a mission school." She had heard a good deal about that motto from Miss Southey and others, and had said to herself, perhaps a dozen times, that she must write a letter to Nettie Belden and tell her what her work had accomplished. On the day of the funeral, she said, going home, "I declare, it is a shame that I have not written to Nettie. Such a wonderful change as her motto has made in the family, and for that matter, in the neighborhood!" She had been talking with Mrs. Perkins for the last hour, while they put the room in order for the home-coming of Vira and her mother.

"It seems hardly possible that one Bible verse could accomplish so much. I will write a long letter to Nettie this very evening; it will comfort the poor little thing to know what she has done."

So the letter was written, long and full. Mrs. Carpenter was an excellent letter-writer. She described Vira on her first acquaintance with her, when she peeped into the Mission after the Christmas-tree had been despoiled, and wanted, instead of cup or dolly, "that picture;" she described the effect it had on her and on her home; she told of George Washington and Martha, and of Jim, and Pete Knowles, and Mrs. Perkins, and her husband and baby, and finally of the poor drunken father, transformed, renewed, and safe in heaven that day.

"There!" she said, when she had finished. "It is a long story, and it makes a very thick letter, if I did write on thin paper; it will give Nettie a good many pleasant half-hours reading it over. I wish I had written it before; it might have helped cheer her a good many times this winter. But better late than never! I shall like to hear what she said when she read about Vira and Jim."

But Mrs. Carpenter never heard what Nettie Beldon said. The letter was posted the next morning, and travelled with all speed over the miles which intervened; and the postman brought it one lovely summer evening, just at twilight, to Mrs. Beldon's door. It was the grown-up daughter, Sarah, who received it; the only letter that came for them that day.

"Oh, mother!" she said, in a tremulous voice. "Here is a letter for Nettie." And then the tears came thick and fast. The letter was dropped on the floor, and Sarah went and hid her head in her mother's lap, and they cried together. For the wheeled chair had been moved, that very afternoon, by thoughtful friends, out of sight. Nettie had no more need for it.

Only that day they had carried her small, fair body, dressed in white, and almost embalmed in flowers, and laid it away in the cemetery, Nettie herself having gone two days before to heaven.

She had been so fond of receiving letters—that little Nettie, —and she had gotten so very few; could the mother and sister help crying when they saw what a thick one had come, too late?

After a while Sarah read it aloud to her mother. She stopped often to brush away the tears and to get better control of her voice. It was such a wonderful story the letter told; and Nettie had so often wondered what became of her motto, and whether anybody really cared for it. If she could only have known a little about Vira! If Mrs. Carpenter, who had known her so long, had only written just a few of these many pages in time for Nettie to read them!

"Mother," Sarah said, stopping to calculate, after she had read about Vira's father, "he must have been in heaven only a few hours when Nettie got there; perhaps she will hear the story from him."

"Perhaps so," said her mother, awed, and her tears held back for a moment by the wondrous possibilities of the life upon which her Nettie had entered. And then the present, with its sorrow and loneliness, and the past, with its pitiful memories, flowed over her again, and she cried out, "But, oh, I wish it had come before, so she could have had the comfort of it here!"

The End

Thank you for reading ☒☒☒ ☒☒ ☒☒☒☒ If you'd like to learn more about Isabella Alden, read free novels and stories, and view a complete list of her published books, please visit:

www.IsabellaAlden.com

Isabella wrote over one-hundred books in her lifetime, as well as short stories and newspaper articles—all for the purpose of winning souls for Christ.

Please turn the page to read a biography of the author and additional bonus content.

BIOGRAPHY OF THE AUTHOR

I sabella Macdonald Alden was born in New York in 1841. Her mother, Myra Spafford Macdonald, was the daughter of a distinguished scholar. Her father, Isaac Macdonald was well-educated and an advocate of social reform. In her younger years, her father tutored her at home instead of sending her to public school. It was her father who gave Isabella the nick-name "Pansy" and encouraged her to write, beginning at a young age. At ten years old, Isabella had a story published by a local newspaper.

When she was old enough to leave home, she continued her education as a boarding student at the Oneida Seminary in upstate New York. There she met Theodosia Toll (later, Theodosia Toll Foster), who would become her roommate, life-long friend, and co-author (under the pseudonym, Faye Huntington). Later, Isabella attended the Seneca Collegiate Institute and finished her formal education at the Young Ladies Institute at Auburn, New York. After finishing her formal education, Isabella took a teaching position at her alma mater, where she met her husband, Reverend Gustavus Rossenberg Alden. They were married in 1866 and had one son, Raymond.

Prior to her marriage, her friend Theodosia (or "Docia," as she was often called) helped launch Isabella's literary career. Docia submitted one of Isabella's novels to a writing contest (against Isabella's wishes). Isabella won the contest and in 1865 the winning novel, *Helen Lester*, was published under her pseudonym, Pansy. Isabella would use the Pansy pseudonym for all her published works.

As a new bride, Isabella devoted her energies to being the ideal pastor's wife. She called on church members, cared for the sick, taught Sunday-school, orchestrated ladies' prayer meetings and mission bands, and developed Sunday-school lesson helps that were widely used by Christian churches across the country.

With her husband, she instituted a weekly magazine for children, appropriately titled, "The Pansy." The magazine was wildly popular. Children from all over the country subscribed and devoured the stories that described God's plan for salvation and reinforced Christian behaviors. Producing the magazine was a family business, with each member contributing stories. Isabella's husband, son, father and sisters all wrote for the magazine, as did her best friend, Theodosia Foster.

Isabella was active in the Chautauqua movement of the late 19th Century. The movement was named for New York's Chautauqua Lake, which was the site of the original assembly in 1874. John Vincent and Lewis Miller began the program as a training camp for Sunday-school teachers. Over the years, the religious focus of the program evolved to include nondenominational lectures and classes, concerts, plays and university-level courses. The program proved so popular that by the end of the century, hundreds of Chautauqua camps had sprung up across the country, offering similar programs.

Her Chautauqua experiences sparked Isabella's interest in the temperance movement of the time. She was an officer of the Women's Christian Temperance Union; and she featured the WCTU's work in her book, *Judge Burnham's Daughters*.

With all her activities and responsibilities, Isabella still found time to write novels. She was prolific, producing an estimated one-hundred books, as well as short stories and articles. Many of her books were based on personal experience or featured characters based on real people in her life. Her childhood friend, Theodosia Foster, was the inspiration for the main character in *Docia's Journal*. Her own life as a teacher and pastor's wife served as the model for Marion Wilbur in the Chautauqua Girls series. In *Wanted* and *Julia Ried*, her heroines boldly speak out in church—a direct and liberating reference to her own upbringing in which her father had a strong aversion to women speaking in public, especially in church.

Her books were translated into several languages, including Japanese, Armenian, Norwegian and French, and sold around the world

After Isabella's son and husband passed away in 1924, she lived with her daughter-in-law until her own death in 1930.

Isabella left behind a legacy of sincere, beautifully written books and stories that tell of Christ's salvation and the joys of living a Christian life with strength and conviction. In her memoirs, she wrote:

"My very first little story books were written with a single distinct purpose in view, given over to the desire and determination to win souls for Jesus Christ. The longer I wrote and the older I grew, that was my central purpose."

"I dedicated my pen to the direct and continuous effort to win others for Christ and help others to closer fellowship with him."

Isabella Alden accomplished much in her remarkable life. Most importantly, she accomplished her purpose of winning souls for Christ through her inspiring stories.

Please turn the page to read additional bonus content.

MY ISABELLA ALDEN TREASURE HUNT

by Christian Fiction Author
Jenny Berlin

I discovered Isabella Alden's books a few years ago on a visit to my favorite antique store. In an old basket, almost buried beneath a pile of vintage table linens was a copy of *Overruled*. At the time, I'd never heard of Isabella Alden, but I liked the cover and the pages seemed to be intact. When I flipped to the back of the book, the final pages captured my attention and made me want to read more. I took *Overruled* home with me.

And it so it began. That book—once buried and forgotten beneath a pile of linen—so touched and inspired me that I embarked on a mission to find other books by Isabella Alden.

Next I found *Julia Ried* and *Wanted*. Then I read the Chautauqua Girls series and I became a genuine fan of this talented writer.

After reading a number of her books, I was surprised to discover that Isabella's reputation was founded as a writer of children's fiction. From about 1866 to 1929, under her pseudonym, Pansy, she produced wildly popular children's novels and short stories that explained Christian values in terms children could easily understand. It's almost forgotten, though, that she was a talented writer of books and stories for adults, as well.

At the time they were published, Isabella's adult novels were also very popular; and, like her children's stories, they addressed adult themes in a Christian context. She often portrayed her main character as a strong woman who—for better or for worse—affected others' lives for Christ or learned to be a better Christian because of the situations she encountered in the story.

Isabella's plots were inventive and interesting, often incorporating current issues of the day. She was a gifted writer of dialog and she used it to instantly define her characters and make them memorable. It didn't take long for me to realize that Mrs. Tyndall's helpful advice in *Julia Ried* is little more than the weapon of a catty and mean-spirited woman; or that the almost ethereally perfect Christian, Marjorie Edmonds, can say exactly the wrong thing to unwittingly incite another's jealousy and desperation (in *Overruled*). Isabella's talents shine in *Four Girls at Chautauqua*, where she skillfully used dialog to make the four main characters come alive, each with her own unique voice, sense of humor and personality.

With all that being said, it's surprising that Isabella Alden is so little read today. In many cases, modern readers know her (if at all) as the favorite aunt of Christian writer, Grace Livingston Hill; but I think Isabella Alden deserves more recognition than that.

In her books for adults she tackled adult subjects: gossip and reputation; pettiness and envy; witnessing for Christ and strength of conviction—and she did it all within the context of explaining God's plan for salvation. The characters in her books may be non-believers who come to accept Christ as Savior by the book's end; or they may be Christians who are tested or enlightened throughout the course of the story's events. No matter the premise, Isabella created true-to-life characters that are easily identifiable with today's reader.

Take, for instance, Estelle and Ralph Bramlett in *Overruled*. Their arguments, hurt feelings, and resentments are so real and so well written, they could easily be transplanted into a 21st Century novel about a bickering couple.

The same can be said of John Stuart King in *As in a Mirror*. Modern readers have no trouble relating to John's disillusionment with his Christian life. Not content with simply going to church, John realizes that the Christian life he leads is not really grounded in obedience to God's Word. What starts out for John as simply an experimental change in his life leads to the revelation that his Christian walk requires a growing relationship with God. With each obstacle placed in his path, John Stuart King—like all Isabella's characters—ultimately overcomes challenges and prevails with God's help.

Isabella included the message of salvation in each of her adult-focused books. As in her children's stories, she used plain-spoken, everyday terms that were easy for readers to understand as she presented simple but effective arguments for accepting Christ's salvation. As she said through a character in *Ester Ried Yet Speaking*:

> Will He not be pleased with even my little bits of
> efforts if He knows that my sincere desire is to save
> souls for his glory?

I think it's clear that her writings were her personal ministry
to others. She was dedicated to using her talent to win souls for
Christ.

She also sought to strengthen the faith of Christians who
read her books. Like her character, John Stuart King, Isabella
believed that simply going to church every Sunday didn't
strengthen the believer's walk with Christ. She encouraged
readers to engage in an ever-growing relationship with Jesus.
Her characters read their Bibles, actively sought work to
perform in His name, and yielded to the Holy Spirit by allowing
God to take unconditional control of their lives.

One of her common themes was the sense of peace we can
attain only through a personal relationship with Jesus Christ.
Peace and rest and freedom from worry were recurring
messages in many of her books, particularly in the Chautauqua
series. One of the Chautauqua girls, Ruth Erskine, thought she
had the perfect life; but inwardly, she simply went through the
motions of her day, feeling nothing, bonding with no one, and
rigidly holding on to her pride and society's dictates. Ruth may
appear outwardly calm, but inside she's restless, spending all her
energy keeping her perfect life in order but pushing away
anyone who might get close enough to see under the surface of
her beautiful but fragile existence. It's only through engaging
with God daily and making Him the center of her life that Ruth

finds peace. Peace with God is a lesson Isabella taught many times in her novels:

> You don't know what a relief it is to go right to the Lord with your worries.
>
> *The Man of the House*

> Go to Him for help, and as sure as the sun shines above these clouds, you will get just what you need.
>
> *The Pocket Measure*

> "Peace with God!" It expresses so much! Peace is greater than joy, or comfort, or rest.
>
> *Ruth Erskine's Crosses*

In my search for information about Isabella, I discovered some critics carelessly group Isabella Alden with "temperance writers" of the late 19th Century. While some of her novels (such as *Overruled, Three People, Judge Burnham's Daughters* and *One Commonplace Day*) included sub-plots that warned of the pitfalls of alcohol abuse, I think it's unfair to label her books as "temperance novels."

She wrote to win souls for Christ. Her characters abstained from alcohol in the same way they abstained from dancing or playing cards. She summarized her position in *The Chautauqua Girls at Home*:

> "It is a question whether we have any right to indulge in an amusement that has the power to lead people astray," Ruth said, grave and thoughtful, "especially when it is impossible to tell what boy may be growing up under that influence to whom it will become a snare."

In *Overruled*, Miss Hannah Bramlett vows to help Jack Taylor fight the temptation of alcohol, no matter what it takes. Later, Hannah's sister-in-law Glyde Douglass comes upon Jack just as he is about to enter a saloon. Their encounter leads Jack to confess to Glyde that he blames God for not making it easier for him to resist alcohol, giving Glyde the opportunity to explain to him the concept of free will:

> "Suppose you had a very pleasant house into which you could put your little boy, and keep him there with locked doors and windows grated, so that it would not be possible for him to escape. You could keep him from a good many wrong roads by that means, couldn't you? He would not be tempted by gambling-saloons nor drinking-saloons; he would not stand around on street corners, nor mingle with men who used evil words—oh, there are a hundred wrong roads from which you could surely shield him! Would you do it? Keep him there all his life, surrounded with pleasant things, books and flowers and birds, and everything that love could furnish, but still a prisoner? Would you do this, instead of letting him go out in the world to choose his own way?"

Vigilance of character and staying true to one's faith were also common themes in Isabella's adult fiction. In *Julia Reid*, the heroine takes a job that requires her to leave home and live in a boarding house run by the attractive Mrs. Tyndall, who describes herself as a Christian and attends church regularly. Julia admires her instantly and falls under the woman's influence before she realizes the woman's behavior to others is far from Christ-like.

Isabella's long-time friend, Theodosia Toll Foster described her as having "great strength of character and an inflexible firmness in matters of duty and right." In her books, Isabella's characters were portrayed as people who must develop that same strength. She challenged her readers to be better people and to nurture a closer walk with God.

She was astonishingly prolific, producing over 100 books, as well as serialized stories and Sunday school lessons for children. In the year 1900 alone, her book sales were estimated at around 100,000 copies per year, and they were published in several languages.

Unfortunately for us, Isabella Alden's books are becoming more difficult to find. While some of her adult books, such as the Chautauqua series, are available to today's reader, other Alden books, like *Enlisted* and *Doris Farrand's Vocation*, are rare.

That's why I'm so pleased to see publishers bring out new editions of her works. To me, Isabella Alden's stories are treasures of inspiration. Each book helps me examine my own walk with God and challenges me to truly experience the abundant life He has promised me.

Isabella Alden's books are as true and compelling today as when they were first published; and they achieve what Isabella wanted most: "to save souls for His glory."

Blessings to you,
JENNY BERLIN

Jenny Berlin is the author of *Ask Me Again,* a contemporary Christian novel. Learn more about Jenny and her books at www.JennyBerlin.com.

Please turn the page to read an excerpt from *Ask Me Again.*

ASK ME AGAIN

A Novel of Faith in Colorado

by
Jenny Berlin

Chapter 1

September
Denver, Colorado

"Mother! I'm home!"

From the far reaches of her expansive back yard, Minda McAllister could hear her daughter's voice echoing through the house.

Mother.

Tracy didn't usually call her "mother" unless she was with a new acquaintance and desperately trying to appear older than her seventeen years. Minda pushed at the wide brim of the gardening hat she wore, squinted up at the early evening sun, and vaguely wondered who her daughter had brought home.

"Mother? Where *are* you?"

"I'm out here! In the garden!"

Minda plunged the hand trowel into the ground, then

carefully levered a weed, roots and all, from her bed of purple asters. She let loose a sigh of satisfaction, content to revel in small victories.

She heard the old kitchen screen door creak open and slap shut. In the next moment, Tracy bounded down the steps and crossed the lawn to stand over her.

"Mom, what are you doing?" Tracy's voice was heavy with censure, as if the sight of her mother on her knees, toiling in the dirt, was something she hadn't seen countless times before.

"Pulling weeds. I haven't tended this garden in weeks and now I'm paying for it." Minda pushed back the wide brim of her gardening hat and looked up, past her daughter's immaculate skirt, past her pristine blouse, and up to her modestly-but-perfectly-made-up face. "I could use some help."

"Are you kidding? I can't pull weeds now." Her tone left little doubt that she questioned her mother's sanity. "There's someone I want you to meet. He's in the kitchen waiting. Are you coming?"

He. That explained the "mother" bit. Since Minda knew all of Tracy's friends from church and school, she wondered who the boy might be. A new student at school? A new neighbor on the block?

She attacked another weed and said mildly, "I'd like to meet him, honey. Why don't you ask him to come on out here?"

"Mo-o-o-m!" Tracy's groan stretched the simple word into multiple syllables. "I'm not going to bring him out *here* to meet you! Not in the back yard!"

"There's nothing wrong with our back yard, Tracy. It's a lovely and serene place that's the envy of our neighborhood.

And if I remember correctly, you've hosted plenty of parties for your friends and church groups on this very spot. Why shouldn't I meet your friend here in the back yard?"

"Couldn't you just come inside?" Tracy pleaded.

Minda rocked back on her heels and looked up at her daughter. The expression on Tracy's face surprised her. Anxiety, happiness, strain—that unique mix of emotions could mean only one thing.

"Tracy, honey, did you bring a . . . a *special* boy home to meet me?"

Tracy stiffened. "He's not a *boy*."

"But he's someone important? Someone you want to make a good impression on?"

"Yeah, well . . . sorta."

Minda didn't know whether to laugh or cry. Tracy had brought boys home before but they'd always been more of the friendship variety. Tracy dated—A girl as pretty as Tracy was bound to attract boys her own age—but she had yet to show any particular interest in any one boy.

Until now.

Minda's spirits lifted as she conjured an image of the special young man. He'd be a little taller than Tracy, with nice eyes and an attractive smile. He'd be a bit gangly, too, like a lot of teenaged boys, but Minda would be able to see the potential for grace in his movements. And, of course, he'd share Tracy's Christian beliefs and together they'd walk in faith, allowing the Lord to guide their relationship.

Minda found herself smiling. She had been almost the same age when she'd become engaged to Tracy's father. She had never regretted marrying Dale McAllister at such a young age, but marrying straight out of high school and having a baby right away—though much loved and wanted—were decisions Minda wouldn't recommend to anyone, especially Tracy. And when Dale had died, leaving Minda to raise their daughter alone . . .

Deliberately, Minda blocked those thoughts. She hadn't even met Tracy's young man, yet her over-fertile imagination was already running rampant to the point of planning their wedding.

She squinted up at Tracy and said, reasonably, "I understand you want to make a good impression, honey, and I suppose I could come into the house and meet the young man you've brought home. But unless your guest wants to wait an hour while I shower and change and do my make-up and hair, he'll have to take me as I am right now. I know I don't look my best, but here—working in the gardens, taking care of this house— this is the real me. And isn't that who you want your guest to meet?"

Tracy didn't look convinced, but she after a moment she said, a little sullenly, "I guess so."

She retreated to the house and Minda turned her attention back to the garden. Again she heard the screen door creak open and slap shut; but this time she heard two sets of footsteps descend the back steps and shuffle across the grass.

Minda suppressed an urge to jump to her feet. Tracy was always telling her that she wasn't like other mothers. Other mothers, according to Tracy, didn't impose strict curfews. They didn't force their children to exist on meager allowances or report which friends they were seeing and when. Other mothers were *cool*.

She wasn't sure how cool she was going to be about Tracy's young man. Certainly, Tracy would want her to be nonchalant, as if bringing a boy home to meet her were an everyday affair.

But it wasn't an everyday affair. It was a singular, important event or Tracy wouldn't be so nervous and jumpy, so insistent that everything be right.

Minda smiled softly. She was witnessing her daughter's first serious crush; no small milestone in a young woman's life. She had a feeling she was really going to really like this boy.

Minda continued to dig away at the soft soil, plying her trowel in a way she hoped Tracy would approve as having just the right amount of coolness.

Two pairs of shoes appeared within the limited view afforded by the broad brim of Minda's hat. She recognized Tracy's sandals. Next to them, the toes of a sizable pair of expensive Italian leather loafers peaked from beneath the cuffed hems of perfectly-creased wool pant legs.

Tracy cleared her throat and said, in her best imitation of a cultured adult, "Mother, there's someone here I'd like you to meet. Mother, this . . . this is Mark Cartier!"

Minda found that a masculine hand was being extended toward her. She dropped the trowel and knew instantly that the strong fingers that gripped hers didn't belong to a boy in high school. This hand held hers firmly and purposefully.

Her gaze traveled up along a tanned forearm, dusted with dark hair. Her gaze traveled higher, past broad shoulders, past a full, tanned neck above a loosened starched collar and tie, up to his face.

This was no high school student.

This was a man.

A man with strong, lean features and the faint shadow of a beard on his face. A man with little laugh lines exploding from the corners of his brilliant blue eyes. Those blue eyes widened for the briefest of moments when they first made contact with hers.

So, she thought, he was just as surprised by her as she was by him. Good. Because Minda was really surprised.

She'd been expecting a teenager. A young man near Tracy's age, but . . . *this?* The man had to be in his late twenties; he might even be thirty. So what in the world was he doing with her daughter?

His pull on her hand was easy and strong, as if setting bemused women on their feet was a task he performed countless times each day.

For a moment she stood practically toe to toe with Mark Cartier, her surprised gaze fixed on his handsome face, her hand in his, as half a dozen disjointed thoughts careened like bumper cars around her brain.

Up close, her initial impression of him didn't change much. He was definitely thirty-ish. He was also definitely good-looking in a polished sort of way that made her think he was used to women fainting dead-away at his feet.

There had to be some mistake.

Minda's eyes flew to Tracy's face. Her daughter was smiling nervously, her expression aglow and shy and anxious all at the same time.

There was no mistake. Minda's heart sank a little.

With her free hand she swept the hat from her head and tried to pull herself together. "It's nice to meet you . . ." His name deserted her. "I'm sorry."

"*Mark*, mother," Tracy hissed. "I told you, his name is Mark Cartier."

"I beg your pardon."

He was still holding her rather grubby hand in his. He didn't seem to mind, though. He flashed a self-possessed smile as he looked her right in the eye. "It's a pleasure, Mrs. McAllister. I've been looking forward to meeting you."

Mrs. McAllister? Who was he trying to kid? He wasn't *that* much younger than she and Minda was thirty-six.

She pulled her hand from his and said, coolly, "If you call me Mrs. McAllister, I probably won't answer. I'd rather you just called me Minda."

"I will. And I hope you'll call me Mark."

If he'd been a seventeen-year-old boy like he was supposed to be, there would have been no question what she would have called him. "Oh, I was planning to," she said, as the shy, gangly teenage boy of her imaginings faded forever away.

He smiled and slipped his hands into the pockets of his trousers. "You have a very lovely home here." His blue eyes scanned the big back yard, from the arbored corner at one end to the tree-hung swing at the other. "Altogether I'd say you have an acre or so of valuable, rich land. I wouldn't have expected to find such a place so close to downtown Denver. It's almost like an oasis of your very own right in the middle of the city."

Minda didn't know whether to be annoyed or pleased. He was standing there so casually, talking about acreage and land as if he were just one of the folks, dressed in overalls with a long shaft of wheat dangling from his perfectly-straight, incredibly-white teeth.

On the other hand, he'd said the very thing that could usually make Minda swell with pride. Her home *was* her oasis. This house and its surrounding land, along with the old commercial building downtown that housed her business, had been in her husband's family for generations. They had come to her when Dale died and meant all the more because they represented all she had left of the things he loved most.

But she wasn't going to tell that to Mark Cartier, nor was she going to stand there and exchange small talk with a man who owed her some big explanations.

She looked from Tracy to Mark and asked deliberately, "Why don't you tell me how you two met?"

"We met at school today." He flashed a gleaming smile.

Minda's heart dropped a little lower. Schoolgirl crushes on handsome young teachers could be the most devastating kind. "I see. What subjects do you teach?"

"Oh, I'm not a teacher."

"A student?" She sounded more sarcastic than she intended, but she had a feeling Mark Cartier was being deliberately uncooperative, making her drag every little bit of information out of him.

Tracy intervened. "Mother, Mark spoke at our school today. It's career week and he was a guest speaker."

Minda plopped her gardening hat back on her head and bent down to pick up her abandoned trowel. "Is that so? Do you regularly make speeches to auditoriums full of teenagers?"

"I don't make it a habit."

"Any particular pearls of wisdom you passed on to them today?"

"Just . . . stay in school." He didn't react to the sharp tone of her questions. "I think a good education is the key to success in life."

She stared at him for a moment. Maybe looking into his eyes would give her a window into his thoughts and help her make sense of the situation.

It didn't help. He simply looked back at her with a calm expression and that too-perfect smile that she was sure was meant to quell any further questions.

But Minda had plenty of questions, and she was beginning to think she wasn't going to like the answers.

She held her palm up in a surrendering gesture. "I think you have me at a disadvantage, Mark. Please make yourself at home while I wash some of my garden off my hands." She looked at Tracy, who was smiling adoringly at the man as if he'd just promised her the moon. "Tracy, would you help me for a minute, please?"

She started for the house without waiting for a reply. She didn't want to hear that man's voice again or look up once more into his self-satisfied smile. In less than five minutes time she'd had her fill of Mark Cartier.

Inside, she went upstairs to her bedroom and it's big, master bath. In its original state, when the house had first been built in the 1920s, the bathroom had been a tiny tiled room no larger than a closet. But years ago, when Minda and her husband had updated the house for late-twentieth-century living, they had converted an adjacent sitting room to a bathroom. Now its large proportions and relatively modern fixtures, combined with a few scented candles and a good supply of bubble-bath, gave Minda one of few opportunities to pamper herself when she felt the need.

She felt the need now. But she hadn't the time. Her seventeen-year-old daughter and her incredibly unsuitable, would-be boyfriend were downstairs behaving for all the world as if nothing were wrong.

Minda hadn't the faintest idea what to do about it.

She knew some fast thinking and ardent prayer were called for. She bowed her head as she turned on the taps at the sink, but a light knock at the door interrupted her.

"Can I come in?" Tracy asked. Without waiting for an answer, she sat inelegantly down on the edge of the tub. Her expression was glowing. "Isn't he great?"

Minda struggled for a moment over how she should reply and offered up a silent prayer for guidance. She pumped a dollop of liquid soap onto her palm. "Oh, he's something, I'd say."

"And he's so handsome. Everybody thought so and practically every girl in the whole school stayed after the assembly to try to talk to him about his speech." Tracy's words came out in a rush. "And whenever one of us would, like, ask him a question, he would, like, ask us our names and stuff. And when I told him my name, he, like, seriously *stared* at me. I was so nervous! And then I asked my question and he said it was the best question any high school student had ever asked him! He said it revealed a good deal of maturity on my part," she added, proudly.

"What was it?"

Tracy frowned. "What was *what?*"

"What was the question you asked him?"

"Mo-o-o-o-m! Who cares what I asked him? I hardly remember myself and, besides, it doesn't matter."

Minda reached for the towel and dried her hands in a slow, deliberate way. "I guess you're right." She hesitated for only a second, then decided to dive right in. "To tell you the truth, honey, I'm a little surprised. To be honest, I think Mark Cartier is—"

"Gosh, me, too! You know what? When he first talked to me, I could hardly pay attention to what he said, you know what I mean? I've never met anybody like him before. He's so good looking and he dresses so perfect and he's like somebody out of the movies or something."

One look into her daughter's face made Minda doubt whether the time was right for a heart-to-heart discussion. Tracy was too full of emotion to see sense; too spellbound by the man waiting downstairs to understand all the reasons he shouldn't be sitting in their living-room in the first place. Minda judged that any conversation they had now would only set Tracy's defenses up and end disastrously.

They'd already had more than their fair share of conflicts during the last year, which their pastor had diagnosed as little more than garden-variety teenage rebellion. But those conflicts had been painful to Minda and she sometimes wondered how much more strained her relationship with her daughter might be if not for Pastor Walker's intervention and counsel.

Minda took a deep breath, determined to wait for God to help her show Tracy the choice she was making was the wrong choice.

She reached down and gently brushed Tracy's hair back from her face. And for the first time in a long time, Tracy allowed her to do it.

"You're right, honey. Men like Mark Cartier don't come our way very often. I guess it's easy enough to be dazzled by a handsome face that looks like it's attached to a big bank account."

Tracy flashed her a sour look. "I'm not *dazzled*, Mom. He happens to be, like, the most perfect guy I ever met."

Minda declined to remind Tracy that her knowledge and experience with guys was limited. "I happen to think you're pretty perfect, yourself."

A reluctant smile tugged at Tracy's lips. "Thanks, Mom. So, do you think I look all right? I mean, do I look pretty? You know, like someone Mark will think is pretty?"

Minda felt a door open in the conversation. "Tracy, honey, the man you're with should like you for who you are, not who you pretend to be."

She made a face. "I know. But I don't want to be just plain, old Tracy McAllister—at least, not when I'm with Mark. It's hard to explain. He's just special. Like, you know, when girls say they've met The One? You know what I mean, Mom? Like when you met Daddy and you just knew you were going to marry him. You know?"

"No, Tracy, it's not like when I met Daddy." Minda felt a danger alarm go off in her head. "Your father was ten and I was eight years old when we met. We had a lifetime to get to know each other and learn what love was about. We didn't just fall in love one afternoon after school—" She stopped short as she realized her voice had carried a tinge of sarcasm. She took a deep breath and said in a voice she hoped was much calmer, "I'm sorry, honey, but it's not the same. You know nothing about this man . . . And I do mean *man*."

"You make it sound like there's something wrong with him," Tracy said, defensively.

"That's because there *is* something wrong. He's too old. You're too young."

"I'm not too young. I'll be eighteen in two weeks."

"But right now you're seventeen. You're too young and the man downstairs is not suitable for you to think of in a romantic way."

"In two weeks it won't matter *what* you think!" Tracy's voice rose a little. "In two weeks I can do whatever I want. In two weeks, I'll be eighteen and *I'll* be the one deciding who's suitable!"

"Tracy, you can't really be interested in that man. What on earth could the two of you possibly have in common?"

In a flash Tracy's arms were folded across her chest. "You mean: what could he possibly see in *me*."

"Honey, that's not what I said."

"No, but it's what you meant. You don't think a handsome and hot guy could ever possibly be interested in me. You refuse to see that I've grown up!"

"Yes, you've grown, but you'll never catch up to *him*. The man downstairs is ten years older than you are, Tracy."

Tracy's brown eyes, that had glared so hotly at Minda only a moment ago, softened a little.

Minda knew that look and her breath caught a little in her throat. "He's *more* than ten years older, isn't he?"

Tracy looked away but a faint tinge of pink stained her cheeks.

Minda sat down on the edge of the tub beside her daughter and clasped one of her hands. "Just how old is he, Tracy?"

Tracy shrugged her shoulders and tried to pull her hand away but Minda wouldn't let go.

"I think he's, like . . . thirty-two," she mumbled, still unwilling to make eye-contact.

After a long moment Minda asked gently, "Honey, do you see that this is a problem?"

"No! You know, Mom, you just don't know him, *that's* the problem."

"And you *do* know him?" Minda challenged. "Okay, then tell me about him." Minda waited expectantly, but Tracy didn't speak. Instead, her chin jutted out to a militant angle as she glared back at her mother.

Minda wasn't deterred. "Is he a Christian, Tracy? Does he go to church? What's his favorite color? What does he like to eat for dinner? Does he have any brothers or sisters?"

Tracy pursed her lips into a straight line.

"The fact is, honey, you really don't know anything about him. So here's my idea: Let's learn about Mark Cartier together."

The look on Tracy's face wavered between hope and distrust. "You aren't going to interrogate him or something, are you?"

"No, I thought I'd ask him to stay for dinner. He can eat pot roast and tell us about himself. What do you think?"

Tracy studied the pattern on the tile floor for a moment. "I *think* it sounds like a good idea, but there must be a catch somewhere."

Minda shook her head. "No catch. No trap. No hidden strings. We'll just have a nice dinner and we'll both get a chance to know our guest better. Maybe I'll find out I was wrong and he's really a great guy who's suitable for my daughter."

"Oh, yeah, right. You're really hoping I'll find out *I* was wrong and I won't like him after all."

"Anything can happen," Minda said, with a slight shrug of her shoulders.

"Not that. Mark's an awesome guy. You'll see. You'll change your mind about *him*."

For the hundredth time in less than thirty minutes, Minda wondered how things could have progressed so far in a single afternoon. Tracy had only met the man a few hours ago, yet she was clearly deep in the throes of a heart-felt crush. Minda truly questioned whether Mark Cartier felt the same moon-eyed, isn't-life-wonderful kind of first love that Tracy was feeling. It didn't make sense that a man as polished and good-looking as Mark Cartier couldn't find half a dozen women his own age to date.

So why on earth was he interested in her daughter?

Minda wasn't going to tease herself over the answer. She made up her mind. She was going to find out what his intentions were and have him out of Tracy's life by the end of the evening.

Tonight would be Mark Cartier's first—and last—meal at the McAllister house.

Chapter 2

Mark Cartier drew another deep breath, enjoying the savory smells coming from the kitchen. With a few well-placed compliments and a little bit of his own brand of charm, he was certain he could get Minda McAllister to invite him to dinner. It had been a long time since he'd had a home-cooked meal and this one smelled particularly delicious. Pot roast, if he trusted his memory, and he'd bet it tasted as good as it smelled.

The aroma of dinner cooking added to the overall hominess of the McAllister place—a home that had initially surprised him when he'd first followed Tracy through the front door. From the outside, he thought it was nothing more than a big, old barn of a house. A yellow clapboard beast.

Once inside, the businessman in him had immediately cataloged its contents with a practiced eye, from the warm tones of the wood mouldings around the windows and doors, to the gently over-stuffed furniture and faded, but still valuable area carpets that were scattered over the hard-wood floors. He figured the place had to be about a hundred years old, yet there was nothing musty or out-dated about it, as he had expected. It was a warm, charming place that was welcoming, yet elegant. A home that was surprisingly serene amid the bustle of downtown Denver.

There were few houses left in the surrounding area. Most of

the old homes had been torn down years before, replaced by office buildings, trendy towers of open-space lofts, and multi-level parking structures. Minda McAllister was one of the few property owners who declined to sell out in the name of progress, but Mark had a feeling he could change her mind about that.

Without thinking, from habit born of practice, he had been sizing up Minda McAllister since the moment he had first caught a glimpse of her. She was, to a certain extent, the enemy. She had what he wanted and he was smart enough to remember that.

Yet she had surprised him, too. He had come to think of the Widow McAllister as just another adversary to be vanquished, another obstacle to be overcome in his quest for success in his career. He hadn't expected her to be so pretty. He certainly hadn't expected that the sight of her—working her garden with tell-tale signs of dirt clinging to her hands and a light breeze gently ruffling her shoulder-length brown hair—could be so attractive.

But those thoughts, he knew, were dangerous. They diverted him from his purpose and distracted him from his goal. Determinedly, he blocked them from his mind, replacing them with a more sensible variety.

He'd spotted a large, old roll-top desk in a shadowed alcove at one end of the living-room. It was an enormous piece of furniture that rivaled the size of the upright piano on the other side of the room, and it looked twice as old.

Alert to any warning sound that Minda and her daughter were coming down the stairs, Mark approached the desk. He saw papers and bank statements neatly stacked on the desktop beside a Bible-study lesson plan. One by one, Mark pulled at the heavy wooden desk drawers. To his relief, they didn't squeak or scrape when he opened them.

He shuffled quickly through the drawers' contents and found nothing to cause surprise: an over-due property tax notice, a clutch of unpaid bills, some church tithe receipts. In another drawer he discovered a collection of probably every single report card Tracy ever brought home from school.

In the wide pencil drawer he found several unopened pieces of mail, including a large envelope imprinted with the familiar return address of his employer: Goble, Haines and Wyman.

His boss, Robert Haines, would have a heart attack if he knew his last best offer had been tossed, unopened, into a desk drawer. Robert Haines would never be able to understand that a woman could be so disinterested in a multi-million dollar offer to buy her property. Mark was having a bit of trouble understanding it himself. If it was some sort of ploy on her part, Mark would get to the bottom of it.

He quickly stuffed the envelope back into the drawer at the sound of footsteps descending the stairs. By the time Tracy and Minda reached the bottom step, Mark was casually sitting on the living-room sofa. He looked up at them and smiled.

Minda smiled politely back. "Mark, I'm about to put the finishing touches on dinner. I hope you'll stay and join us."

"I appreciate the invitation," he said, smoothly, "but I don't want to impose."

"In that case, maybe you'd feel better about staying if you worked for your supper. *You* can set the dinner table."

He actually smiled then. Not that plastic, movie-star smile that was meant to charm her into doing his will, but a genuine smile that lit his blue eyes and transformed his expression.

Slowly, Mark left the sofa and rose to his feet. He stood almost toe-to-toe with her, his size towering over her petite frame.

She didn't back up and she didn't flinch. She looked him full in the eyes for a moment that seemed to last a lifetime.

The light in his eyes intensified. "In that case, I'd love to stay."

Thank you for reading this excerpt. *Ask Me Again* is available in print and e-book formats. Visit your favorite book retailer to purchase *Ask Me Again* or learn more about the book.

www.ingramcontent.com/pod-product-compliance
Lightning Source LLC
Chambersburg PA
CBHW031706170626
46808CB00005B/1637